FIRST AND ONLY

Peter Flannery

BLACKHEART BOOKS

FIRST AND ONLY

A BLACKHEART BOOK : 978-0-9570919-0-0

First published for Kindle by Blackheart Books in 2011

PRINTING HISTORY

Blackheart Edition 2011

Contact:

Twitter: @TheFlanston

Website: peterflannery.co.uk

Peter Flannery lives in the Scottish Borders with his wife and two young boys. He worked in horticulture for several years before setting himself up as a sculptor for the toy and hobby industry. While working for a design studio in Edinburgh he moved from sculpting to writing, producing background stories for the company's models and games. He is now an independent writer working on a range of titles for both adults and children. First & Only is his first published novel.

To Julie

For her love and support

and for letting me know when I lost the plot!

Author's Note

The James Randi Educational Foundation is a genuine organisation and while it features in this book I would like to make it clear that all the occurrences are entirely imaginary. Likewise the words spoken by the characters James Randi and Jeff Wagg are entirely imagined by me and cannot be taken as quotes. I would however, like to thank Mr Randi and Mr Wagg for taking the time to read through the relevant chapters of First & Only and correcting me on several key points.

Those wishing to learn more about the JREF and the million-dollar challenge can visit their website at: http://www.randi.org/site/.

The image of the 'Safemaker II' push dagger on the back cover is used by the kind permission of Mr Lynn C. Thompson of Cold Steel Blades. Anyone wishing to know more about their products can find them at: http://www.coldsteel.com/

First and Only

PROLOGUE

Newspaper cutting

Fourteen years ago

TORTURE

Police have confirmed that the man's body, found earlier this week in Didsbury, Manchester, showed signs of torture. They have refused to comment on the nature of the injuries and defended their lack of progress in finding the killer.

The lighting in the church was pleasantly subdued. Flames flickered through sconces of red glass and the still air carried the familiar smells of furniture polish, burning candles, incense and stone.

It was time for evening confession in the parish church of St Joseph's. Two tradesmen worked quietly from a tower of scaffolding, fitting new lights above the statue of the Sacred Heart but apart from them the church was almost empty. Just two people waited silently in the pews. One was a woman in her sixties with her faded blue raincoat and dull grey hair; the other was an eight-year-old boy who sat in the pew with his head bowed and his hands twisting in his lap.

His name was Psimon, and he was terrified.

Every week he came to evening confession, not to confess his sins but just to speak to Father Kavanagh, the gentlest, most understanding man he had ever known. He enjoyed the game of pretending they did not know each other and the fact that the priest was bound by a sacred oath never to reveal a word of what was told to him. But tonight was different. Tonight something was going to happen; something from his dreams, from his nightmares. The church appeared serene and safe. There was nothing to portend the presence of evil but somehow Psimon knew.

Somehow Psimon always knew.

To the right of the pews were the two doors of the confessional each leading to a small rectangular room and joined by a pierced screen of polished brass. Psimon glanced up as the light above the penitent's door went out and an elderly man emerged clutching a flat cap and a walking stick carved in the likeness of a Jack Russel terrier. He gave Psimon a smile and a conspiratorial wink before making his way to the doors at the back of the church. The light above the other door remained lit, indicating that the priest was still in residence. The grey haired woman turned to look at Psimon but he bowed his head and the woman gave a weary sigh before rising from her pew.

As the woman disappeared into the confessional Psimon looked up at the workmen. Except for them the church was now empty. There was no one else waiting to see Father Kavanagh. He drew a breath. Maybe he was wrong... maybe the old priest would be all right after all. He glanced eagerly at the confessional light. The grey haired woman would not take long, she never did. He was edging towards the end of the pew when he froze. He felt a prickling sensation across the back of his neck and an unpleasant chill surged through his body. Someone had entered the church behind him and Psimon knew that his fears were true.

His small hands gripped the pew as the stranger came closer until he could hear their heavy footfalls on the brown ceramic floor tiles. And there was something else… a noise; a confusion of whispers that sounded almost like a voice, or many voices. Psimon did not know if the whispers were coming from the stranger or just echoing within the confines of his own head. He tried not to listen. He did not like the voices.

The stranger was almost level with him when the confessional door opened and the grey haired woman stepped out into the aisle. From the corner of his eye Psimon saw the woman check herself at the sight of the stranger. He noticed how she flattened herself against the wall to let the stranger pass.

Psimon's eyes flitted fearfully to the side. He saw a tall youth with long black hair falling unkempt about his face. His posture was hunched and brooding but his broad shoulders spoke of the powerful man he would soon become. Without hesitation the stranger opened the door to the penitent's confessional and disappeared inside. Psimon glanced at the grey haired woman who gave him a brief look of concern before hurrying away, the harsh click of her heels receding until she left the church and the main door closed with a soft percussive boom.

An ominous silence descended in which Psimon could hear his own shallow breathing. He could just hear the tradesmen atop the scaffolding talking in low respectful voices. And now he could hear the stranger's voice... harsh, unpleasant and made all the more sinister by the incessant presence of the whispers; whispers that were almost words. He did not want to hear it but he could not shut it out.

'Forgive me Father for I have sinned...' the stranger said. 'But then I told you I was going to, didn't I?'

The stranger snorted in response to some reaction from the priest.

'Yes. Your lost sheep has returned to confess his sins.'

There was a pause and Psimon could sense Father Kavanagh's shock and fear.

'So who needs a confessor now, priest? He who committed the sin or he who let it happen?' The stranger spoke in a mocking tone, and in the background the voices whispered with dark malevolence.

Father Kavanagh did not answer but somehow Psimon could sense his breathing, heavy and laboured, and his heart, thumping, thumping... Psimon wrapped his arms around his chest as his own body began to mirror the old priest's anxiety.

'You knew I'd do it, didn't you Father?'

Still Father Kavanagh said nothing and Psimon winced, hunching forward and struggling to breathe through the pain that was crushing his chest.

'What's the matter priest... taken a vow of silence?'

Fighting against the pain Psimon raised his head, looking up at the workmen who were oblivious to what was happening.

'***He*** wasn't silent when I put him to the torment.'

Psimon's eyes grew wide. He did not know what the stranger was talking about but he knew that something terrible had happened, that the stranger had done something terrible. He was about to call to the workmen when he heard a heavy thudding sound coming from the priest's confessional. Before he knew what he was doing Psimon dashed across the aisle and pulled open the priest's door. Father Kavanagh had slipped from his chair and was slumped in the corner of the small room; his hands knotted in his cassock, clutching at his chest.

'Stop it!' said Psimon. 'Stop it, you're hurting him.'

'Who's there?' said the stranger and suddenly the voices ceased their whispering and coalesced into words...

'A witness... a witness in the house of Jehovah...'

'Father, are you all right?' cried Psimon. 'Father Kavanagh, please...'

'Who the fuck is that?' snarled the stranger.

'No one must know...' hissed the voices.

Psimon crouched down beside the stricken priest. He jumped at the sound of the penitent's door flying open and he knew the stranger was coming. Pressing his face against Father Kavanagh's chest he began to cry but when the stranger grabbed the handle and tried to open the priest's door Psimon held it shut.

'Open this fucking door priest,' growled the stranger, and the whispers made his intentions terrifyingly clear...

'Silence the witness...'

'Cut out his tongue...'

'Fill his mouth with dirt...'

Psimon knew that Father Kavanagh was dead. There was nothing he could do. He was just eight years old and he was utterly terrified. The stranger pulled at the door, tearing at the handle with all his animal strength but Psimon closed his eyes and held it shut. If that was all he could do then he would do it. He would hold the door shut. Keep the stranger out.

'Silence the witness...'

'Cut out his tongue...'

'Fill his mouth with dirt...'

Psimon sobbed against the priest's chest. He was losing his battle with the fear and his grip on the door was failing.

Hold the door shut...

Keep the stranger out...

'Hey!'

The shout came from the workmen on top of the scaffolding and the assault on the door came to a sudden stop. The two men began to climb quickly down the ladder and the stranger stepped away from the door. 'What the hell are you doing?' they demanded as they reached the floor but the stranger was already heading towards the back of the church. 'Stop... What've you done? Stop!'

The stranger started to run, racing down one aisle while the workmen gave chase down the other. Oblivious to the presence of the traumatised boy they sprinted for the main doors and the stranger fled before them.

Psimon heard the men charging through the church and, trembling with fear, he pushed himself away from the body of Father Kavanagh. He opened the confessional door and peered round the church now quiet and peaceful as if nothing had happened. With a last tearful look at his friend and confidant he left the confessional and crossed over to the sacristy where there was a side door that was always unlocked. Grasping the heavy iron ring he hauled the door open and gasped as the night air cooled the tears on his face. He was halfway through the door when he heard footsteps coming back into the church. Having lost the stranger in the dark suburban streets the two workmen returned to discover the body of Father Kavanagh.

'Christ!' said one as they opened the door of the confessional. 'Do you think that guy killed him?'

'Either that or he had a heart attack trying to hold the door shut.'

'Don't know how he managed that...' said the other. 'There's no handle on this side.'

The two men looked at the brass plate on the inside of the door. There was no lock, no handle, no way of holding it shut.

Quiet as a ghost Psimon closed the sacristy door. He squeezed his eyes shut and rested his forehead against the cool thick oak. He tried to tell himself that it was over but he knew that it was not; he knew that one day he would meet the stranger again only then there would be no escape. Struggling against the fear that had engulfed his soul he tried to drive the stranger from his mind but all he could see was the vast shadow of a man and the name by which the stranger knew himself...

'Lucifer!'

Psimon sank to his knees and sobbed in fearful silence.

'Lucifer!'

The stranger's name was Lucifer.

Chapter 1

Tuesday March 1st
The Present Day

MISSING

There is still no word on the whereabouts of the eminent psychologist Dr Marcus Bryant who went missing last week near his home in Sefton Park, Liverpool. Police are reluctant to link this latest incident with the murder of several other individuals over the last few years, all of whom worked in the field of mental health. Questions about the existence of a serial killer have been deemed unhelpful.

Psimon watched as the gravediggers levelled the soil over his mother's grave. They arranged the flowers around the headstone and placed a small posy in the centre of the low mound. The foreman turned to him and touched the peak of his cap in respectful salute. Psimon nodded and offered a small smile of thanks then waited as they loaded their tools into the barrow, put on their coats and sauntered away.

The graveyard was quiet. The last of the mourners had long since taken their leave and Psimon was alone at last. It was raining slightly and the air was filled with the loamy scent of earth. Breathing in the smell he moved forward to stand at the foot of the grave. He let out a sigh as the expression on his face turned inwards, the grief softened by a smile of love and enduring fondness. His mother's death had come as no surprise and yet, after twenty-two years of her constant presence, it was difficult to accept that she was gone. He felt the sadness welling up inside but he also felt relief that she had not lived to see him suffer. She was down there now with his dad; together again at last. They were at peace and he was free to do what he had to do. Wiping the tears from his eyes his mind drifted back to the last conversation he had had with his mum.

'Will you tell anyone?' she had asked.

Psimon nodded.

'Who?'

'Everyone.'

She smiled but her smile was tempered with a mother's concern. 'They will fear you.'

'I will help them understand.'

'They will try to control you.'

'Yes...' he replied. 'They will try.'

'And is there someone you trust; someone who can help you?'

'Possibly… Yes.'

'Good… That's good.'

She had closed her eyes a final time. 'Take care of yourself, my love...' she breathed. 'Do what you have to do…'

Psimon nodded at the memory of his mother's final words. Crouching down beside the grave he kissed his fingers and pressed them into the soft mound of earth then he withdrew his hand and rose to his feet.

'Now,' he thought. *'Now I can begin.'*

He had five days to decide his fate, five days before the end. But would it be slow or would it be quick...

'Let it be quick,' he thought. *'Please God... Let it be quick.'*

He lifted his face to the sky and blinked away his tears then he made his way back to the path and turned in the direction of his flat. He paused. Heading that way would take him past the church; past the place where it had all begun. For a moment he wavered. He was not sure he could face it. But the church was just a building… a place of memories.

Lucifer was not there; Lucifer was elsewhere.

Psimon took a breath and began to walk. The light was fading when he reached St Joseph's. He stopped and turned to peer over the black iron railings, his mind leaping back to that terrible night fourteen years ago... the lifeless body of Father Kavanagh, the unsettling sound of whispers and the fury in Lucifer's voice when he realised that someone had overheard his confession. As the memories faded Psimon found that he was gripping the railings. Slowly the tension went out of his body. He let go of the railings and his eyes took on a more determined glint. He shook his head to clear his thoughts then with a final look at the church he continued on his way.

Navigating the leafy suburbs of Manchester it took him another twenty minutes to reach his flat. He opened the front door of the converted Victorian house and climbed the stairs to a second door on the first floor. Opening it he placed his keys on a small unit in the hall. He took off his jacket, loosened his black tie and proceeded down the hall to his spare room. The room was almost empty but there was a chair and a white table beside the door. On it was a pot full of pens, a sprawl of paper and various rolls of adhesive tape. There was also a white padded envelope, a mobile phone and a small black notebook with a thin pencil pushed down into the spine. The notebook looked old and well used.

Psimon picked it up and turned to the first entry...

October 1997. The entry was made some fourteen years ago in the scrawly hand of an eight-year-old boy. Under the date was a name... ~~Father Kavanagh~~. The old priest's name was crossed out and beneath it Psimon had written... I'm sorry.

He flicked through the pages, through the long list of crossed out names, to a page that was divided into six days. In the space for today's date there were two names noted down.

The first was, *mum*. Gently Psimon crossed out the word and drew a single *X* beside it. The second name was, *Dr Marcus Bryant*. He put the tip of the pencil to the name and shook his head in a gesture of regret then slowly his eyes moved across the page to Thursday and another name... *Dr Patrick Denning*. Finally he reached the space marked for Sunday, just five days from now. Here was written a single word, the last word in his little book of death. Here, he had written, *me*.

For several seconds he stared at the word as images of pain and death swam through his mind. He tried to make sense of them, he tried to see beyond them but as he did so he began to sweat. His hands shook, his jaw clenched and his breathing grew ragged until dark spots appeared in his vision and the images were swallowed up in the black shadows of his fear.

Slowly the crippling anxiety faded as Psimon conceded to his fate. He could not stop it; he could not change it. The end was close but before it came there were things he had to do. He reached across the table for the mobile phone. The world needed to know that he existed, or at least that someone like him *could* exist. He had five days in which to tell them and it would start with a phone call.

CHAPTER 2

International Liaison for National Security

The Blenheim Suite

MI5

London

Richard Chatham spoke into the phone as he turned to the computer on his broad walnut desk. 'Thank you Ambassador. I'm just retrieving the files now.' He covered the mouthpiece with his hand and breathed a deep sigh of relief. He had just succeeded in averting an international crisis but it had taken the entire weekend *and* the first day of his long-awaited vacation, and his wife was not amused. The high security network flashed up on his monitor and he entered his password...

T H E R M O P Y L A E 1 3 4 6

Locating the necessary files he entered the ambassador's details, verified the digital signature, and clicked send. 'That's it,' he said, speaking once more into the phone. 'The files should be with you now.' There was a brief pause and Chatham smiled. 'Not at all, ambassador. Thank *you* for being so understanding.' He put down the handset and pressed the red button on the base of the phone to call his aide. A few seconds passed and a tall young man leaned in through the door of Chatham's office.

'You've done it then?' asked the young man.

'Yes, Stokes,' said Chatham. 'You can tell upstairs to stand down.'

Stokes lingered in the doorway. 'Your wife phoned again...' he said. 'She wants to know if you plan on joining her for the rest of your holiday.'

Chatham rolled his eyes but his face took on a guilty flush as his eyes flicked down to his desk and the small black and white photograph of his wife.

'Well you did stand her up at lunchtime,' said Stokes.

'There was an accident,' said Chatham, fixing his aide with a disapproving eye.

'I know, said Stokes. 'She was just upset that you didn't call...'

'I...'

'Lost your mobile phone... I know,' said Stokes. 'I told her...'

'And what did she say?'

'She said that was 'convenient'.'

Chatham sighed. He could not blame his wife for being annoyed. It had been eighteen months since he had last taken a holiday and this one had been murder to arrange. With annoyance he waved Stokes out. 'Just tell them upstairs,' he said.

'Yes sir,' said Stokes and with that he left the room.

Chatham took an exhausted breath. He was just reaching out to call his wife when a phone began to ring. And not just any phone but *the* phone.

He paused. Maybe he had heard wrong. Maybe it was just his desk phone that was ringing. The phone rang again and now there was no mistaking its distinctive tone. Chatham turned to look at the old-fashioned phone that sat on the bureau in the corner of his office. In the seven years he had held this post that phone had rung only five times and none of them was an occasion he was eager to recall. He stared at the large black phone as if it were a Pandora's Box he feared to open but the prospect of ignoring it was not an option. Only a handful of people in the world were cleared to use that line and ignoring any one of them was absolutely unthinkable.

The phone rang a third time but still he hesitated. His wife would never forgive him if he ruined the rest of their holiday. Almost without thinking he got up from his desk, and went to stand over the bureau.

The phone rang a fourth time.

Four times was tardy; five would be downright rude, and if the phone was left to ring six times Chatham would be getting a call from his superiors. There was no doubt about it… this call was going to screw up his week but Richard Chatham could not abide rudeness. He picked up the phone. 'Blenheim Suite, Chatham speaking,' he said, following the accepted protocol.

'My apologies for ruining your holiday, Mr Chatham.'

In an instant Chatham went from professional resignation to icy alertness. That was not a conventional reply and the voice was not one that he recognised. The accent was English but not the Prime Minister's Eton English; this was more northerly, Manchester maybe…

'Who is this?' he demanded.

'This is not the time for introductions, Mr Chatham. I just need you to listen.'

The voice was self-assured but despite that there was a distinct note of weariness to it.

'How did you get this number?' Chatham was playing for time, trying to collect his thoughts. He was still reeling from the fact that an unauthorised individual had managed to get access to this line. Stepping away from the bureau he reached across his desk and began to stab at the red button on the base of his normal desk phone.

'I'm sorry Mr Chatham. I'm not in a position to answer your questions at the moment. But I do need your attention.'

Chatham waited impatiently for Stokes to answer the buzzer. At the same time he tried to glean as much detail about the caller as possible.

He was male… young… early-twenties…

The door to Chatham's office opened and Stokes poked his head into the room. 'Sir?' The frantic beeping of the intercom had effectively communicated the urgency of the summons.

Chatham made a rapid circling motion with his finger and pointed to the handset held to his ear. He also mouthed the words, *'Trace this call!'*

Stokes looked down at the phone on Chatham's desk. He seemed puzzled by the fact that the handset was still in place. Chatham covered the mouthpiece of the phone he was holding. 'Not that one you idiot... This one!' He pointed to the phone sitting on the bureau.

Stokes looked at the old-fashioned phone and comprehension finally dawned. He disappeared rapidly from the doorway and Chatham returned his full attention to the caller on the line.

'Are you still there, Mr Chatham?' said the caller as if he had been waiting for Chatham to finish.

'Yes, I'm still here. Now who the hell is this? This is a restricted…'

'Please, Mr Chatham. I do not have time to explain. Now, do you have a pen and paper?'

Needled at being cut off like that Chatham grabbed a pencil from a rosewood desk-tidy and flipped open his leather-bound diary. He glanced anxiously at the door to his office, wondering how Stokes was coming along with the trace. It would not be an easy task. This was a clean line… no computer screening, no automatic recording, no network and exchange software. The people who used this phone had to know that their words were treated with the utmost confidentiality.

'Go ahead,' said Chatham trying to sound calm when in truth he was deeply unsettled by this breach of security. If someone had managed to get hold of this number then he wondered what other sensitive information they might have access to. He was about to find out.

'Please write down the following letters and numbers as I call them out,' the caller directed.

Chatham's pencil hovered over the page. *'What kind of perverse game is this?'*

'T…' the voice said.

Chatham wrote a capital T at the top of the page.

'H… E… R…M… O… P…Y… L… A… E…'

A chill ran down Chatham's spine as he recognised the first part of his password for accessing the classified files of the Blenheim Suite. As a student of history Chatham had combined two famous battles to make up his password. The first was the battle of Thermopylae from the Greco-Persian Wars, the second was the battle of Crècy which took place on the 26th of August 1346.

'1… 3… 4… 6…' the voice on the line continued.

Thermopylae1346… Chatham's password to information that could undermine the United Kingdom's relations with half the countries in the developed world.

Chatham felt sick.

'Who is this?' he asked in a voice that was all but robbed of breath.

'As I indicated, Mr Chatham. I am not going to tell you my name at this time. I apologise for the secrecy but for the moment it is necessary. I have contacted you because I believe I can trust you. I hope in time you will learn to trust me but for now I just need you to write down the names of the following people.'

Chatham's brain was buzzing with so many thoughts that he barely registered what the caller had just said.

'Mr Chatham?'

'Yes…' said Chatham. 'Yes, I'm ready.' Chatham's mind raced as he began to write. *'Who **is** this? What do they want?'*

'First of all, there's Greater Manchester's Chief Coroner, Sir Daniel Coombs.'

'Has somebody died?' asked Chatham.

'Not yet, Mr Chatham. Now please, just note down the names.'

Chatham bridled at being spoken to like this but he wrote the name down all the same.

'Then there's the German psychiatrist... Heinrich Döllinger.'

'How did he get this number?' thought Chatham. *'And how the **hell** does he know my password?'*

'Yale's Professor of Neurology... Harvey Osler,' the caller added.

The list ran to seventeen names and included scientists, doctors, military personnel and even religious leaders from at least thirteen different countries. Scanning the list Chatham wondered what they could possibly have in common and what the caller wanted him to do with the list.

'Do you have them noted down?' the caller asked.

'Yes,' replied Chatham. 'But I don't see how they concern me. I deal in the political arena.'

'Oh, you're too modest, Mr Chatham,' the caller chided. 'You deal in far more than that.'

Chatham remained silent. True, his remit was largely political but the methods he used to achieve his ends had more in common with a spymaster from the era of the Cold War. But Chatham was not a high profile member of the security services. He worked behind the scenes, the oil between the cogs of power. If Chatham was doing his job properly then he should not be noticed at all. 'That's as maybe,' he said. 'But what is it you want from me? Why this list of people? Do you *have* information? Something that could help the British government?'

'Not exactly.'

'Then what?' said Chatham with growing exasperation. 'What is it you want me to do?'

'I want you to send them an invitation.'

'An invitation to what?'

'I'm afraid that will have to wait for another time.'

'What do you mean, *another time*?' said Chatham, sensing that the caller was bringing their conversation to a close.

'We will speak again, Mr Chatham,' the caller said in a tone of certainty that Chatham found far from reassuring. 'For now, I think your colleague has some information for you.'

'Wait!' said Chatham as Stokes reappeared in the doorway.

'Goodbye, Mr Chatham. And once again I am sorry for ruining your holiday.'

The caller hung up and the buzz of the disconnected line was like the bewildered buzzing of Chatham's mind. *'What the hell had just happened? What the hell was all that about?'* Slowly Chatham lowered the handset from his ear. Then he looked up at Stokes whose expression suggested that he had never seen his boss this unsettled before. 'What have you got?' asked Chatham in a voice that made his young aide shrink behind the door.

Stokes hesitated.

'Tell me you got something,' said Chatham. 'The guy was on for ages, you must have got something!'

'Yes, we got something,' said Stokes. 'But you're not going to like it.'

Richard Chatham leaned heavily on his broad walnut desk. It seemed that one crisis was over but the next had only just begun. Someone had done the unthinkable. They had successfully breached one of the upper tiers of MI5 security. They had undermined the integrity of the Blenheim Suite and they had ensured that he would be working every hour God sent until he had some answers. He screwed up his face in frustrated anguish and glanced at the black and white photo on his desk. Of all the questions flooding through his mind there was one that stood out more starkly than all the rest…

How the hell was he going to tell his wife?

CHAPTER 3

Psimon's hand shook as he lowered the mobile phone and pressed the button to end the call. He had tried to sound calm and confident while in truth he had felt sick with nerves. But that was it. That was the first call, the crucial call that set everything else in motion. Now he just had to see it through, if he could.

Reaching across the table he picked up the padded envelope and dropped the mobile phone inside. He sealed the envelope and turned it over to check the address.

Richard Chatham
International Liaison for National Security
The Blenheim Suite
MI5
London

He hoped that Mr Chatham would be relieved to get his phone back but he suspected its return would only add to the sense of futility that the poor man was undoubtedly feeling. Still, he could not suppress a wicked little smile at Chatham's bewilderment. Putting the package down he picked up a black marker and approached the far wall of his spare room which was covered by a mass of notes, newspaper cuttings and pictures, most of them concerning abductions and gruesome, unsolved murders. There were photographs of individuals alongside travel schedules, maps and obscure technical blueprints. And everything was covered with interconnecting lines and arrows. It looked like the obsessive wall of a madman.

Psimon moved to the left-hand-side of the wall, where a small piece of paper bore the words 'Richard Chatham MI5'. He underlined the name and gave it a self-satisfied little tick. Only one picture lay to the left of Chatham's name and Psimon brushed the photograph of his parents lightly with his fingertips.

With a sigh of exhaustion he stepped back from the wall. What he really needed now was sleep but he found himself hovering, his eyes drawn to a small piece of fluorescent orange paper bearing a mobile telephone number and the name **'Steve Brennus'**. This piece of paper lay at the centre of the wall with numerous lines and arrows radiating from it. Pinned to the wall beside it were a Virgin Airlines envelope and a receipt from a local florist for a bouquet of flowers and a 'large, stuffed Nemo'.

Psimon continued to stare at the piece of paper, his hand aching as he gripped the marker in his fist. His heart began to pound and beads of sweat stood out upon his brow. To acknowledge that piece of paper was to acknowledge the very worst of all his fears.

'Not just now,' he breathed.

This deferment was enough and the tension went out of his body. With a deep breath he turned away from the wall. He put the marker back on the table and was about to leave the room when a sense of overwhelming fear rose up inside him. An image sprang into his mind; the image of a man standing bound and naked on the stone floor of a crudely built chapel. A dark figure loomed over him. It was the dark figure of Lucifer.

Psimon's face grew pale and fixed with terror then his head was snatched back as if someone had hit him in the face with something hard. With a choking cry he was sent reeling back against the wall. He raised his hands as if to fend off another blow. 'No! Please no…' he gasped although he was completely alone in the room. Another invisible blow smashed into the side of his knee and with an agonised grunt he fell to the floor. 'Not again! Please…' He cowered against the wall, his trembling hands still trying to shield his face.

The blows had ceased and Psimon looked up as if someone were speaking to him. He began to cry, shaking his head in hopeless denial. He knew what was coming next. His eyes grew wide with horror then his body convulsed in agony as a spatter of lesions appeared on his face.

He screamed as the burning began.

'Yes!' he cried. 'Yes... I confess!' But it was too late. Even now he could feel the shroud closing around his body. 'No,' he sobbed. 'No…' And then he spoke no more. His words were choked off and his eyes began to bulge. The muscles in his face and neck strained with desperate futility but the blackness was closing in around him, his vision shrinking down to a dark, diminishing tunnel…

And then… as suddenly as it had materialised, it was gone; the pain was gone.

Psimon drew a shuddering breath. His entire body shook as he glanced around the room as if trying to convince himself there was no one there. Finally he let out a tremulous sigh and leaned back against the wall. He sat for a minute or two in shock then rose unsteadily to his feet. With trembling fingers he plucked the small piece of orange paper from the wall then, stumbling across the room, he collapsed into the chair at the table beside the door. With one hand he wiped the tears from his face, with the other he reached for his small black note book. His hands shook as he turned to the page marked for today then he took out the thin pencil and crossed out the name of Dr Marcus Bryant. Beneath it he wrote, I'm sorry. He squeezed his eyes shut as a tight knot of guilt twisted inside him. Once again Lucifer had taken a life and once again *he* had been unable to stop him. He closed the notebook and stared at the small piece of orange paper.

'No,' he breathed. 'I can't do this alone.'

Reaching inside his jacket he took out his own mobile phone then he closed his eyes and took a few deep breaths to compose himself. When he was ready he raised the phone and entered the number. There was no need for him to check it; he knew the number by heart.

*

Steve Brennus stood in the front room of his parents' Welsh cottage, a mobile phone held to his ear. He dropped a beautifully prepared business plan on the coffee table and slumped into the armchair by the window as his accountant confirmed what he already knew.

He was screwed.

'I'm sorry Steve. But they've already extended the deadline twice... Unless you can come up with twelve thousand pounds by next Thursday the bank will take possession of the house.'

Steve put a hand to his head.

'I still can't believe it's all gone?' said his accountant after a pause. 'Three hundred thousand pounds is an awful lot to lose in one night.'

Steve snorted bitterly. 'Apparently Christine's brother has a gift for losing money.'

'Have you spoken to her?'

'No. Not since she phoned from the hospital.'

There was an awkward silence.

'They'll want you back,' said his accountant. 'They just need a bit of time.'

'Sure,' said Steve.

'You should call her...'

'No. She'll call me when she's ready.'

Another uncomfortable pause.

'Listen Steve,' began his accountant. 'Jenny and I have got more shares. We could easily...'

'No, Mike, really...' said Steve. 'You've already done more than enough.'

'Don't worry about that... Things'll work themselves out. You'll see.'

Steve couldn't bring himself to answer. 'I have to go...' he said

'Okay. You take care of yourself. And call me if you need anything...'

Steve ended the call and put his phone down on the coffee table. Looking through the rain-streaked window he gazed at the vast, dim shapes of the Welsh mountains. Even on a dismal evening like this they managed to look glorious, indomitable, like the Welsh spirit, his mate Paddy would have said. He glanced at a photograph on the mantelpiece, five hard-faced young men in combat fatigues, sitting together on a sand-coloured Landover. Their uniforms bore no sign of the SAS regiment in which they served but Christine had cut out a picture of the famous 'winged dagger' and stuck it in the corner of the frame. Steve shook his head, a nostalgic smile creeping onto his face.

Grabbing a bottle of water from the coffee table he went to stand before the mantel piece. At the centre was a picture of Steve with an attractive woman and a beautiful young girl. His smile broadened but then his eyes closed and his face contorted with a frown of regret. 'What a fucking mess,' he said softly to himself.

Shaking his head he took a mouthful of water and placed the bottle on the mantel piece then he went to get the rest of his things from the car. The rain was getting heavier so he grabbed his father's waxed-cotton jacket from the peg in the hall. His father had been every bit as tall as Steve although not as solidly built. The jacket felt tight but Steve liked to wear it when he came to the cottage. He found the smell comforting.

In the living room Steve's mobile phone began to ring.

'Christine,' he breathed and some of the weight seemed to lift from his face as he dashed back into the front room of the cottage. His heart was suddenly racing but his face fell as he picked up his phone. There was no sign of Christine's name on the phone's screen and he did not recognise the caller's number. With a heavy sigh he pressed the button to accept the call. 'Hello.'

'Hello, Mr Brennus.'

The caller sounded shaken up and for a moment Steve thought it was Christine's brother, Paul, calling to apologise for ruining his life. But no, this guy sounded younger.

‘Who is this?’ said Steve as he shrugged himself into the waxed cotton jacket.

‘My name is Psimon and I would like to employ your services.’

‘As what?’ asked Steve becoming suddenly wary.

Psimon paused. ‘As a chaperon, I suppose you might say.’

‘You mean bodyguard,’ said Steve with annoyance. ‘You want a bodyguard.’

‘In a sense, yes.’

‘I’m not in the security business anymore. Haven’t been for years. Besides, I’m not really trained for personal protection. If you need a specialist I can…’

‘I don’t need an expert,’ said Psimon. ‘I need you.’

‘Thanks a lot!’ thought Steve. His thumb twitched to end the call but he was curious to know how this guy had got hold of his number.

‘Who put you on to me?’ he asked. ‘How did you get this number?’

‘That’s not important,’ said Psimon. ‘What’s important is that I need your help… and you need mine.’

Steve’s attention was now fully engaged. ‘In what way can you help me?’

‘I will pay you three thousand pounds a day for five days employment. Plus expenses,’ said Psimon.

Steve’s eyebrows lifted in surprise. Fifteen thousand pounds was enough to prevent the bank foreclosing on the house. However, going back into the field of personal security held no appeal for him, and Christine would never approve. ‘Not interested,’ he said.

‘Are you sure?’ said Psimon. ‘Fifteen thousand pounds...’

‘Money isn’t everything.’

‘No... But the love of a wife and daughter is.’

‘What the hell do you know about my wife and daughter?’

'I know that you didn't mean to hurt her,' said Psimon. 'And that they will miss you when you don't come home.'

Steve spun round in the small living room of the cottage. He was suddenly anxious, confused and furious. Was this guy threatening him? He said he wanted to help. What the hell was going on?

'Mr Brennus,' said Psimon. 'I have no desire to add to your troubles. I wouldn't be calling you at all if I didn't think it was necessary.' He paused allowing Steve to absorb what he was saying. 'But I really do need your help. And I'm not trying to intimidate you either… I really can help sort things out with your wife and your little girl.'

'How do you know about this?' said Steve. 'No one knows about this… Are you a friend of Paul's? Did he put you up to this?' Steve knew he was ranting and he hated the sense of being in the dark; of feeling so unnerved.

'No one put me up to this, Mr Brennus,' said Psimon. 'I will explain in more detail when we meet.'

Steve gave a hollow laugh. 'And what makes you think I'm willing to meet you?' He was suddenly calm and more annoyed than ever.

'You will agree to meet me because you will want to know what I know. And…' said Psimon. 'You really could do with the money.'

There was a long and deeply uncomfortable silence in which Steve tried to think of any way he could possibly ignore this strange and infuriating guy on the other end of the telephone. After almost a minute he knew there was not.

'Where?' he said… 'When?'

*

Psimon put the phone down and breathed a deep sigh of relief.

There, he had done it. He had made the call; faced his fear.

It was the fear that made him uncertain. It was the fear that clouded his view. For all his insight the fear was like a black shadow that engulfed his mind. There were gaps in the shadow and glimpses of what might lie beyond but the gaps were filled with pain and what lay beyond seemed insubstantial. More like wishful thinking than concrete reality. He drew his hands over his face. The trauma of the mysterious attack was still evident in his trembling limbs but that was not the first time he had experienced violence like that and he knew, with sickening certainty, that it would not be the last. However, the growing intensity of the attacks was almost more than he could bear. But bear it he must, for the next five days at least. One way or another that would decide it.

Decide the manner of his death that is…

Psimon rose from the chair and limped through to the bathroom to examine his face in the mirror. His left eye was badly swollen with a livid red mark across his temple. The spattering of pockmarks was still intensely painful but even now they were beginning to fade. A wave of exhaustion swept over him and he leaned heavily on the hand basin. He had to remain strong; he had to remain focussed. It had taken many months to plan the next five days, he could not lose it now. He was frightened and tired and needed to get some sleep because tomorrow he was going to meet Steve Brennus.

Steve Brennus, the man that he hoped would kill him.

CHAPTER 4

Lucifer was satisfied.
Lucifer was sated.
One less voice of heresy in a world of lies.

Dressed in the filthy cassock and cotta of an altar server Lucifer gazed at the inverted crucifix that hung battered and splintered from the bare stone walls of his chapel. He was filled with the glory of the chorus but slowly the ecstasy lifted from his mind. He looked at the body of the heretic lying at his feet; the broken face, the shattered knee, the smoking flesh. He bent down, removed the hose from the shroud and sealed it with a plastic tie before lifting the body from the slick and sticky paving stones. Soft hues from the stained-glass-window fell across his massive form as, with apparent ease, he raised the man's grotesquely wrapped corpse high above the altar. The sleeves of his cassock fell back to reveal powerful arms covered with a hatch work of scars, and lines of scripture crudely tattooed or burned into the skin.

With something closer to control than care, Lucifer laid the limp body on the altar. He pinched out the thick tallow candles and stepped back from the great slab of marble. He genuflected in the aisle between the short rows of crudely made pews then he rose from his knee, crossed himself and retired.

CHAPTER 5

Wednesday March 2nd

TORTURE

Police have refused to confirm that the body of a man found earlier this morning on the outskirts of Liverpool, is that of the missing psychologist, Dr Marcus Bryant.

They have also refused to comment on the cause of death or the nature of Dr Bryant's injuries, although witnesses at the scene have reported signs of apparent torture.

Steve Brennus picked his way up the wooded hillside of Alderley Edge. He knew the Edge well and had been surprised that his mysterious caller had chosen this particular location for their meeting. The path levelled out and Steve paused beside a sandstone outcrop at the foot of which was a shallow stone basin filled with water. Above the basin an inscription had been carved into the rock, now weatherworn and barely visible but Steve knew what it said...

Drink of this

and take thy fill

For the water falls

by the wizard's will

Above the words one could just make out the image of a wizard's face. Steve smiled as he continued along the woodland path. He had always loved the legend of Alderly Edge…

A hundred enchanted knights lying beneath the hollow hill, sleeping in wizard-induced slumber. And beside each knight a milk-white steed. A hundred knights, ready to ride out and defeat evil in the hour of Britain's greatest need.

Steve had spent endless days as a child exploring the rocks and caves of the Edge searching for the secret gates beyond which the knights were said to lie. He and Christine had brought Sally here. They had raced down the forest tracks, stopping at every rock face to rap on it with their 'staffs' to see if the golden gates of magic would appear. They never did of course but the magic was not diminished.

A spasm of regret gripped Steve's chest at the thought of his wife and daughter. Waking without them had been the most miserable experience but he did not know how to fix what he had done, and he would not go back until he did. With an effort he pushed them from the forefront of his mind and brought his attention back to the reason why he was here.

'Stormy Point, five o-clock,' the man called Psimon had said.

Stormy Point was a famous prominence on the Edge where a jumble of sandstone boulders forged an opening in the forested slopes to reveal the wide expanse of the Cheshire plain.

Another half mile saw Steve drawing close to the agreed meeting place. Following his military training he left the path and circled round through the undergrowth to come at the Point from the opposite direction. If this guy was actually there he wanted to get a good look at him before he made his presence known. Moving slowly now he scrambled up a bank and, using a stunted holly bush for cover, he peered out through a cleft in the rocks.

A young man sat on the rocks some fifty yards away staring out across the plain, a mobile phone held to his ear. Dressed in jeans, light walking boots and a brown corduroy jacket, he looked too normal to be Steve's mystery caller, too pleasant. Cautiously Steve shifted his position to see if there was anyone else there…

Nope, no one.

He glanced down at his watch…

Five o-clock dead.

Steve looked back up and felt his balls tighten with the cold chill of discovery. The young man was staring directly at him, a strange smile on his 'pleasant' face. Steve cursed himself as he realised he had just broken one of the primary rules of engagement… never underestimate the enemy.

Forsaking any vestige of stealth Steve came out from his hiding place and made his way across the open space.

The young man put away his mobile phone and stood to meet him.

'Psimon?' said Steve as he came within a yard or two. His manner was gruff almost menacing. Their phone conversation was still fresh in his mind. This man had made mention of his family and Steve was here to make damn sure that he meant them no harm.

Psimon held out his hand.

'Mr Brennus,' he said. 'Thank you for coming.'

Steve stepped forward and hesitated before taking the young man's hand. 'You left me little choice,' he said.

Psimon smiled apologetically. He released Steve's hand and invited him to take a seat on the rocks. 'Forgive me,' he said. 'I wanted to make sure you would come.'

Steve remained standing for a moment. Whatever he had been expecting this was not it. He placed great store on first impressions and his instincts told him that this 'Psimon' was all right… a typically nice guy. Slender build and tall, though not quite up to Steve's six-two. He wore his sandy brown hair casually long, and with his prominent cheekbones and grey eyes he was essentially a good-looking young man. His face was discoloured with some nasty bruising but that looked to be a week or two old and would soon be gone.

No, not what he had been expecting at all.

Despite the unsettling intrigue of that first phone call Steve found Psimon's demeanour to be gentle, almost timid. Only his eyes suggested that there might be more. There was a strange intensity to Psimon's gaze but there was something else too; something that Steve had seen many times before; something with which he was all to familiar… fear.

Much of Steve's apprehension leeched away and he sat down on the bare ground just a few feet from Psimon. Whatever trouble this kid was in Steve suspected that he would not have to sell his soul to keep him safe. *'What was it?'* he thought. *'Borrowed money from the wrong people... selling dope on some thug's turf in Manchester... some kind of corporate trouble maybe...'*

'Do you believe in psychics, Mr Brennus?' asked Psimon suddenly.

'What do you mean?' said Steve momentarily thrown by the unexpected question. 'Bending spoons or talking to the dead?'

'Mediums claim to be able to speak to the dead,' clarified Psimon. 'While bending spoons comes under the heading of 'macro-psychokinesis.'

'As opposed to micro…'

'Psychokinesis,' Psimon finished for him. 'Yes.'

'Which is?' queried Steve playing along for the sake of it.

'The ability to influence things on a small scale… computers, electrical circuits, that kind of thing.'

'You're talking ESP.'

'Yes.'

'Moving things with your mind… reading people's thoughts… prophesying the future.'

'They call it precognition,' said Psimon.

'No,' said Steve.

'No, what?' asked Psimon.

'No, I don't believe in psychics,' said Steve with annoyance. *'If this was some kind of wind-up, some kind of scam...'*

Psimon looked at Steve with his deep grey eyes. 'You've never had something happen to you that you can't explain?' he asked.

'Course I have,' admitted Steve. 'But that doesn't mean it was supernatural.'

'True,' agreed Psimon.

There was a moment's silence between the two men.

'My dad claimed to have had psychic experiences,' said Steve, somewhat irritated that he had been drawn into this ridiculous conversation.

'Are you calling your dad a liar then?' challenged Psimon.

'No,' replied Steve. 'I believe what he said happened. We just reached different conclusions about how it happened.'

Psimon gave a satisfied nod. He reached into his jacket pocket and pulled out a brown envelope. He reached across and laid it on the rock within arm's reach of Steve.

'What's that?' asked Steve.

'There's three thousand pounds in there, Mr Brennus,' said Psimon. 'I will pay you another three thousand pounds a day if you will accompany me while I go about my business and keep me safe for the next five days.'

'What happens in the next five days?' asked Steve.

'I die,' said Psimon and the fear that Steve had perceived in him earlier was suddenly brimming in his eyes.

'What do you mean?' asked Steve not at all certain that he wanted to know the answer.

'I have two visions of my death, Mr Brennus,' said Psimon, his voice strained with the effort of speaking about something which quite obviously terrified him. He looked away before going on…

'One in which I drown in agony and despair…'

'And the other?' asked Steve with a sudden sense of foreboding.

Psimon turned back and there was a kind of pleading in his eyes. 'In the other... you stab me in the face with a short-bladed knife.'

Steve felt a chill run down his spine. 'Not a chance,' he stated with angry conviction.

But still Psimon looked at him.

'Listen,' said Steve rising to his feet. 'I can see you're in trouble. I can see you're frightened.' He held out the envelope of cash. 'But my days of hurting people are over,' he said, wishing with all his heart that that was true.

'But that's why I need you,' protested Psimon. 'Because I don't want anyone hurt over the next five days.'

'You just said I was going to fucking kill you!' snapped Steve, beginning to lose his composure.

Psimon's eyes pleaded with him for a moment longer then with a tremulous sigh he lowered his eyes.

'Listen,' said Steve suddenly, his distrust finally giving way to sympathy for this frightened kid. 'You don't need me... the police maybe or a doctor.'

'You mean a psychiatrist,' said Psimon and the expression in his eyes changed to one of disdain.

'Well I don't know,' said Steve sheepishly. 'You seem a little...'

'Nuts,' said Psimon.

'Well... yes,' admitted Steve.

Psimon suddenly smiled and the haughty expression faded from his eyes. The two men glanced at each other furtively for a minute or two. Finally Psimon turned away looking out once more over the rural landscape below them. Steve hovered beside him. Not wanting to stay but not wanting to seem too hard-hearted either. The envelope of money felt uncomfortable in his hand so he laid it down beside Psimon.

'What if there was?' asked Psimon still staring off into the distance.

'Was what?' asked Steve.

'Someone with genuine psychic ability.'

'Are you saying you're psychic? Is that how you seem to know so much about me?' said Steve, making no attempt to disguise the scorn in his voice. He was still annoyed about the references Psimon had made to his family during the previous day's phone call.

'I'm not saying anything,' replied Psimon. 'But what if there really was someone in the world who could read people's thoughts, see into the future, move things with their minds…'

Steve looked down at Psimon. His bearing was suddenly more upright than it had been, his jaw set more determinedly. He seemed somehow more mature than Steve had first given him credit for.

'I don't know,' said Steve. 'I guess I've never really thought about it.'

'I have,' said Psimon looking up at Steve. 'I've thought about it a lot.'

Despite his misgivings Steve had the growing feeling that he had misjudged this guy Psimon entirely. He had been trying to figure out the kid's angle, to identify the catch that he would later come to regret. But he was finally becoming convinced that Psimon was on the level. That there was no hidden agenda…

'Other than the fact that he thinks you're going to kill him,' Steve reminded himself.

Steve suddenly found himself feeling sorry for Psimon. Not in a patronising way, more in the way he might have looked out for a rookie soldier in their first real firefight. With a sigh of resignation Steve sat down once more.

Psimon glanced across at him. 'Thank you, Mr Brennus,' he said softly.

'Steve… Call me Steve.'

Psimon smiled shyly and gave him a small affirmative nod. The relief in his eyes was unmistakable.

'Hold your horses,' thought Steve. *'I haven't said yes yet!'*

Psimon's smile broadened and his gaze drifted back out over the plain. There followed another, more companionable pause. Finally Psimon broke the silence. 'How would you feel if there was someone who could read your mind?' he asked.

'Nervous,' replied Steve with an appropriately nervous laugh.

'And how would the Prime Minister feel?' asked Psimon turning to look at Steve. 'How would a president feel?'

Steve's eyes narrowed as he met Psimon's intense gaze, the hairs on the back of his neck rising unpleasantly. He knew the havoc that a wayward email could cause a government let alone someone who could read their most damaging, their most sordid secrets.

'And what if you had committed murder and you lived a hunted life of violence and deceit?' asked Psimon. 'How would you feel then?'

'Terrified,' said Steve in a voice that was little more than a whisper.

The intensity slowly faded from Psimon's eyes but he continued to hold Steve captivated. 'So what do you say, Mr Brennus…' he said at last. 'Will you help me? Will you be my guardian angel for the next five days?'

For the longest time Steve just looked at Psimon, trying to make sense of all the things they had been talking about. The fact was he did not believe in psychic phenomena. And that just left a frightened young man who, at worst, seemed to be suffering from some kind of delusion. Maybe he had convinced some paranoid and dangerous individual that he really could disclose their dirty little secrets. In which case his life could well be in danger. And if that were so then Steve could certainly help him. In the end he went with his gut instinct. The kid was frightened and needed help; the kind of help that Steve could provide. Besides, as Psimon himself had said… he could do with the money.

'Yes,' said Steve at last. 'But no more of this 'I'm going to kill you malarkey'… deal?'

'Thank you Steve,' said Psimon and a single tear rolled down his cheek.

Steve looked away awkwardly and together they took in the twilight view from Stormy Point on Alderley Edge.

‘So what about you…’ asked Steve with a sideways glance at Psimon. ‘Do you think there’s a person out there with genuine psychic powers.’

‘Out there…’ said Psimon and his gaze swept across the Cheshire plain as if he were taking in the entire world.

‘No,’ he said. ‘Not a single one!’

CHAPTER 6

Richard Chatham put down the old-fashioned handset and reset the newly installed monitoring equipment. He had been wryly amused when his mobile phone had turned up at his office earlier today. Phoning him on his own mobile phone had been a neat trick but now the mysterious phone-thief had called back and this time he had not been so clever… not by half.

The phone he had used this time belonged to a woman. Admittedly it was a woman who had recently died but every new piece of information now added to the file that would, sooner or later, lead them to their man.

'But what would they find,' thought Chatham. He looked over the data that had been accumulated.

Male… Caucasian… mid twenties… British native… South Manchester accent… moderate levels of stress… no indication of deception…

Chatham had already gleaned much of this information himself but it was reassuring to have it confirmed by the voice analysis software. But now, in addition to the growing profile, they had a name…

Psimon

Having spoken to him a second time Chatham no longer felt the overwhelming sense of shock that had so unnerved him during their first call. In fact, despite some serious misgivings, he was convinced that 'Psimon' meant them no harm, *them* being MI5 and the British government in general. In fact, if the information that he had provided turned out to be reliable, he could just be the most valuable informant that Chatham had ever dealt with.

Chatham had no idea how Psimon could know the things he did but however he managed it this guy was frighteningly accurate; a quality that the security services prized above all else. So at least some things were becoming clear...

Psimon wanted to make a deal.

He had something that was of considerable value to MI5 but he also wanted a couple of things in return. The first was certainly possible to arrange. Indeed Chatham already had the 'guest list' from their first phone conversation. A symposium at the Dstl, the Defence Science and Technology Laboratory at Porton Down in Wiltshire, the UK government's most secure research facility. The second request was for something that Chatham was not at all sure he could provide... legal immunity for a Mr Steven Brennus, and not just standard immunity...

Class A Transactional Immunity... the highest level of immunity that it was possible to award.

This would effectively place the recipient outside, or rather beyond the law, granting them immunity not only from any form of prosecution but also from any form of detention by law enforcement agencies. Such a status could only conceivably be granted to someone who possessed information of imminent and critical importance to national security. Someone who knew the location and deactivation sequence of a nuclear bomb in the heart of London... that kind of thing.

'Check it with the Chancellor,' Psimon had said. 'He can get authorisation from the Prime Minister.'

'I'm not about to phone the Chancellor of the Exchequer,' Chatham had said.

'You won't need to,' said Psimon with annoying confidence. 'He'll call you.'

Chatham had laughed at his mystery caller's certainty but something told him that his laughter would soon ring hollow. Now, as he sat there pondering their second conversation Chatham wondered just what could be so important that it might require legal immunity, so compelling that Psimon expected some of the most eminent minds in the world to attend a symposium at his bidding. He looked down at the title that Psimon had given him for the week-long seminar…

First and Only

'*First and only what?*' thought Chatham, sitting back in his chair with a sigh of frustration. And yet, in spite of the fact that this 'case' was playing havoc with his personal life, he was already looking forward to the next call from Mr First and Only. He smiled and opened his laptop to update his ongoing report.

For the first time in seven years Richard Chatham was enjoying his job.

CHAPTER 7

For as long as he could remember Psimon had been afraid. But now, as he followed Steve Brennus down the forest track, he felt… not safe exactly but protected; protected from the violence, the madness, the unrelenting hatred of the man that haunted his dreams and stalked his every waking thought.

'Was it enough?' thought Psimon. *'Would it be enough?'*

The truth was he did not know. He had never been able to face 'the fear'; never been able to see beyond it. It lay like a poisoned knot in his mind, confounding any attempt to penetrate it. But now at least he had done what he could. He had walked the enchanted paths of Alderley Edge and come away with a knight of his own.

He was content.

He watched the way Steve walked over the slippery uneven ground, never losing his footing, moving with the economy of motion that came from years of physical training. Beneath his bulky, waxed-cotton jacket and brown denim jeans lay a lean and muscular physique. Despite the flecks of grey hair that peppered Steve's temples one might have taken him for an athlete or a boxer but not necessarily for the soldier that he was. The soldier that he once had been.

Steve Brennus, ex-para, ex-SAS… now failed entrepreneur and ex-happily married family man.

His face was all hard lines and rugged edges and might have been considered ugly but for the warmth of his brown eyes. Steve had the kind of face that could stop a fight before it began but it was also a face that fell easily into a smile, an honest smile that softened his harsh features and put people at their ease. Psimon liked his face and found himself looking at it whenever Steve glanced back to make sure he was okay.

'What are you looking at?' asked Steve as he became aware of Psimon's scrutiny.

'Nothing,' said Psimon feeling caught out.

'You're not gay are you?' asked Steve.

'Why, would that be a problem?'

'Not in the slightest,' said Steve. 'Just seemed like you were checking me out.'

'Appraising, maybe,' suggested Psimon.

'Huh,' said Steve. He stopped on the path and turned to face Psimon. 'And how do I measure up?' he asked.

Psimon looked him up and down.

'Well, you're smaller than I expected,' he said, the corners of his mouth twitching.

'Cheeky bastard,' said Steve turning away and heading back down the path but Psimon had seen the beginnings of a smile on his face.

The ground levelled out as they neared the road and Psimon could see a dark BMW parked up in a lay-by where the path emerged from the woods. Steve reached into his pocket and a moment later the BMW gave a little beep-beep, its indicators flashing in recognition as Steve pressed the button on his key.

'Nice car,' said Psimon.

'Not for long.'

Psimon grimaced apologetically and made no further comment. Then at Steve's invitation he opened the door and settled into the passenger seat pushing his bag down between his feet.

Steve took off his jacket and threw it onto the back seat before getting in beside him.

'Okay,' he said. 'First things first…'

Psimon took a deep breath and readied himself.

'Who am I protecting you from?'

Psimon had been expecting the question but it still felt strange now that it came to it.

‘I don’t know,’ he said, cringing slightly at the vagueness of his answer.

‘What do you mean you don’t know?’ asked Steve.

‘Well I’ve never *actually* met him,’ admitted Psimon. ‘I don’t know who he is.’

Steve looked across at him. ‘So somebody’s threatened you from a distance,’ he said. ‘Letters, phone calls…’

‘No,’ said Psimon. ‘We’ve never actually spoken, not really.’

‘But you have had some contact,’ pressed Steve. ‘Some reason to think he might want to hurt you?’

‘Oh yes,’ said Psimon in a voice of dark intensity.

‘Right,’ said Steve with obvious relief. ‘So when did you last have contact?’

‘Fourteen years ago,’ said Psimon.

Steve shifted round in his seat to look directly at Psimon.

‘Let me get this straight,’ he said. ‘You want me to protect you from a guy you’ve never ‘actually met’, never ‘actually’ spoken to; a guy you’ve not had any kind of contact with for *fourteen years*!’

‘I wouldn’t say no contact exactly,’ said Psimon enigmatically, his eyes flashing up to meet Steve’s exasperated gaze.

‘Okay,’ said Steve making an effort to remain patient. ‘Why don’t you start from the beginning.’

Psimon looked down at his hands. He said nothing for a while, then…

‘I was eight years old,’ he began. ‘I’d gone to church to talk to our parish priest. He was a friend of mine,’ he added as if this was important.

Steve said nothing, only settled back in his seat to listen.

‘Father Kavanagh was taking confessions when a man came into the church.’

Any impatience drained away from Steve. He could see that this was not easy for Psimon.

'The man went into the confessional and started abusing Father Kavanagh.'

'Physically abusing him?'

'No,' said Psimon. 'Just talking through the screen, saying things… horrible things.'

Steve waited for him to go on.

'Father Kavanagh wasn't well,' resumed Psimon. 'His heart was weak. The man's abuse was too much for him. He collapsed… I went to help him.'

'Did the guy hurt you?' asked Steve when Psimon didn't continue.

'No,' said Psimon. 'I told him to stop it… to leave Father Kavanagh alone. But he didn't. When he heard me there he went wild, threatened to kill me. He tried to get at me but I held the door shut, I kept him out.' This last was said with tight-jawed conviction and Steve could see this memory was still alive and vivid in Psimon's mind. Something Steve could relate to. He too was plagued by images that lost none of their intensity with the passing of time.

'So why did he want to hurt you?' asked Steve.

'It was what I heard,' said Psimon. 'It was what he told the priest.'

'You heard his confession?'

'He wasn't there to confess,' scoffed Psimon. 'He was there to gloat and to drag Father Kavanagh into the filth of his crime.'

'And you heard this?' asked Steve. 'You heard him boasting about his crimes.'

At last this was starting to make some kind of sense.

'Yes,' said Psimon. 'I heard him.'

'And what makes you think he's after you now, after all this time?' asked Steve. 'Has he been released from prison? Does he know who you are?'

'No,' said Psimon. 'He was never caught.'

'Then what makes you think you're in danger?'

To Steve's mind they were coming back to Psimon's paranoid, unreasonable fear.

'I can feel him getting closer,' said Psimon staring fixedly at his wringing hands. 'I can feel the lines of our lives converging. At some point in the next five days our paths will cross again. Only this time I won't be able to keep him out.'

Steve leaned back in his chair. This was all getting a bit too Mystic Meg for his liking.

'So what you're telling me is that you want me to protect you from a man that you *feel* is going to hurt you?'

'Going to kill me,' corrected Psimon.

'But you have no proof,' said Steve. 'No death threats, no crazed stalker at the bottom of your garden.'

'Depends what you mean by proof,' said Psimon.

'We're back to this psychic thing, aren't we?' said Steve with renewed frustration. He was not about to take serious money off someone just to protect them from an imaginary bogey man that had frightened them as a child.

'Yes, I suppose we are,' said Psimon with a note of disappointment.

'And I've already told you, I don't believe in psychics.'

Psimon's hands ceased their nervous agitation. He closed his eyes and let out a long slow breath. And there it was again, that sense of him being more mature, more knowing than his years might suggest.

'If I can convince you…' said Psimon without looking at Steve, 'that I know things I couldn't possibly know. Will you take me at my word and honour the contract that we agreed on the Edge.'

Steve was right on the verge of saying no and letting Psimon out of the car. And yet despite himself he was curious, almost amused to see what Psimon might say. He and the lads had once visited a palm reader in Kabul; a spindly old man who told Steve he had the spirit of a tree and would sire five children.

'Load of old bollocks!' he had thought then and he thought about the same right now. But still he wondered what Psimon might have to say… He was Virgo maybe, or that he

suffered from self-doubts and should pursue his dreams, that his love life would soon improve and did he know anyone by the name of Anthony or Andrew or Andrea...

'What the hell,' he said finally. 'I've nothing to lose.'

'Thank you,' said Psimon. Then he hesitated looking sideways at Steve. 'But please, don't be frightened… don't be angry…'

Steve's eyes narrowed at the genuine note of concern in Psimon's voice.

Psimon did not close his eyes. He did not go into a trance. He did not look at Steve's palm or take out a pack of tarot cards. He simply looked Steve straight in the eye and said…

'You wouldn't have hesitated if you'd known they had RPGs.'

'What did you say?' said Steve, his spine turning suddenly to ice.

'You wouldn't have hesitated if you'd known they had rocket propelled grenades,' said Psimon. 'You gave yourself a count of ten just to compose yourself, to steel your nerves. You would not have hesitated a heartbeat if you'd known they had RPGs.'

Steve's heart was suddenly hammering in his chest. He was no longer in the driving seat of his comfortable BMW; he was back in the searing heat of the Iraqi desert, his bloody back pressed against the rough blocks of the shattered house and his C8 carbine assault rifle held diagonally across his body. Bullets slammed into the wall behind him chiselling chunks of concrete from the edge of the doorway and filling the air with clouds of gritty dust that stung his eyes and crunched unpleasantly between his clenched teeth.

'Jesus, that was close.'

The village was supposed to have been cleared and only the tedious procedures of the unit had saved them from walking into an ambush. They had identified thirty marks, neutralised seventeen but that still left at least thirteen kalashnikovs trying to drill through the walls to get at them. He was just relieved that they were armed with nothing more than rifles.

In his current position Steve was relatively safe but the rest of the unit were pinned down and would soon be outflanked. He knew he had to break cover to allow them to relocate. It was all about mobility, keeping the initiative, not allowing the enemy to dictate the sequence of events. The moment you stopped moving was the moment your options began to dwindle.

Steve bit down on the pain from his back. The bullet had torn through his flesh and taken a chunk out of his shoulder blade before burying itself in the sand. Not critical but it hurt like a bastard, made his head swim. Blinking the sweat from his eyes he slung his rifle and pulled three fragmentation grenades from the webbing at his waist. He swallowed hard doing his best not to throw up. He just needed a second to clear his head, to stop the ground from tilting.

He would give himself a count of ten. Then he would break the lads out and give these bastards a lesson in close-quarters combat.

'1… 2…' He got as far as seven when the explosion sent a cloud of dust and jagged chippings blasting towards him.

'Fuck, they've got RPGs!' thought Steve with a new kind of sick feeling in his stomach. Without a second thought he pulled the pins from the three grenades and lobbed them round the doorway towards the enemy.

Pop… pop… pop…

Pause…

BOOM… BOOM… BOOM…

Steve moved on the 'B' of the final BOOM! He switched his carbine to full automatic and charged headlong in to a storm of violence.

The first bullet grazed his thigh, the second nicked his upper arm but he was moving now, pushing forward, regaining the initiative. And then behind him came the staccato crack of small-arms fire. M16s and C8s like his own, rising in lethal chorus as the rest of his unit broke from cover and took the battle to the enemy…

Boom, Boom, Boom… went Steve's heart as he looked at Psimon as if from a great height and distance.

'You gave yourself ten seconds to gather your composure,' said Psimon softly. 'Ten seconds to keep from passing out. And still you think of yourself as a coward because you hesitated.'

Steve swallowed the burning lump in his throat and turned away from Psimon.

'If I hadn't hesitated…' he began huskily.

'Paddy wouldn't have lost his left foot,' Psimon finished. 'He wouldn't have lost two foot of bowel. He wouldn't have to wear…'

'Enough!' snapped Steve holding up his hands to ward off any more unwelcome images.

They were silent for a while. Then…

'How do you know?' Steve began. 'No one knows about that… no one. How do you…?

'I have no idea,' replied Psimon quietly, head bowed, eyes focussed once more on the hands in his lap. 'I just do.'

'Jesus,' breathed Steve, still not quite sure what to make of what he had just heard. Having those memories dragged from his past and held up before his eyes had provoked a fierce reaction. He felt angry, frightened, threatened. But now as he looked at Psimon he found those feelings seeping away just as they had on the Edge. There was something vulnerable about Psimon, something desperately lonely. It took the heat out of Steve's anger and aroused within him a kind of fraternal instinct, which as an only child, Steve found surprising.

'Okay,' said Steve when his heart had stopped trying to beat its way out of his chest. 'I'm impressed.'

Glancing up at Steve Psimon felt a wave of relief. There was no sign of the defensive paranoia that he might have expected.

'Yes,' he thought to himself. *'I was right to phone him.'*

He had never known a man of such contrast… a man capable of such destructive violence and yet possessed of a gentle nature and understated empathy. He had chosen his knight well.

'So, what else can you do?' asked Steve in a tone that lightened the mood.

'Well,' said Psimon, and here he held up the envelope of cash that Steve had returned to him on the Edge. 'How would you like to trade the fifteen thousand pounds for tonight's winning lottery numbers?'

'I said I was impressed, not stupid,' said Steve, snatching the envelope from Psimon's hand and deftly slipping it into the covered compartment between their seats.

Psimon's smile broadened.

Steve let out a deep breath and ran his hands down over his face. He inserted the car keys, checked his mirror and flicked on the lights as it was already getting dark.

'Okay, freak,' he said. 'Where to first?'

'Did you bring the things I told you to?' asked Psimon, finding the light-hearted insult strangely pleasing.

'In the boot,' said Steve referring to the travel bag and passport that Psimon had instructed him to bring during their phone call. He reached round to grab his seat belt and when he turned back Psimon was holding up two airline tickets. Steve reached across and turned up the flap of the envelope to look at the destination.

'Manchester to Fort Lauderdale via Orlando (MC0),' the tickets read.

'So what's in Florida?' asked Steve.

'The James Randi Educational Foundation,' replied Psimon.

'And what do they do at the James Randi Educational Foundation?'

'They challenge claims of paranormal phenomena,' said Psimon.

Steve looked at Psimon with a 'you've got to be kidding' expression on his face.

'There's a million-dollar prize for anyone who can demonstrate genuine psychic ability.'

Steve's expression changed to one of the 'Oh really?' variety.

'We have an appointment with the testing panel tomorrow afternoon at two-thirty.'

'Oh, we do, do we?' challenged Steve.

'Yes,' replied Psimon.

'And I suppose you want me to protect you from all the nutters in America?'

'No,' said Psimon and his voice was suddenly serious once more. 'I need you to get me out.'

CHAPTER 8

Dr Patrick Denning left the lecture in buoyant mood. 'Silencing the Voices' was far and away the most successful book he had ever written. That was the third lecture this week and every one sold out. The psychiatrist smiled to himself as he dwelt on the crowd of enthusiastic faces at the signing, each one eager to share their own ideas and insights into the world of schizophrenia. But it was he who held court, he who could grant or deny them the few minutes of attention that they craved. Now it was off to the restaurant for another free dinner at his publisher's expense.

He turned off the main road and headed for the short-cut via the canal. It was too dark and wet to take the towpath tonight but he was running late and nipping over the bridge would still save him a few minutes.

The orange glow from the street lamps faded as he made his way up the narrow cobbled road. The white lamp that normally illuminated the bridge was out but it was only a short span of darkness and Dr Denning was not concerned.

He was not concerned because he did not know that darkness of an altogether different kind waited for him upon that narrow arc of shadow… darkness in the form of a tall and powerfully built man. A man who had listened with sublime fury as the psychiatrist had preached his lies.

Now ***He*** was here to teach the heretic the error of his ways.

Dr Denning climbed the short humpback bridge over the canal but as he reached the summit a dark hulking figure stepped out in front of him. Fear clutched the psychiatrist's bowels as the stranger raised his arm, something black and shiny in his outstretched fist. Dr Denning started to cry out but the lightning exploded in his chest, seizing his heart in an unyielding grip and tightening every muscle in his body to the point of snapping. His legs gave out and he might have injured himself on the cobbles had ***He*** not caught him… Had ***He*** not carried him away…

He who called himself Lucifer…
He whose name was Legion,
For ***He*** was many.

CHAPTER 9

Steve was surprised at how easily he had slipped back into surveillance mode. Even now, as he scanned the bookshelves in WH Smiths for something to read on the plane, he had one eye on Psimon and one on the bustling flow of people heading for the check-in desks. His mind was in a heightened state of awareness, primed for anything out of the ordinary. Someone hesitating where there was no reason to stop. Someone moving too quickly or too slowly, and of course anyone who came close to Psimon. He knew that the chances of anything happening in an airport terminal were pretty slim, especially in these days of increased security but he had accepted responsibility for keeping Psimon safe and that was exactly what he intended to do.

He suddenly became aware that Psimon had ceased trawling through the magazines and had stopped in front of the newspaper stand and was gazing down at tonight's copy of the Manchester Evening News. Steve noticed the tension in Psimon's body and moved to stand beside him.

'You okay?' he asked.

Psimon said nothing, only continued to stare at the paper's headlines.

Steve glanced down at the front page of the newspaper and his eyes were immediately drawn to the emotive word...
TORTURE

This was the article that held Psimon entranced.

'Pretty grim,' said Steve referring to the series of brutal murders that had been in the news a lot recently.

Psimon said nothing. He did not appear to have heard Steve at all.

'This doesn't have anything to do with…' Steve began but Psimon had turned away heading out of the shop.

'Wait a minute,' said Steve as he hurried to catch up with Psimon. He tried to slow him down but Psimon shrugged him off.

'Is this the guy?' persisted Steve. 'The killer… is he the one?'

'I need a coffee,' said Psimon brusquely. He pulled away from Steve heading for the coffee shop round the corner.

Steve caught up with him at the Costa Coffee counter.

'Double shot cappuccino,' snapped Psimon in a sharp tone that Steve would not have expected. Psimon paid the young woman behind the counter and moved along to the collection point where several other people were waiting for their orders.

'Just a coffee,' said Steve when she turned to him.

Moving more slowly now Steve went over to stand beside Psimon.

'Is it him?' he asked quietly while they waited for their drinks.

Psimon turned away but the expression on his face was answer enough.

'Then why don't you go to the police?' Steve asked gently. 'Tell them what you know. You might be able to help them.'

'I don't know anything,' said Psimon despondently.

'But you could tell them what happened to you,' said Steve. 'Tie that to the current spate of murders.'

'It wouldn't help.'

'But you could help them in other ways,' suggested Steve. 'You obviously have some kind of gift. Why don't you use it to help the police find this guy.'

'I can't,' said Psimon.

'Why not?' pressed Steve. 'The police use mediums… psychics. When they've got nothing else to go on,' he added. 'Why not…'

‘Cos I’m afraid,’ snarled Psimon rounding on Steve. ‘I’m afraid,’ he repeated more quietly looking embarrassed as people turned to look at them.

Steve just looked at Psimon feeling a mixture of sympathy and exasperation.

‘One coffee, one double-shot cappuccino,’ said a young lad serving up their order.

Steve reached for their drinks but stopped as he saw Psimon’s face suddenly screw up with pain. His lips drew back from gritted teeth and his fingers curled tightly into claws. Psimon’s body seemed unnaturally rigid, then as his legs buckled Steve grabbed hold of him and held him up against the counter.

‘Psimon,’ he said. ‘Psimon can you hear me?’ but Psimon was insensible, his body twitching with vicious spasms.

Steve lowered him to the ground and cradled his head against his chest.

‘What the fuck is this?’ he thought. *‘Some kind of seizure?’*

He was about to call for help when Psimon drew a ragged breath.

‘It’s all right…’ he gasped to Steve’s great relief. ‘I’m okay,’

Slowly Steve helped Psimon get to his feet watching him closely.

‘Is everything all right?’ asked a woman in a Costa Coffee uniform.

Steve glimpsed the manager’s badge on her shirt. ‘Yes,’ he said sounding less than convinced himself. ‘Just a nasty bout of indigestion.’

The manager asked one of her staff to help them with their drinks as Steve led a still-shaky Psimon to an empty table.

‘Thanks,’ said Steve as the young lad set their drinks down on the table.

He guided Psimon into a chair before taking a seat beside him. The manager returned with a glass of cold water and, with a nod of thanks, Psimon reached out a trembling hand to take a sip.

Steve waited for Psimon to regain his composure. 'So what was that all about?' he asked gently when some colour had returned to Psimon's cheeks.

'He's taken someone else,' said Psimon.

'Who's taken someone else,' asked Steve but Psimon only looked up, a dark haunted look in his eyes.

'The killer?' whispered Steve. 'That guy in the paper?'

By way of an answer Psimon lowered his eyes staring into the glass of cool clear water in his hand.

Steve was struggling with this. Picking out an incident from his past he could just about get his head round but some kind of psychic link with a deranged serial killer was a step too far. 'How do you know?' he asked trying not to sound too sceptical.

'I always know…' replied Psimon without raising his eyes.

'This has happened before then?'

'Many times,' said Psimon.

'How many times?' asked Steve warily.

'Fourteen.'

'Fourteen!' exclaimed Steve.

'Not counting Father Kavanagh,' Psimon added.

Steve sat back in his chair, stunned. His worldview was struggling to accommodate the new insights being thrust upon him.

'This can't be possible,' he thought. *'None of this is possible!'*

'And he's getting angrier…' said Psimon ominously. 'More voracious.'

'What do you mean?'

'That's two in a week,' said Psimon. 'The time between confessions is growing shorter. If we don't stop him soon…'

'But you said he was going to kill you,' argued Steve. 'Surely we want to stay away from this guy.'

'We have no choice,' said Psimon. 'Our paths will cross. All that matters is how it ends.'

'You mean if I kill you,' said Steve in a low scornful tone.

'All I know,' said Psimon looking up at Steve. 'Is that if he kills me then it's over, that's the end… but if you kill me then everything will be all right.'

'Some fucking choice,' muttered Steve under his breath. Then to his surprise Psimon smiled. It was a strange smile of sympathy and understanding that made Steve feel like he was the younger of the two men.

'Not easy, is it?' said Psimon.

'What, being around you?' said Steve. 'No... not easy at all.'

Psimon's smile warmed but then he suddenly turned as if he had heard something that caught his attention.

'What?' said Steve sensing the alertness in Psimon's manner. 'What is it?'

'He's here,' said Psimon rising from his seat.

'The killer!' exclaimed Steve.

'No,' said Psimon as if Steve were a particularly dim-witted student. 'Commander Douglas Scott.'

'Who the hell is…' began Steve but Psimon was already heading out of the coffee shop.

Steve took a quick scalding gulp of his coffee, though he suspected he was going to need more than caffeine to keep up with his changeable and distinctly irritating new charge. When he emerged from the Costa Coffee front Psimon was walking quickly towards an area of the check-in desks right next to security control; an area that was roped off from the general public. Steve jogged to catch him up.

'What's going on?' he asked Psimon as he strode along beside him.

Psimon did not answer. His eyes were searching for someone among the line of people beyond the cordon.

Steve looked at the people moving through the separate check-in area and despite the fact that they were dressed in civilian clothes he immediately recognised them as military personnel.

'Navy,' thought Steve. It was strange how each branch of the armed forces had their own recognisable air.

The screen above the desk listed the flight for Glasgow but Steve noticed more than one monogrammed label that bore the name 'HMNB Clyde'. Her Majesty's Naval Base Clyde, one of three operating bases for the Royal Navy and home to the United Kingdom's nuclear submarine force.

Steve caught Psimon's arm as he approached the looping rope that corralled the military personnel from the general public but Psimon pushed his hand away, his face animated and focussed. There was no trace of the shaken young man that Steve had helped into a chair only minutes before.

'Douglas,' shouted Psimon suddenly and before he could stop him Psimon had ducked under the rope.

'Psimon!' hissed Steve making a grab for him as he strode into the restricted area, heading towards a man near the back of the queue. Steve cursed Psimon's stupidity. The police were now routinely armed in British airports and two of them had noticed this infringement of security and were closing in on Psimon, their HK submachine guns angled ominously across their bodies.

'Dougie,' shouted Psimon once more making no attempt to conceal his approach.

Upon hearing his name Commander Douglas Scott turned to see who was calling him. He did not recognise the young man striding towards him but the young man certainly seemed to know him.

'Douglas,' said Psimon holding out his hand. 'Didn't expect to see you here.'

Somewhat tentatively Commander Scott reached out to shake Psimon's hand. He glanced at the police officers closing in from the sides giving them a slight nod to say that everything was all right. The officers held their ground but kept their eyes on Psimon.

'Do I know...' began Commander Scott.

'How are you doing?' interrupted Psimon all smiles and geniality. 'How are Anne and the boys?'

'They're fine,' said Commander Scott, his face a picture of puzzlement as he tried to figure out where this stranger knew him from.

'And Gregor's leg... is he back to playing rugby yet?'

'It's mending well...' replied Scott still struggling to put a name to this face.

'That's good... that's good,' said Psimon and here he reached up with his left hand to clasp Scott's hand in both of his. He said nothing for a second or two, his gaze becoming suddenly intense as he looked directly into Commander Scott's eyes.

Scott began to frown under the intense scrutiny but before he felt compelled to pull his hand away Psimon released it with a smile.

'Well,' said Psimon as a gap opened up in the queue ahead of Commander Scott. 'I won't keep you. Give my best to Anne.'

Commander Scott seemed relieved that Psimon was going but before Psimon turned away he looked at a young man standing behind Scott in the queue, fixing him with the same penetrating gaze.

'How's it going Mike?' he asked to the young man's obvious surprise. Then before anyone could challenge him or seek clarification he turned away and headed back towards the cordon.

Commander Scott's eyes followed Psimon as he ducked back under the ropes then he turned to speak to the young man called Mike standing beside him.

Steve watched them talking quietly, doubt and confusion written on their faces. The young man shook his head in response to a question from his commanding officer. They glanced at Steve as Psimon came to stand beside him then shuffled down the line as it shrank towards the check-in.

'Where do you know him from?' asked Steve.

'Never met him before in my life,' said Psimon. Then, 'Come on,' he said. 'We should make our way through to the departure lounge.'

Steve gaped at him in frustration but Psimon just gave him one of those infuriating smiles and headed off towards security control.

To Steve's relief they passed through security without any more surprises. Now they were finally able to sit and enjoy a coffee before their flight was called out. Steve had bought a newspaper and a couple of magazines and was attempting to read an article on bird-flu while Psimon had found a pen and was studying the sudoku at the back of the paper. Behind him a television mounted on the wall was playing Saturday evening telly giving Steve a depressing glimpse into the normality of life that he seemed to have left far behind.

'Aren't you going to phone them?' asked Psimon suddenly.

Steve glanced up becoming increasingly convinced that Psimon really could read his mind. Psimon was looking at him. He seemed to have given up on the sudoku and was now sitting there, one hand in his jacket pocket, the other holding his half-finished cup of coffee.

'They'll be in the middle of the bedtime routine,' said Steve trying not to sound as miserable as he felt.

'Still,' said Psimon. 'It might be nice to get a quick message.'

'Just leave it!' snapped Steve. It was clear that he did not appreciate Psimon commenting on his private life.

'But what would you say if you did call?' asked Psimon with annoying persistence.

'I'm not telling you that,' snorted Steve turning his body away from Psimon as if to emphasise his irritation. But in his mind he was kissing his wife and daughter goodnight.

'Good night darling,' he thought. *'Give Nemo a kiss for me...'*

Faced with Steve's broad, obdurate back Psimon remained unperturbed. And in his pocket, where he held his mobile phone, his thumb moved to the little green button and pressed 'Send'.

Steve gave up trying to read his article. He sat forward and drained his cup of coffee. Then he reached across and snatched up the paper from where Psimon had laid it on the table. He turned it over to see how far he had got with the sudoku.

'Hopeless!' thought Steve with satisfaction when he saw that the numbers Psimon had entered were not even close to being right, *'The seven doesn't go there.'*

He took up the pen to correct Psimon's efforts. Meanwhile on the wall behind Psimon the picture had just changed to the lottery draw with a shot of colourful balls bouncing around inside a clear perspex sphere. A plunger suddenly lifted a single numbered ball clear of the chaos and tipped it down a curving wire track. It was the number seven. The plunger descended before rising to select another number. It repeated the procedure six times but Steve was paying no attention. He was too busy correcting Psimon's mistakes.

'And the two and the eight can't go there...' he almost sniggered.

And the bonus ball is…

Psimon sipped his coffee and smiled to himself as he waited for the tannoy to announce that the flight for Orlando Florida was ready for boarding.

CHAPTER 10

Steve woke midway across the Atlantic. He woke with a start in response to some kind of impact. Squinting through the disorientation he focussed on his surroundings. They sat just behind the wing on the starboard side of the Virgin Atlantic 747. Psimon was sleeping soundly in the window seat beside him. The aisle seat was empty.

Steve was shifting round in his seat when the plane suddenly kicked up beneath him before dropping away just as suddenly. An overhead locker made a hollow clunking sound and Steve could see a small rucksack lying nearby in the aisle. He looked round as a flight attendant drew level with his seat. She retrieved the rucksack and reached up to stow it back in the locker. She tucked in the straps and gave the door a healthy slam to make sure it did not pop open a second time.

'Where are we?' asked Steve.

'We've a few hours to go yet,' replied the attendant. 'Can I get you anything?'

Steve shook his head. 'I'm fine, thanks.'

'Don't worry,' said the attendant comfortingly. 'We'll be through this in a minute.'

Steve did his best to look reassured. *'You should try a low altitude insertion through the boiling thermals of the Colombian jungle,'* he thought.

The attendant gave him a parting smile and returned to her duties.

Steve sat up in his seat and straightened the blanket over his legs. The plane gave another lurch and the fold-down tray on the seat in front dropped open coming to rest against his shins. He pushed it back into place and settled back in his seat but a moment later the tray was rubbing against his legs once more. With an irritated sigh Steve reached forward and slammed the tray back up with more force than was necessary and in his mind he saw his fist make contact with the door to his living room, with a good deal more force than was necessary…

It was five-thirty in the morning and Christine had just returned from the police station. Her brother had been picked up earlier that morning for a breach of the peace outside a casino. The police had called to say that, while he was not hurt, he *was* in a state of some considerable distress, and would she come and collect him.

Christine had left, leaving Steve in the house with Sally.

When, after a couple of hours, Christine had still not returned Steve phoned her on her mobile.

'Is everything all right?' he asked. 'How's Paul?'

'Paul's fine,' Christine had replied but Steve could hear the tears in her voice.

'What's the matter?' he asked, bracing himself in anticipation of bad news.

'I'm heading home now,' said Christine. 'I'll see you in a few minutes.'

The very fact that Christine had dodged the question told Steve more than he wanted to know.

'Okay,' he said, a cold, sick feeling spreading through his stomach. 'See you then.'

The next ten minutes felt like an hour as Steve waited for Christine to return. Finally her car pulled onto the drive and Steve went to meet her at the door. Christine was obviously upset but instead of seeking comfort in Steve's embrace she pushed past him into the living room. Steve followed, the sense of foreboding growing ever stronger. His wife stood in the middle of the room, her back to him, her hands held up to her face.

'Christine?' said Steve reaching out to her but before he could touch her Christine let out a sob.

'It's gone,' she cried. 'It's all gone.

'What's gone?' asked Steve warily.

'The money, Steve… the money. It's all gone!'

Now Steve knew *exactly* what she was talking about. She was talking about the capital they had raised for the launch of their new business venture; the three hundred thousand pounds that represented every last penny of their assets.

'That's not possible,' said Steve, unwilling to accept what she was telling him. 'I spoke to the bank manager only last week… it's not possible.'

Christine rounded on him, the bitterness etched on her tear-streaked face. 'This is Paul we're talking about. Believe me it's possible.'

Steve felt as if the ground had been torn from under his feet. The room seemed to suddenly tilt around him. 'But that's all the money we have,' protested Steve.

'I know,' said Christine.

'That's the money my father left me…'

'I know,' said Christine in a low moan.

'That's the house, Christine… we borrowed money against the house.'

'Steve!' shouted Christine in frustration. 'I know!'

'Sshh!' said Steve in response to the raised voice. 'We'll wake Sally.'

He pushed the living room door to but it never stayed closed and even as he turned back to the room it swung open several inches.

'Oh God' said Christine raising a hand to her mouth and turning away.

'Jesus,' swore Steve softly as the enormity of what she was telling him sank in.

They were four weeks away from signing a deal that would see the bank matching their money; four weeks from the start of production on the first of nearly two hundred orders, and each one worth the best part of five thousand pounds. They were four weeks away from ensuring the financial security of their family and proving that Steve could do something worthwhile in life other than fighting for Her Majesty's armed forces.

'What are we going to do?' said Christine sinking into a chair.

'But how?' asked Steve still wondering how Paul could have gone through three hundred grand in less than a week.

'Oh, you name it…' said Christine angrily.

Steve shook his head, the shock giving way to anger.

'I knew we shouldn't have trusted him.'

'So this is my fault!' challenged Christine. 'For talking you into it…'

'No,' said Steve somewhat taken aback.

'But if I hadn't talked you into it…'

'That's not it at all,' protested Steve.

'But I did Steve. I did talk you into it.' Christine was back on her feet. 'Oh, he's fine for a night down the pub. Great for a laugh… great with Sally…'

'Christine, don't,' said Steve taking a step towards her.

'No!' snapped Christine pulling away from him. 'You never trusted him, not really. If I hadn't persuaded you that he deserved a second chance… that the responsibility would do him good…'

'You didn't talk me into it,' said Steve. 'We made the decision together.'

He made another attempt to comfort his wife but she just kept turning away from him. 'I like Paul… I always have. I knew the way he was… I just never believed he was capable of something like this.

'But maybe I did,' cried Christine and the guilt in her voice was more than Steve could bear.

'Christine, please…' he began but she cut him off.

'Steve, what are we going to do?'

Now it was Steve who turned away. He could not believe that Christine was blaming herself after all that she had done.

'Enough…' he said quietly. 'Just let me think.'

'We have no money…'

Steve sighed wearily. As much as he had always liked Paul, he hated him at this moment. He hated him for his selfishness, for his weakness… he hated him for what he had done but most of all he hated him for what this was doing to his family. He and Christine never argued, not really, and he hated to see his confident, resourceful wife reduced to self-doubt and despair. Steve raised his hands to massage the growing ache in his temples, while behind him Christine paced back and forth sounding off the miseries that lay ahead of them.

'The mortgage is due next week and we're already three months behind…'

Steve could hear the blood rushing in his ears. *'How could he do this?'*

'Then there's the loan for the research costs…'

Steve's heart was pounding in his chest. *'He knows what this means to us… He knows what this will cost us.'*

Steve's hands withdrew from his throbbing temples; the joints of his knuckles cracking ominously as they tightened into fists.

'The car will have to go back… We won't be able to get Sally to school…

'How could he do this?'

'Steve, what are we going…?'

'I don't know!' shouted Steve and, lashing out, he punched the half-open door.

Even in the grip of angry frustration Steve knew that something was wrong. His awareness had registered two sounds, two impacts… His fist denting the solid wood of the door and then, a fraction of a second later, a second impact. And there had been something else… the tiny, choked off whimper of a little girl.

Steve stood there, frozen to the spot, as Christine moved past him to open the door.

There, lying insensible on the hall carpet, was Sally their five-year-old daughter. There was blood on her face and her perfect little nose looked misshapen and nudged to one side.

'Oh God!' whispered Christine kneeling down beside her daughter.

'Oh Christ!' breathed Steve as he looked down on the two people who meant everything in life to him.

Sally stirred as Christine bent to check on her. She tried to open her eyes but her left one would not open, the previously unblemished flesh starting to redden and swell.

'Lie still baby,' said Christine as Sally began to cry.

'Steve,' said Christine in a voice of cold necessity. 'Get me a damp cloth and the first aid kit from the kitchen.

As a trained nurse Christine knew what to do but Steve just stood there. Years of combat and training to deal with crisis situations had not prepared him for this.

'Steve, a cloth, please!' said Christine in that same harsh tone of control.

Steve started towards the kitchen.

'And phone for an ambulance,' Christine called after him. 'I want to get her checked out.'

Steve grabbed the first aid kit from the kitchen cupboard and rinsed a clean cloth under the tap. *'Oh my God,'* he thought. *'I've put my daughter in an ambulance... my little girl... Oh my God!'*

Steve's vision was blurred with tears as he made his way back to the hall. He handed Christine the first aid kit and cloth then went back into the living room to call for an ambulance. 'They'll be here in a few minutes,' he said in a hollow voice when he returned to the hall.

Sally had stopped crying but she still snivelled and moaned while Christine tried to keep her from getting up.

'Is she okay?' asked Steve. The paralysis of shock was starting to leave him and he went to crouch down beside Sally but Sally recoiled from him in confusion and fear and Steve backed away in dismay. He had never had a reaction like that from his little girl before. But until now he had never given her reason to fear him, never given her reason to doubt his love.

'Just leave her,' said Christine, her tone softening a little as she nodded Steve back towards the living room.

Feeling more lonely and worthless than he ever had in his life Steve went and sat in his comfortable living room. He listened to his wife's gentle voice as she soothed and reassured their daughter. He listened as the ambulance arrived and Christine briefed the paramedics on Sally's condition.

'I think she's okay,' Steve heard her say. 'But she did lose consciousness and she's complaining of a sore neck. I didn't want to move her…'

'You did exactly the right thing,' one of the paramedics told her as he bent down to examine Sally. 'Now, what happened?'

Steve had passed through the brutal psyche evaluation of the SAS selection process, where would-be recruits are placed under severe psychological stress to simulate what they might experience during interrogation by the enemy. Psyche week was notoriously difficult to endure… this was worse.

Steve had watched the ambulance drive away. He had waited until the police arrived with a social worker in attendance to take a statement from Steve and assess whether remaining in the family home represented a danger to Sally. He had waited until Christine phoned to say that Sally was going to be okay. She had a broken nose and a badly bruised face but there was no serious damage done and her nose would soon be just as perfect as it always had been.

'Kids mend remarkably well,' Christine had said.

'Kids shouldn't have to fucking mend!' Steve had rebuked himself.

'When can you bring her home?' he had asked.

'We're going to stay at mum's tonight,' said Christine tentatively. 'Sally doesn't want to go home just now.'

'Sally doesn't want to come home just now.'

The words had echoed in Steve's mind as he felt himself shrinking away to nothing. 'Listen,' he said at last. 'I'll go up to the cottage for a few days. You come home when you're ready. Give me a call when Sally is ready to see me.'

'Okay,' Christine had said.

Not, '*Okay darling*'. Not, '*okay, I love you. See you soon'*... just, '*Okay*'.

Steve had never felt so miserable, so hopeless, so guilty in his life. He had packed a bag, grabbed the keys to the cottage and stalked out the front door walking straight into the florist who was delivering a big bunch of flowers and a large, incredibly cute, Nemo cuddly toy.

'Delivery for Brennus,' said the florist brightly but one look at Steve's stony expression and the smile faded from her face.

'Fucking typical,' Steve fumed to himself. Typical of Paul to think that a bunch of flowers and Sally's favourite Disney character could make up for ruining their lives. 'Just leave them in the hall,' Steve had said ungraciously. 'Close the door when you leave.'

And with that he had climbed into the BMW and driven away. Had he paused to read the note that came with the flowers he might have been less harsh in his manner; more puzzled perhaps but certainly less rude. But he did not read the note; he had only assumed that the flowers were from Paul.

But they were not.

If Steve had bothered to read the note he would have seen that the flowers were, in fact, from him.

And that was that. Steve had spent the rest of the day talking to bank managers, lawyers and his accountant trying to see if there was any way out of the hole that had swallowed them. There was not. It all came down to money. When you had it your options were limitless, when you did not those options dwindled to zero. Now it was all about damage control. Retaining the house, salvaging as much of their lives as possible but this too came down to money. Steve had to find a way of earning money and earning it fast, and he could think of no way quicker than three thousand pounds a day for the next five days...

Steve pressed the tears from the corners of his eyes and tried to get comfortable in his seat. He pulled the blanket up over his chest and closed his eyes, searching once more for the oblivion of sleep. For another thirty minutes he fidgeted and wrestled with his blanket, his body mirroring the churning anxiety within him. And even when his breathing finally grew deep and regular his blanket refused to lie across his body and the frown of worry refused to leave his face.

And as sleep finally brought relief to Steve, Psimon opened his eyes. He looked across at his sleeping companion, an unreadable expression in his eyes. Then he reached across and pulled the blanket up around Steve's shoulders.

He envied Steve the refuge of sleep as he waited in frightened anticipation for what he knew was soon to come… for the next confession to begin. He waited for the pain and fear of the latest victim to become so great that it burst, unbidden, into his mind. He closed his eyes once more. He was tired and the distant sound of the aircraft's engines had a soothing, soporific quality to it but still the repose of slumber eluded him.

There would be precious little sleep for those condemned to die.

CHAPTER 11

Thursday March 3rd

MISSING

There is growing concern for the welfare of psychiatrist Dr Patrick Denning who disappeared last night after giving a public reading of his new book 'Silencing the Voices'.

A police spokesman has said that it is too early to conclude that anything untoward has happened to Dr Denning and they are continuing in their attempts to ascertain his whereabouts.

There is as yet no evidence to link this disappearance with the abduction and murder of Dr Marcus Bryant, the psychologist whose body was found earlier this week.

The main terminal of Orlando International Airport was lofty and bright. The facetted glass ceiling allowed the early morning Florida sun to flood in, bathing the homogenous airport facilities in a flattering light. Psimon and Steve sat in the food court, just across from the Krispy Kreme Doughnuts counter, while they waited for their connecting flight to Fort Lauderdale.

'How can you eat those for breakfast?' asked Steve nodding towards Psimon's second blueberry doughnut.

Psimon said nothing as he licked the powdered sugar from his lips but his eyes flicked to the empty McDonald's packaging that lay beside Steve's coffee cup. Both men felt tired and somewhat crumpled after the long transatlantic flight but the coffee was finally starting to take effect and the brightness of the day made it easier to function.

Steve drained the last of his coffee. 'Shouldn't we be making a move?' he said.

'We've got a few minutes,' said Psimon.

'Not many,' said Steve looking at his watch. 'We still have to get over to the airside terminal.'

But Psimon was not really listening. He was staring past Steve towards the south side of the terminal where people were coming through from the check-in desks.

'Come on,' said Steve pushing back his chair. 'We're going to miss our flight…' He reached down to grab his bag but when he straightened up Psimon was no longer in his seat.

Steve felt a moment's alarm at Psimon's sudden disappearance but he soon spotted him striding away across the terminal. With an exasperated sigh he shouldered his bag and started after Psimon. He had just about caught up with him when Psimon called out to a middle-aged man in a smart, blue suit.

'Captain Kern,' said Psimon in a tone of friendly deference. 'I thought it was you…' He held out his hand to the somewhat baffled looking man.

'Christ, not again!' Steve said to himself swerving away from Psimon and trying to appear casual as he hovered nearby.

Captain Kern turned a puzzled stare on Psimon.

'I'm sorry, I don't…' he began, shifting his bag as he automatically reached for Psimon's outstretched hand.

'King's Bay, last June,' said Psimon. 'I never got chance to thank you for smoothing things out with Commander Tully.'

Captain Kern looked none the wiser for this information, although he smiled stiffly as he tried to place the young man in front of him.

'I hope he didn't hold you to that promise,' Psimon went on in a knowing tone. 'I don't think Stephanie would appreciate having him down at the lake for a whole weekend.'

Captain Kern's smile looked more strained than ever.

'Well,' said Psimon. 'Best not keep New London waiting.'

At this Captain Kern's eyes narrowed in suspicion and, a few metres away, Steve's ears pricked up.

'Thanks again Captain,' said Psimon, bringing his other hand up to clasp Kern's. And there it was again that fleeting spike of intensity as Psimon's eyes pinioned the older man.

Captain Kern was clearly mystified but even as his lips parted to formulate a question Psimon let go of his hand and began to move away.

'Goodbye Captain…' he called over his shoulder. 'Say hello to Commander Tully for me…'

And with that Psimon walked away heading for the AGT station and the train that would transfer them to the airside terminal.

Steve lingered for a few seconds, watching as Kern turned to follow Psimon with his eyes. He could see the indecision on Kern's face. Would he let this strange encounter pass? Would he call Psimon back? Would he call airport security to find out how this young man knew he was flying up to New London?

'Naval Submarine Base New London, Connecticut' thought Steve, the submarine capital of the world. *'What the hell was Psimon playing at?'*

Finally Captain Kern turned away from Psimon and, with his brows still knitted together in thought, he continued on his way.

Steve let out a sigh of relief and hurried to catch up with Psimon.

'Don't tell me…' said Steve falling in beside Psimon on the AGT platform.

'Never seen him before in my life,' said Psimon with a sideways smile as the train pulled up in front of them.

Steve gave Psimon a withering look as the doors slid open and they stepped onto the train.

'What's going on?' asked Steve taking a seat beside Psimon. 'Two naval captains on opposite sides of the Atlantic. That's not a coincidence… Just what are you playing at?'

For a moment Psimon looked at Steve as if he were a stranger who was not entitled to know such things. Steve was surprised at the hardness in his eyes. Then his expression softened.

'Just a little trick I learned from the Trojans,' said Psimon and the smile came back to his eyes as he turned to look out of the window.

Steve raised his eyes to heaven wondering just what he had got himself involved in.

The flight to Fort Lauderdale was just a short hop of an hour but it gave Steve a chance to pose a few questions. And this time he would not settle for stony silence. These questions concerned their security… 'I need you to get me out,' Psimon had said.

Steve would have his answers.

'So what makes you think we might have trouble leaving the country?' Steve asked quietly when they were airborne.

'Just a feeling,' replied Psimon.

'Yeah, well your feelings are starting to give me the creeps.'

Psimon offered a wry smile. 'Welcome to my world,' he said.

Steve gave a gentle snort. He could not believe that he was starting to believe this whole psychic thing. 'Seriously,' he said. 'If there's some reason why we might have trouble getting out I need to know.'

Psimon nodded his understanding and began.

'The James Randi Educational Foundation is a world renowned institution that actively challenges claims of a pseudo-scientific or supernatural nature; anything that can not be demonstrated to be true.'

'Spoon bending mediums,' interjected Steve.

'Exactly,' said Psimon.

'But some of them are pretty convincing,' argued Steve. 'There's this guy in America, John something... He's a medium... gets pretty close to the truth a lot of the time.'

Psimon raised an eyebrow at Steve's familiarity with daytime television programmes.

'And do you believe he can talk to the dead relatives of people in the audience?' he asked.

'Of course not,' said Steve.

'And that's the point,' said Psimon. 'If he were able to demonstrate his ability in a reliable way; if he were able to prove that he really can talk to the dead then it wouldn't be a matter of belief, it would be a matter of fact.'

Steve nodded and Psimon went on.

'The same goes for bending spoons, reading people's minds, prophesying the future.'

'They call it precognition,' said Steve with a glint in his eye.

'Quite,' said Psimon with a smile. 'But the same thing applies to all of them.'

'Namely?'

'That it's not possible to demonstrate they are real.'

'Not to sceptics, you mean,' challenged Steve.

'Not objectively,' clarified Psimon. 'Not to people with an open mind.'

'Would people with an open mind not be prepared to accept that it ***might*** be true?' asked Steve.

'Yes,' admitted Psimon. 'But having an open mind also means being prepared to accept that it is ***not*** true.'

'So none of these claims are actually true,' stated Steve.

'That's right,' said Psimon.

'Because they can't be proven objectively?'

'Exactly.'

'So…?' urged Steve hoping that all this was heading somewhere.

'So why do governments around the world spend serious money on paranormal research?'

Steve just looked at Psimon.

'The Americans, the Russians, the Chinese, even the Europeans. They all believe there might be something in it. Or at least, they cannot afford to dismiss it out of hand.'

Steve felt a chill run down his spine. Even during his military reconnaissance training they were taught never to look directly at the subject. There was this enduring notion that the target might somehow feel the eyes of the enemy upon them.

'Imagine someone who could break the White House's 'lost leaf' code system,' Psimon went on. 'Or someone who could bring down an F-22 Raptor using nothing but the power of thought.'

For the first time in his life Steve was starting to appreciate the ramifications of a true psychic existing in the world. 'So what are you saying?' he asked.

'I'm saying that the 'powers that be' cannot afford to ignore the possibility that someone somewhere, with genuine psychic abilities, might one day exist.'

Steve's eyes narrowed.

'I'm saying that they are working to find them. And that they keep at least half an eye on the kind of places where someone might just turn up.'

'You're saying that the Randi Foundation is being watched?' asked Steve, finding the idea somewhat less than credible.

Psimon nodded.

'So, what…' asked Steve. 'Is the place bugged? Do they have a man inside?'

'Let's just say one of the JREF staff members has been… 'approached'.'

'Christ,' said Steve. 'I feel like I'm in an episode of the X-Files!'

Psimon's smile did nothing to undermine the seriousness in his gaze.

'Okay… Let's say I buy into your conspiracy theory,' said Steve, although his expression suggested otherwise. 'Who exactly would be watching? …the police? …the FBI? …the media?'

'Let's just call them an agency,' replied Psimon.

Steve raised a hand to his forehead. 'Please don't tell me you want me to protect you from the fucking CIA,' he said in a hushed tone. Despite what people might like to believe the CIA were not the bumbling incompetents that they were often portrayed to be in the media. If the CIA did not want them to leave the country then that would be that… end of story.

'No,' said Psimon, much to Steve's relief. 'Let's call them a private surveillance agency that happens to have certain government organisations on their books.'

'So what kind of resources might they have?' asked Steve going through the automatic procedure of gathering intelligence.

'Cars…' said Psimon. 'Cell phones… standard surveillance equipment…'

Steve's anxiety was steadily diminishing.

'Some latitude with the law enforcement authorities…'

Steve's anxiety stepped up a notch.

'And helicopters…' added Psimon as if it were an afterthought.

'Helicopters?' repeated Steve.

'Well *a* helicopter,' amended Psimon. 'But I thought I should mention it as it might make it difficult for us to get back to the airport without being followed.'

'Damn right!' snapped Steve.

He could not believe that Psimon had not told him all this before they left the UK. Being away from Christine and

Sally for a few days was one thing but being held in America as some kind of threat to national security was something else entirely. Steve took a deep breath and tried to get things in perspective.

'Okay,' he said. 'These guys are not linked to the police.'

'Not officially,' said Psimon.

'And they're not CIA or FBI?''

'No,' Psimon reassured him. 'Not directly,' he added.

Steve gave him a severe glance before sitting back in his seat.

'So we're talking about some kind of freelance security firm carrying out a passive surveillance operation.'

'Precisely,' said Psimon.

'And what are they waiting for?' asked Steve.

'Why, for someone to succeed in the challenge,' said Psimon as if it were obvious.

'What challenge?' asked Steve.

'The million-dollar challenge,' said Psimon. 'A standing prize to anyone who can demonstrate genuine psychic ability.'

'And how many people have tried?' asked Steve.

'Oh I don't know,' said Psimon. 'A couple of hundred maybe.'

'And they all failed.'

'Every one.'

'And you think you can succeed?' asked Steve.

'Well if I can't,' replied Psimon. 'I won't need you to get me out of the country, will I?'

*

Much to Steve's relief their arrival at Fort Lauderdale airport had been pleasantly uneventful. Now they stood at the Avis car rental counter just across from the terminal building.

The woman behind the counter looked up from her computer screen.

'And how long will you be needing the vehicle for?' she asked.

‘Oh, just the da…’ began Psimon.

‘A week,’ interjected Steve. ‘We’re heading up to Cape Canaveral later today,’ he added, giving Psimon a ‘let me do the talking’ look.

Psimon raised an amused eyebrow and stepped back to let Steve complete the booking.

‘Thanks,’ said Steve a few minutes later when the woman handed him a paper wallet containing all the details of the rental.

‘You’re welcome sir,’ she said sunnily. ‘Have a nice day.’

Steve started to turn away. ‘Oh,’ he said suddenly. ‘Do you have a road map… something listing parking lots in the city?’

‘It’s all in the GPS unit, sir,’ said the woman.

‘I prefer the old-fashioned paper kind,’ insisted Steve.

The woman smiled politely and pointed to a series of shelves at the far end of the counter. ‘The green one should have everything you need.’

‘Thank you,’ said Steve.

Steve helped himself to one of the maps, opened it briefly and gave a small nod of satisfaction. ‘Let’s go,’ he said to Psimon heading out to the forecourt where a metallic-blue Chevy Cobalt was waiting for them. ‘Where to now?’ he asked, adjusting the seat and mirror to his satisfaction. ‘Are we going straight there?’ He was a little surprised to feel a flutter of excitement in his belly.

‘No,’ replied Psimon. ‘We still have a few hours to kill. I’ve booked us a room so that we can freshen up and relax for a while.’

‘Where abouts?’ asked Steve switching on the GPS unit and working his way through the menu.

‘I thought you preferred the paper kind.’

‘Just tell me where we’re staying psyche-boy.’

Psimon smiled and gave Steve the name.

*

'Not exactly the Royal Palms, is it?' said Steve as he grabbed his travel bag from the back seat of the car.

The Bridge hostel was a small complex of apartments used mainly by yacht crews from the innumerable craft moored up in Fort Lauderdale.

'It's clean and comfortable,' said Psimon as they climbed the short flight of steps to the upper floor of the pink coloured building. Their apartment was basic but more than adequate for their means, two bedrooms with a shared bathroom and a small kitchen-dining area.

Steve took a shower first while Psimon grabbed the chance to lie down on a proper bed for a while. He lay on the comfortable mattress and closed his eyes. Here in the bright Florida sunlight he could almost convince himself that he was safe. But he knew that he was not. Distance was no bar to the evil that stalked him. Still, the temptation to forget the James Randi Foundation and stay in the US for as long as possible was incredibly strong. And yet he knew he could not do it… knew he would not do it. If he *was* to die then the world should at least know that he had existed, that someone like him had existed. No, he would go back… he would just close his eyes for a while…

Psimon started from sleep.

'It's all yours,' said Steve, tousling his hair with a towel and bending over the street map that was laid out on the breakfast bar.

Psimon felt a strange kind of disorientation as he picked up the towel from the end of his bed and made his way through the apartment towards the bathroom.

Steve now had his elbows on the map and was tracing a route with his finger. 'Yep,' he said pensively. 'That will do nicely.'

He tapped the map with his fingertips and walked over to his jacket. He did not notice the distracted expression on Psimon's face or the stiffness with which he held himself.

'Here are the keys to the apartment,' he said, laying them down on the counter. 'Lock the door when I go out and don't open it for anyone but me.'

'Where are you going?' asked Psimon in a voice that seemed to echo in his ears. To Psimon the room was growing suddenly darker as someone on the other side of the world was waking up from a deeply troubled sleep. And with consciousness came the fear; fear so great that it eclipsed everything, even the brilliance of the midday Florida sun.

'To rent a car,' said Steve as he opened the door to the apartment.

'But we already have a car.'

Psimon began to tremble.

'You concentrate on the million-dollar challenge,' said Steve checking his wallet for the money he would need. 'Leave the escape and evasion to me.'

He tucked his wallet back into his pocket and grabbed the handle of the door.

'You look wrecked,' he told Psimon. 'Get yourself a shower, I won't be long.'

And with that he shut the door and left.

Psimon just stood there, unable to move as the fear crept like a foul smell into his world. 'Steve…' he breathed in the barely audible voice of a frightened little boy. 'Steve…' he said again as the tears rolled down his cheeks.

But Steve was gone…

Psimon was on his own.

CHAPTER 12

He was naked.
He was cold.
He was terrified.

The psychiatrist tried to get up but found that he could not. His hands were tied behind his back and his feet too were bound. A wire gag had been drawn tight across his mouth forcing him to breathe through his nose in short, shallow gasps, and the presence of a soggy, unidentifiable mass in his mouth made him want to retch. He was lying on his side on bare flagstones that felt cold, dank and tacky against his skin. Beside him lay a copy of his book, 'Silencing the Voices'. The front cover was missing.

Struggling up through the cloying mire of unnatural sleep he tried to focus his eyes on his gloomy surroundings. He appeared to be in some kind of church or chapel.

There were church pews, the aisle between them leading to a studded wooden door with a black cross carved into it. With painful torpidity he craned his neck round to look behind him… an altar, a heavy marble altar… a large unlit candle at either end. In the wall behind the altar a stained glass window, the fractured panes of colour rendered dull and lifeless by the meagre light of distant street lamps. And there, on the bare stone walls, hung a large wooden crucifix. But something was wrong. The crucifix looked wrong…

The psychiatrist stared at the crucifix but his strained vision and groggy mind could not make sense of it. All he knew was that this symbol of love and deliverance brought him no comfort, no comfort at all. He was still staring at the crucifix when a door opened. Not the large main door but a small postern door to the side of the altar.

The psychiatrist twisted round, his mind igniting with hope and fear in equal measure.

Hope vanished, the fear remained…

A man had entered… a large, broad-shouldered man, dressed like a church acolyte in a black cassock and white, lace-trimmed cotta. He approached the altar, head bowed, one hand shielding the small flame of the taper that he carried close to his chest. He reached the central aisle, turned to face the altar and genuflected, his trailing foot coming within inches of the terrified psychiatrist. He rose and, stepping up to the altar, he lit the right-hand candle. Then he genuflected once more before crossing the altar to light the candle on the left. He blew out his small waxed taper and placed it on a wooden table to the side of the altar. Then, from the table he lifted a small silver bell and gave it a little shake; the bright, tinkling refrain sounding strangely obscene in the grim confines of the chapel.

The psychiatrist was shaking uncontrollably, arching himself round, trying to keep the sinister acolyte in view.

The acolyte came to stand beside the prone figure of the psychiatrist who cowered at his feet, too frightened even to look up at his captor. Then suddenly the acolyte bent down and grabbed the psychiatrist by the arms, hauling him from the floor to stand awkwardly before the altar.

The psychiatrist cried out in pain as the cord around his wrists bit into the flesh, tearing the skin. He felt blood running down his hand, dripping from his fingertips. But he felt something else too. He felt the cord slip in the wetness, felt his swollen hand squeezing through the lubricated grip of the ligature.

From the corner of his eye the psychiatrist saw the acolyte make the sign of the cross.

'Amen,' said the acolyte in a deep guttural voice.

There was a short pause in which the psychiatrist tried to free his hand without drawing attention to it.

'And also with you,' said the acolyte as if in answer to the blessing from an absent priest.

With a small mutinous jerk the psychiatrist's hand came free. He flicked a fearful glance to his side as he tried to work some feeling back into his numb fingers. Then, knowing he had only one chance he clenched his fingers and formed a bloody fist.

Beside him the acolyte bowed his head and closed his eyes

'I confess to almighty God, and to you, my brothers and sisters…' he began.

The psychiatrist held his breath, tried to adjust his balance.

'…that he has sinned through his own faults, in his thoughts and in his words, in what he has done, and in what he has failed to do…'

The psychiatrist struck with all the force of desperation. His fist made solid contact with his captor's jaw, snatching the acolyte's unsuspecting head to one side. The psychiatrist swivelled his bound feet and struck again, another good blow striking home. He aimed a third, feeling the hope well up in his naked chest but his hope was crushed, as were his fingers, by the massive hand that closed around his fist. He tried to strike with his other hand but the acolyte caught hold of his wrist and drew himself up to his full, intimidating height. The psychiatrist looked up into eyes that were as black and expressionless as coal. He was paralysed by the utter darkness of the man's gaze.

For a terrible moment the acolyte looked down upon the psychiatrist with his dead, black eyes. Then with savage speed he smashed his head down into the psychiatrist's face. The psychiatrist collapsed under the brutal attack as his nose and the orbit of his left eye were broken. The acolyte dragged the semi-conscious man across the floor to the foot of the wall beneath the inverted crucifix. Then he stepped back and disappeared through the small postern door.

Now, struggling to breathe through the gag and his broken nose, the psychiatrist began to cry, the tears seeping out from his badly swollen eye. With his good eye he looked around to see where his tormentor had gone, praying that he would not return.

His prayers went unanswered.

The acolyte returned, and what he carried in his hands made the psychiatrist recoil in horror. In his right hand the acolyte carried a large black hammer; in his left a fistful of long, thick nails. Pathetically the psychiatrist tried to shuffle away but the acolyte caught hold of him and pushed him to the floor. He knelt on his wrist and put one large nail in the centre of his palm.

The psychiatrist let out a stifled cry, trying in vain to pull his arm free. With his free arm he battered ineffectually at the acolyte's head and shoulders, then he screamed as the hammer came down and the nail punched through his hand giving a muted ring as it struck the hard paving stones beneath. The psychiatrist began to lose consciousness as the acolyte moved to his other hand. He gave a tortured moan as the hammer fell a second time.

The acolyte grabbed the psychiatrist's right arm and pulled him up until his hand was level with the crosspiece of the large wooden crucifix. With one huge hand he held it steady while, with the other, he drove the nail deep into the thick piece of solid oak. He repeated the procedure with the psychiatrist's left hand and stepped back.

The psychiatrist was now unconscious once more. Hanging limply from the inverted crucifix his body formed a grotesque mirror to the depiction of Christ that hung on the wall above him.

Lucifer looked at the heretic, the imagery not going unnoticed. He put down the hammer and returned to his place before the altar. Then he bowed his head and continued with the service that had been so inexcusably interrupted.

*

'I thought I told you to lock the door,' said Steve as he re-entered the apartment carrying a bag of food that he had picked up from a nearby store.

He shut the door and looked round the room. Seeing no sign of Psimon he started for the bedroom, then he stopped in his tracks, the brown paper bag falling from his grasp.

'Oh shit!' cursed Steve as he caught sight of Psimon.

Psimon was leaning unnaturally against the wall, head bowed, arms stretched out wide, the backs of his hands pressed flat against the wall. And in the centre of each hand a blood-black bruise that looked fresh and intensely painful.

'Psimon,' said Steve coming to kneel before him. 'Psimon, can you hear me?'

Steve reached up to help Psimon into a more comfortable position. His legs were not even straight beneath him and Steve could not see how he was holding himself up. He put his hands under Psimon's armpits and began to take his weight.

As Psimon's hands came away from the wall he drew a rasping breath and collapsed into Steve's embrace.

'It's okay,' said Steve lowering him gently to the floor.

Psimon began to sob.

'Psimon, it's okay. I've got you now,' repeated Steve trying to reassure him but Psimon clutched at Steve's chest, turning his face up to look at him.

'Jesus,' breathed Steve at the sight of Psimon's face. He looked as if he had taken a good beating. His nose and brow were badly bruised; his left eye almost closed with the swelling.

'He crucified him,' sobbed Psimon. 'Oh, God, Steve… he crucified him…'

'Who, Psimon?' he asked. 'Who did this to you?'

'Not me,' protested Psimon trying to push away from Steve. 'Him!' he said with conviction. '**He** crucified *him*!'

Steve felt his blood run cold. Despite his years of dealing with violence he felt suddenly out of his depth.

Psimon slumped back against the wall while Steve knelt before him.

'He's going to kill me,' said Psimon with dreadful certainty.

'No!' said Steve reaching out to gently cup Psimon's chin. He stared at Psimon, looking directly into the clear grey depths of his unblemished eye. 'No, he is not.'

'Then you must,' said Psimon.

Steve's jaw bunched and he closed his eyes. *'Not this again,'* he thought.

'But you would,' pleaded Psimon. 'If it was the only way to save me from him… you would, wouldn't you Steve?'

Steve opened his eyes to look at Psimon once more. He said nothing. He still refused to accept this nonsense about killing Psimon and yet there was a hardness and unflinching resolution to his gaze that seemed to offer Psimon some comfort

'Thank you,' said Psimon and finally his breathing began to calm.

*

'You can't,' said Steve a half-hour later when he had tended to Psimon's injuries and they were sitting together at the breakfast bar.

'Yes I can,' said Psimon, putting down the ice pack and stuffing the last piece of a cinnamon and raisin bagel in his mouth. He winced as he brushed a few crumbs from the bandages that Steve had applied to his bruised hands.

'Just call them. Tell them you've had an accident.'

Steve could not believe how quickly Psimon had recovered from his earlier state of distress. He also found it impossible to believe that Psimon's injuries were the result of something that had been done to someone else on the other side of the Atlantic Ocean. And yet…

'No,' said Psimon draining his can of Pepsi and rising somewhat unsteadily from his stool. 'We take the million-dollar challenge in…' he looked at his watch. '…just over half an hour.'

'You're sure?' pressed Steve.

'Absolutely,' insisted Psimon. He reached for his canvas bag but Steve shouldered it for him.

'Besides,' said Psimon with a glint in his one good eye. 'I can't wait to see James Randi's face when he signs over that cheque.'

Steve shook his head as they started for the door. 'You've a wicked streak in you, young man,' he said.

'You have no idea,' replied Psimon with a smile.

'How can you smile?' asked Steve. 'With all this going on… how do you stay so damned cheerful?'

Psimon stopped in the doorway and looked back at Steve.

'Have you ever known someone who lived with constant pain?' he asked.

'Yes,' said Steve remembering his mum in the last few years of her life.

'And did she ever smile?'

Steve closed the door to the apartment.

'All the time,' he said as he turned the key in the lock. 'All the time.'

Psimon smiled and nodded gently. Then together they descended the steps, climbed into their hire car and headed for the James Randi Educational Foundation, an institution whose very existence was based on the premise that true paranormal phenomena could not be shown to exist.

They were about to learn otherwise.

CHAPTER 13

'We should have turned right there,' said Psimon turning in his seat to look down Davie Boulevard on which the Randi Foundation was situated.

'Chill out,' said Steve watching the road ahead of them. 'We're just taking a small detour. We've plenty of time.'

There was a note of confident satisfaction in Steve's voice that Psimon found pleasing. He settled back in his seat content to leave his fate in Steve's hands. He felt no desire to *know* where they were going. He was enjoying the fact that Steve knew what he was doing. That was enough.

For a few minutes they continued north up South Andrews Avenue before taking a right and stopping outside a multi-storey car park. Steve pulled into the side, unbuckled his seat belt and dug in his pocket for some loose change.

'I'll just be a minute,' he said, looking at Psimon to make sure he was okay with that.

Psimon gave him a nod of reassurance and Steve climbed out of the car. He walked quickly towards the parking lot and disappeared inside. Psimon waited. He saw two cars enter the lot and one emerge from the exit, the security barrier rising smartly to let it pass. Then before he knew it the car door opened and Steve swung inside. He opened a small compartment in the dashboard and tucked a printed card inside. Then he started the car and checked his mirror.

'Okay, Uri Geller…' said Steve, pulling a neat one-eighty in the middle of the road, '…time to do your stuff.'

*

The foundation was smaller than Steve had been expecting. He had anticipated something on the scale of a university or hospital but it turned out to be fairly modest building with white walls and a terracotta tiled roof. There was a large red sign to the side of the building…

201 James Randi Educational Foundation

They were met in the reception area by a tall man in a red shirt.

'Psimon?' ventured the man glancing down at his watch. 'You're right on… Jeez, what happened to you?' he exclaimed when he raised his head to look at Psimon properly.

Steve interjected before Psimon could say a thing.

'Kids and motorbikes… what can you say?' he said with an awkward laugh.

'Yeah, sure...' said the man distractedly. Then to Psimon, 'Are you okay? Can we get you anything?'

'No. Thanks. I'm fine,' said Psimon. His smile looked painful and lopsided, his black eye and swollen nose gave him the appearance of having been recently mugged. He held out one bandaged hand. 'It's Jeff isn't it?'

'Yes,' said Jeff shaking Psimon's hand somewhat gingerly. 'Jeff Wagg. I'm the General Manager here at JREF.'

'This is Steve Brennus,' said Psimon. 'He'll be accompanying me for the challenge.'

'Steve,' said Jeff turning to shake Steve's hand. 'Welcome to Florida.' Then turning back to Psimon he said, 'Are you sure you're okay? We can always postpone the challenge…'

'No, I'm fine, really,' insisted Psimon. 'We can go ahead as planned.'

'If you're sure,' said Jeff adjusting his glasses.

Psimon nodded and Jeff finally allowed himself to be convinced.

'Well come on in then,' he said ushering them into the building.

Psimon and Steve followed Jeff into a large room lined with well-stocked bookshelves. There was a sign beside the doorway that read 'Isaac Asimov Library'. A large glass table dominated the centre of the room and the far wall featured a brick and tile fireplace surmounted by what looked like certificates or awards and pictures of people that Steve did not recognise.

'Grab a seat,' said Jeff indicating a couple of chairs at the near end of the table. 'Make yourselves at home.'

Psimon and Steve hovered by the chairs.

'Now, can I get you a coffee or anything?' asked Jeff.

'Coffee would be great,' said Steve. 'Thanks.'

Jeff was barely gone a minute when he returned with a tray carrying a flask of coffee and two cups. In addition to this he had a clipboard tucked under one arm. He placed the tray on the table before them.

'Randi will be here in a few minutes,' he said filling the two cups. 'He's just finishing up with a call.'

Psimon nodded as Jeff placed a cup of steaming coffee in front of him.

'He's quite keen to meet you, Psimon,' continued Jeff. 'In fact you've created quite a bit of interest here.'

'Oh?' said Psimon raising his cup to take a sip.

'Absolutely,' said Jeff. 'This is the first time that anyone is *actually* going to take the challenge. No one else has ever got past the preliminary testing stage.'

'Psimon passed the preliminary tests?' asked Steve.

'Not exactly,' clarified Jeff. 'But we were sufficiently impressed to agree to these special conditions.' Here he tapped the clipboard that he had placed on the table.

'Really?' said Steve giving Psimon a meaningful look.

'That's right,' said Jeff looking at Psimon. 'Even the 'Amazing James Randi' couldn't figure out how you did it. I think that's why he's so keen to sit in on this one.'

Psimon just smiled innocently.

'Psimon,' said a voice suddenly from the doorway.

Psimon and Steve turned as a bald man with glasses and a bushy, stark white beard entered the room. He walked with a slightly hunched gait but seemed animated by a youthfulness that belied his stately years.

'Mr Randi,' said Psimon putting down his coffee and rising from his chair.

'Please, just Randi' said Randi shaking Psimon's hand gently.

His gaze took in, assimilated and decided not to comment on Psimon's injuries with startling swiftness.

'You must be Steve,' said Randi turning to greet Steve. 'Psimon said you might be joining him.'

'That's right,' said Steve resisting the urge to cast an accusing glance at Psimon. He reached out to take Randi's hand and as he did so he looked into the man's vaguely familiar face, a friendly face with a mischievous twinkle in his shrewd eyes.

'Please… take a seat, finish your coffee,' said Randi gesturing everyone towards the table. 'I have to tell you I've been looking forward to this afternoon… hoping you'd be able to make it.'

To Steve, Psimon seemed strangely self-conscious and he wondered if he was having second thoughts about the challenge.

'I must admit to being more than a little intrigued,' said Randi, taking a seat at the table. 'Your performance over the phone was really quite impressive.'

Psimon smiled.

Randi nodded sagely, a small smile on his lips and Steve did not need psychic abilities to know what that smile meant... It was one thing to hoodwink someone over the phone but to do it face to face, under carefully controlled conditions, was something else entirely. Steve hoped that Psimon was not about to make a fool of himself.

'Well,' said Randi as the pause in conversation began to stretch. 'We're just waiting for Lionel, the JREF lawyer, to get here. Then we can begin.' He turned to Jeff. 'Is that the protocol?'

'That's it,' said Jeff. He pushed the clipboard across the table as he too took a seat.

Randi took the clipboard and scanned the first page, nodding as he quickly read it through. He turned to the second page and shook his head as he laid it down. 'Most interesting,' he said taking his glasses off to give them a quick polish. 'Most unusual.'

Steve did his best not to seem too intrigued.

Seated on the opposite side of the table Jeff Wagg nodded in agreement with the JREF's founder and picking up on Steve's curiosity he offered a brief explanation. 'Normally people state the psychic ability that they are going to attempt,' he said.

'And Psimon hasn't told you?' asked Steve, glancing at Psimon and back to the other two men.

'Psimon gave us a choice of about ten so-called psychic powers,' said Randi, shaking his head and laughing softly at Psimon's audacity. 'He invited *us* to choose one for the challenge.'

Steve turned to stare at Psimon and the expression on his face could not have been clearer... *'Are you mad!'*

'And which one did you choose?' asked Steve wondering how they could get out of there before the embarrassment began.

'We call it the spoon-bender's nemesis,' said Randi.

Steve ran his fingers across his brow. He glanced at Psimon who gave him a small shrug that seemed to say... *'Don't look at me... I didn't choose it!'*

Jeff reached into the top pocket of his shirt and pulled out a small glass tube, maybe ten centimetres long, sealed at either end with a red plastic stopper. Inside the tube was a metal rod of almost the same length as the tube. Jeff handed the tube to Randi.

'Bending spoons is one of the easiest 'psychic' feats to explain,' said Randi. 'But there are still plenty of believers out there.' He held up the glass tube so that everyone could clearly see it. 'This challenge is simple,' he went on. 'To bend the metal rod without touching it, using only the power of your mind.' He gave the tube a little shake. 'The fact that it is enclosed in a sealed glass tube tends to put most people off.'

Steve exchanged another loaded glance with Psimon.

'Ah, Lionel,' said Randi suddenly as a grey-haired man in a smart suit was led into the room by a younger member of the JREF staff.

Randi got up from his chair and introduced the foundation's lawyer to Psimon and Steve.

'And this is Tony,' Randi went on. 'Rich normally videos the tests but he has another engagement this afternoon so Tony will be recording the challenge for us today.'

With a brief nod of introduction Tony turned on the video camera and moved to the corner of the room to get the best angle for covering the challenge. As he did so Psimon caught Steve's eye and the meaning in his eyes could not have been clearer…

'He's the one!'

Trying not to make it too obvious Steve gave Tony a more appraising glance. So this was the mole in the JREF camp. He nodded his understanding to Psimon and sat back down on the couch. There was no pulling out now… the game was afoot!

'Okay,' said Randi when everyone was seated at the table.

He pushed the clipboard back to Jeff who pulled a pen from his shirt pocket and offered it to Psimon.

'If you could just read this through,' he said. 'Everything should be as we discussed… One challenge, one psychic ability of our choosing.'

Psimon took the clipboard and gave the form a cursory once over as Jeff continued.

'The rod is currently straight as a die,' said Jeff taking the tube back from Randi and holding it up for everyone to see. 'If at the end of fifteen minutes the rod remains straight then the challenge will be deemed a fail.'

Psimon looked up from the clipboard and gave Jeff an affirmative nod.

'If, after fifteen minutes, the rod has been bent, to the satisfaction of representatives from JREF, without Psimon ever having touched it, then the challenge will be considered a success and the million dollar prize will be transferred to the claimant's account.'

Jeff paused for everyone to absorb this summary of the agreed conditions.

'As requested by today's claimant...' he held out his hand to indicate Psimon. 'In the event of a successful challenge the results of the challenge will not be disclosed by JREF for the period of five days from today. After which, representatives from JREF will be invited to attend a press conference at the BBC studios in Manchester, England; a press conference at which the claimant may or may not be present...'

Here Steve looked pointedly at Psimon. In this, at least, he was the only person in the room to fully appreciate the finer points of this clause.

While Jeff read out the particulars of the protocol Randi watched Psimon with a penetrating gaze. He had seen all manner of people turning up to attempt the million-dollar challenge but he had never met anyone quite like Psimon. There was no bravado, no apparent nervousness, no suggestion of excuses or misgivings creeping into the procedure. Psimon just sat there holding the clipboard while Jeff read out the particulars. Despite his absolute conviction about the truth of paranormal phenomena Randi's sense of anticipation had never been greater.

'So, Psimon,' said Jeff in conclusion. 'If you could just sign both copies of the protocol... here and here...'

Psimon signed his name and handed the clipboard back to Jeff.

'And I will sign it on behalf of JREF,' said Jeff adding his name to the contract. 'Then we can begin.' Jeff looked round at all those present to check that everyone was in agreement, then he set the glass tube down on the table in front of Psimon and settled back in his chair. 'It is now two-fifty pm,' he said. 'Psimon, when you're ready...' Here he looked at Psimon who gave him a simple nod. '...you have fifteen minutes.'

With that Jeff pressed the timer on his watch and all eyes fell on the glass tube and the metal rod that lay sealed within… the spoon bender's nemesis.

CHAPTER 14

For a minute or so Psimon just sat there. No one was looking at him; all eyes were on the small glass tube and the metal rod that lay inside. He felt a faint shiver of nervousness, not uncertainty or doubt, more like a kind of stage fright; a singer who was just about to give a public performance, where before they had only ever sung alone. He found himself wishing that his mum and dad were here. And although he did not believe in life after death he could almost feel their presence beside him.

'Do what you have to do...'

Well this was part of it. There would be no going back from this. Psimon was about to give up his anonymity, about to expose himself to the perilous vagaries of public opinion.

As the minutes went by and nothing happened people began to glance up at him, their expressions betraying a mixture of anticipation, doubt and sympathy. And yet interestingly to Psimon there was no sense of condescension, no sense of judgement. At one point Psimon caught Randi's eye and the two men held each other's gaze for a moment...

Another minute went by and the camera, operated by Tony, began to focus more and more on Psimon. Lionel, the JREF lawyer, had settled back in his chair clearly convinced that nothing was going to happen and Randi's face seemed to convey something akin to disappointment.

He could put it off no longer.

Psimon took a breath.

From the small glass tube there came the tiniest of sounds; the barely audible *tick* of a seal being broken. Suddenly all eyes were glued to the table. There followed a collective suspension of breath as the red plastic stopper began to ease its way out of the tube.

'Fuck me!' breathed Tony quietly as he adjusted the camera's zoom to make sure he did not miss a thing.

Then everyone jumped as, with a small *pop*, the plastic stopper came free. Hardly able to believe his eyes Steve looked up at Psimon who was calmly gazing down at the table. Then Steve's eyes were drawn down once more as the metal rod began to move.

The rod slid clear of the tube and lay, unmoving on the table. The JREF lawyer was no longer lounging back in his chair. Like everyone else he was sitting forward, straining to catch any movement, no matter how small. Then, without anyone touching it, without anyone coming near to touching it, the metal rod began to bend.

Steve's heart was pounding in his chest. Once more he looked up from the astonishing scene unfolding before them only to find Psimon staring directly at him. He was not even looking at the rod. Psimon was doing the impossible and he was not even looking at it! And then it occurred to Steve...

'This is easy for him...' he thought. *'He's doing the impossible and it's easy...'*

Psimon just held his gaze. And now, for the first time, Steve understood the expression that lurked behind Psimon's eyes. That knowing, self-assured expression that made him seem so much older than his years.

'God,' thought Steve with sudden understanding. *'He's never told anyone... What kind of person does it take to live with something like this... and to never tell a soul? He must be the loneliest person alive.'*

For a few seconds more the two men just looked at each other. Then slowly they became aware of people talking excitedly and Psimon lowered his eyes. The James Randi million dollar psychic challenge had been accomplished and the world would never be the same again.

*

In the hubbub of excitement that followed Steve found himself becoming increasingly annoyed and protective of Psimon...

‘How did he do it?’

‘Would he take another test?’

‘Could he really perform all ten of the psychic abilities he listed?’

‘Was there any way he could extend his stay in Fort Lauderdale?’

But as the pressure increased it was James Randi who came to their rescue.

‘Enough,’ he had said with quiet authority. ‘That’s enough…’

‘But Randi,’ said the JREF lawyer.

‘No,’ said Randi.

‘But we can’t just…’ began Tony.

‘Gentlemen, please,’ said Randi more firmly, ushering his colleagues to the far end of the room. He turned to Psimon and Steve. ‘A moment, please,’ he said with a wry smile.

Psimon nodded and sat back down at the table. Steve remained standing. ‘What do you think is the problem?’ he asked quietly.

Psimon looked down the room to where the members of the JREF staff were talking in hushed, and occasionally heated, voices. Every now and then one of them would glance up at the two British men before returning to the huddle.

‘They’re trying to decide if they can honour the contract,’ replied Psimon.

‘You mean they’re not going to pay up!’

‘No,’ said Psimon. ‘The money isn’t the problem.’

‘Then what is it?’ asked Steve.

‘Keeping a lid on this for the next five days,’ explained Psimon.

‘That’s what they agreed to,’ said Steve with annoyance.

‘Easily done, when you don’t believe it will happen,’ said Psimon.

Steve’s derisive snort told exactly what he thought of people who reneged on a deal.

Finally Randi broke from the group and returned to Steve and Psimon who stood to meet him.

'Please accept my apologies gentlemen,' he said as he approached. 'It would seem that the extraordinary events of the day almost got the better of us.'

He stepped up to Psimon and reached out to take his hand holding it gently in both of his.

'I've spent a good many years inviting people to prove the existence of paranormal phenomena. I never believed they would,' he said.

Psimon gave a small apologetic smile.

'It is my deepest privilege that you came *here* to prove me wrong, and I am profoundly honoured… thank you.'

'You're welcome,' said Psimon shyly.

Randi nodded. The smile and the twinkle had returned to his eyes. He turned to the members of his staff. 'Tony, if you could put the disk from the camera in a sealed envelope and pass it to Jeff, he will place it in the company safe.'

A disgruntled Tony seemed suddenly protective of the camera but he nodded his agreement as he left the room.

'Jeff, I wonder if you could check out flights to the UK. I understand there's a press conference being held at the BBC that we wouldn't want to miss.'

Finally he turned to the JREF lawyer.

'Lionel, if you please… I believe we have some formalities to attend to. I trust you brought the necessary papers.'

'Yes… yes,' said Lionel reaching for his briefcase. He opened the case and withdrew several official looking documents.

'Psimon, if you please,' said Randi inviting Psimon to join them.

Steve stepped back as Psimon went to join the two men at the far end of the table.

'Basically…' said Lionel laying the documents out on the desk, 'we just need your signature and the details of the bank account into which you would like the money to be paid.'

Steve could not suppress a smile as he watched Psimon bend forward to sign the 'claimant's' document. He felt strangely proud of Psimon; pleased for him but at the same time he felt unbelievably foolish. Something he had said just two days ago kept repeating itself in his mind...

'And I've already told you... I don't believe in psychics!'

He laughed softly and looked down at the empty glass tube that still lay on the table. And beside it a metal rod; a metal rod that was not only bent but had been formed into a perfect circle. Steve reached down and picked up the circle of steel. He weighed it in the palm of his hand and as he did so the smile faded from his face. He turned to look once more at Psimon. If this one unbelievable thing were true... then how much more of what Psimon had told him was also true?

At some point in the next few days a serial murderer was going to kill Psimon...

...unless Steve killed him first.

*

Tony sat at the computer in his office, the video camera cradled in his lap, a mobile phone pressed to his ear. 'No, I'm not joking...' he hissed into the phone. 'I just saw it with my own fucking eyes!'

Tony cast a nervous glance at the door, clearly anxious that no one should hear him making this call.

'So the prize has been claimed?' said a man's voice on the other end of the line. 'The foundation is actually paying up?'

'They're signing the paperwork as we speak,' said Tony quietly. 'I'm telling you... this is for real.'

'And you've got it all on film?'

'On disk, yes,' said Tony. 'I'm making a copy right now.'

Tony's computer was all set to copy the disk from the camera but, despite Tony repeatedly pressing the eject button, the camera wouldn't give up the disk.

‘Okay…’ said the man on the other end of the phone. ‘Do you know where they’re staying?’

‘No,’ said Tony in growing frustration at the uncooperative camera. ‘They said something about heading up to the Cape.’

‘All right… try and keep them there as long as possible.’

‘There’s nothing I can do to stop them… just send a car as soon as possible.’

‘There’s one on its way but it’s not that simple. We can’t detain them without authorisation.’

‘Authorisation from who?’ asked Tony.

‘Our client,’ came the evasive reply.

‘Whatever,’ said Tony. ‘They’re driving a blue Chevy Cobalt. It’s parked right outside the JREF but I don’t know how long they’ll be here.’

Tony struck the camera with the heel of his hand. The damn thing just wouldn’t open.

*

‘What is it?’ asked Steve when Psimon hesitated in the foundation’s foyer.

For the last few minutes Psimon had seemed distracted and distant.

‘It’s Tony,’ said Psimon quietly. ‘He’s trying to make a copy of the disk.’

‘What!’ exclaimed Steve. ‘We should stop him… tell Randi.’

‘It’s okay,’ said Psimon with a smile. ‘He’s having a little trouble with the camera.’

For a moment Steve just looked at him. Then… ‘No…’ he said incredulously.

‘It’s just a simple electrical switch,’ said Psimon as if this explained everything.

‘But you’re not even in the same room,’ protested Steve.

‘Same room… same city. Distance doesn’t really matter.’

'What...' said Steve. 'You can see through his eyes?'

'Not exactly,' replied Psimon. 'But having met him... having made that connection... it almost allows me to be present in the room.'

The intensity of Steve's frown adequately portrayed the difficulty he was having with these new revelations. He just kept thinking...

'This is not possible... none of this is possible.'

*

Tony's head snapped up as Jeff entered the room.

'Is there a problem?' asked Jeff suspiciously when he saw the guilt written on Tony's face.

'No,' said Tony, his face flushing. 'Just can't seem to get the disk out.'

Jeff stepped forward and held out his hand. With visible reluctance Tony surrendered the camcorder to Jeff who turned it over and pressed the eject button. There was a small click and the caddy popped smoothly open.

'A case,' said Jeff nodding to the stack of DVD cases on Tony's desk.

Tony opened a case and held it out to Jeff who slipped the disk inside and folded it shut. Then he handed the camera back to Tony and left the room.

*

Back in the foyer Steve watched as Psimon's face relaxed into a smile.

'Can we go now?' he asked.

'Yes,' said Psimon. 'We can go.'

Steve shook his head muttering under his breath but Psimon caught the words.

'Bloody psychics...' Steve cursed as they made their way out to the blue Chevy Cobalt in the car park.

CHAPTER 15

The silver Volvo pulled up a hundred metres from the entrance to the James Randi Foundation. The windows were darkly tinted but apart from that there was nothing to mark this vehicle out from several others parked in driveways along the road. The two men inside sat back in their seats. They had made good time getting there and they were relieved to see that the blue Chevy was still in the car park. It was an Avis rental, standard low-end model. Following it should be a piece of cake. They made a note of the licence plate, called it in to control, and settled down to wait.

'I don't get it,' said the younger of the two men.

'We don't have to get it,' said the older man. 'We just have to follow them.' He had the hard, serious face of an ex-cop.

'But really,' persisted the younger man. 'Even if this guy can bend spoons without touching them. I mean… so what? We can tail him all the way to the Cape if need be. I don't see why we need the chopper.'

The ex-cop seemed irritated by the simple act of having to make conversation.

'You wear a Ruger SR9 on your hip,' he stated without looking at his colleague.

'Yeah,' said the younger man. 'So what?'

'So you'd be happy sitting next to a man who could discharge that firearm just by looking at it.'

The younger man looked up sharply, his hand resting suddenly on the pistol at his waist.

'The contact said he could bend metal with his mind,' he objected. 'He said nothing about firing guns.'

'If he can bend a steel rod into a perfect circle,' snapped the ex-cop. 'He can, sure as shit, slip a safety catch and apply the half ounce of pressure required to shoot you in your ass.'

'Shit! I never thought of that.'

'And who's to say he couldn't fuck with a car's engine… or an airliner's?'

'Jesus!' swore the younger man looking at the blue Chevy with considerably more intensity than before.

'There's no telling what this guy is capable of,' said the ex-cop. The conversation seemed to have annoyed him and the look his colleague gave him did nothing to improve his temper. 'You think I'm paranoid,' he said, taking in the younger man's sideways glance. 'I'm nothing compared to our client. They'll be none too pleased if we let this guy get away. *That's* why we need the chopper. To make sure there are no fuck-ups.''

'So you really think they'll authorise us to detain him? I mean… they're not even American citizens.'

The ex-cop just stared out of the Volvo's windscreen.

'Once they're convinced he's for real? Yes, they'll give us authorisation. After all,' he continued. 'It never stopped them with Wernher Von Braun. And just think where we'd be without him.'

'Who?' asked the younger man but the ex-cop was no longer listening.

He fired up the engine.

'Here they come,' he said.

*

'I see it,' said Steve as he pulled out of the James Randi car park.

He did not need to be psychic to pick out the silver Volvo down the street. Intuition was enough. He pulled onto Davie Boulevard, heading west.

Psimon felt a strong urge to turn round to see if the car was following them but he contented himself with watching Steve's face as he kept a sharp eye on the rear view mirror.

'Here they come,' said Steve when he saw the Volvo falling in behind them. He pursed his lips and gave a small nod of approval.

'What is it?' asked Psimon.

'They're really keeping their distance,' said Steve. 'Whoever's driving the car has done this before.'

'Can you lose them?'

Steve looked across at him. Psimon almost seemed to be enjoying this.

'This isn't going to be some high octane car chase,' he said. 'Besides…' he added. 'I don't want to lose them just yet.'

Still driving calmly Steve turned north onto South Andrews Avenue, heading away from the airport where, in just over two hours, they were due to catch a flight back to the UK. He continued north for about a mile, crossed over the river, then stopped at the traffic lights signalling right.

'I take it you do know where you're going?' asked Psimon.

'Just chill out,' said Steve bending forward at an awkward angle to look in his wing mirror. 'We need to see if your information is accurate.'

'Information about what?'

'About that,' said Steve ominously. He reached out, adjusting the angle of the mirror to give him a better chance of keeping the approaching helicopter in sight.

The lights changed to green and Steve went with the flow of traffic, palm trees and tall, pristine buildings lining the road.

'I take it there's some point to this magical mystery tour,' said Psimon.

Steve shot Psimon a sour look.

'First off,' he said, as if he were lecturing some rookie on their first patrol. 'I need to make sure we're dealing with just the one tail. Plus,' he added. 'I need to confirm that this chopper really is here for our benefit; that it's not just some network bird covering downtown Fort Lauderdale…'

Psimon smiled. He was not worried… not about this at least.

*

'Chopper's on the scene,' came the female voice over the Volvo's radio.

'Thanks, control,' said the ex-cop. 'We still have a visual on the target. Any word on authorisation from the client.'

'That's a negative, car 1,' stated the female voice firmly. 'Brief remains, shadow and observe only.'

'Roger that, control. Car 1 out.'

The younger of the two men gave an unimpressed grunt.

'Would have been better if the contact had got a copy of that disk.'

'Well he didn't,' said the ex-cop. 'Just keep your mind on the job in hand. This guy seems like he's on some kind of sightseeing tour.'

They followed the Blue Chevy as it meandered leisurely through Fort Lauderdale's more affluent districts. Then…

'Heads up!' said the ex-cop suddenly. 'I think he's made us.'

*

'Okay,' said Steve. 'That should do it.'

Psimon felt himself pressed gently back in his seat as Steve suddenly accelerated away from the junction, not breaking the speed limit, just driving with more purpose than he had been for the last ten minutes. They turned south and headed back over the river. The Volvo had now closed the distance in response to their increased speed and still the chopper circled overhead. But Steve did not seem concerned. He knew what he needed to know.

Psimon became aware that they were heading back to where they had started from. Up ahead was South Andrews Avenue, and there, coming up on the right was the multi-storey parking lot that Steve had disappeared into before they went to the James Randi Foundation. With a quick glance in his mirror Steve indicated right and turned into the lot. As they turned in Psimon took a quick glance behind them. The Volvo had come up fast and was now right behind them.

*

'Quick,' said the younger man. 'We don't want to lose them in there.'

The ex-cop said nothing. He had already gunned the accelerator. As he watched the Chevy enter the lot ahead of them he wondered if the subjects were going to make a run for it on foot. Through the tight turns and gloomy interior of the lot he kept the Chevy in view at all times but instead of taking one of the numerous available spaces the Chevy just headed straight for the exit. The Volvo followed.

*

Psimon did not like the claustrophobic feel of the parking lot and was relieved when Steve headed for the exit. The Volvo was right on their tail. Any pretence about whether or not they were being followed had been abandoned.

The chase was on…

Or not… as it turned out.

Steve braked suddenly as they reached the security barrier at the exit. He reached forward to the dashboard, opened the small compartment, and took out the printed card that he had placed in there earlier. Then, with a wink at Psimon, he lowered his window and inserted the card into the column beside the car. The security barrier lifted before them and Steve drove slowly through, only speeding up when the barrier dropped down behind them.

*

'Shit!' cursed the ex-cop when he saw the security barrier rise up for the Chevy.

'Where did he get that ticket,' protested the younger man. 'We didn't see him stop.'

'He didn't stop, you moron!' snapped the ex-cop. 'He'd already paid for the ticket.'

The younger man seemed puzzled as the security barrier came down in front of them. For a second the ex-cop considered breaking through the barrier but in addition to the barrier he spotted a steel panel crossing the driveway ahead of them. They might get past the barrier but that steel plate would flip up and stop the Volvo in its tracks. With an animal growl he slammed the car in reverse only to find that two cars were now sitting behind them waiting to exit the lot. One of them honked its horn impatiently.

'For the love of God!' swore the ex-cop.

Then, rummaging in his pocket, he fished out a handful of cash thrusting it at the younger man who seemed stunned at how quickly they had got themselves into this predicament.

'Go find a ticket machine!' he commanded. 'And make it fucking quick!' he added as the younger man jumped out of the car.

With a groan of angry frustration the ex-cop thumbed the radio on the dashboard.

'Car 1 to control…' he began.

'Go ahead, car 1,' said the familiar female voice.

'Control… we've lost them,' he said heavily. 'I repeat… we've lost them.'

*

'Smooth, Mr Brennus… Very smooth,' said Psimon as they accelerated away from the parking lot.

'It helps when your intelligence comes from a bona fide psychic.'

'Quite,' said Psimon.

'Of course,' Steve went on. 'That's the point where we'd normally open up with the M16s and a truckload of claymore mines. But in this case,' he added with a self-satisfied smile. 'I thought a well designed security exit would do the trick.'

The two men glanced at each other and laughed out loud. Then Steve caught sight of the chopper in his mirror and a more serious mood descended once more. They were not in the clear yet.

*

'Control to helicopter N27484, come in please.'

'2-7 here control, go ahead.'

'Ground unit has lost visual on target. Stay tight on target until car 1 can reacquire.'

'Will do, control. Any word yet on authorisation to detain.'

'None as yet, 2-7. The Director has been informed. We should have an answer in the next few minutes.'

'Jesus!' swore the helicopter's co-pilot. 'They've gone right to the top… This must be the real deal.'

'Will do, control,' said the pilot into his microphone. 'Target has just turned onto West Broward Boulevard. Looks like he's heading for the highway.'

'Understood, 2-7. Control out.'

*

Steve turned north onto highway 95 driving as fast as he could without drawing any additional unwanted attention. Beside him Psimon was craning his neck round in an attempt to see the chopper.

'Do you think we've lost it?' he asked.

'Not a chance,' said Steve. 'But we need to before that Volvo can get back on our tail.'

'And can we?'

'Oh yes,' said Steve with a smile which, despite the concern on his face, told just how much he was enjoying this.

'How?' asked Psimon.

'Patience, boy,' said Steve. 'Just another mile.'

A few minutes later and Steve switched to the inside lane, while ahead of them loomed a vast ten-lane overpass.

Psimon had a sudden insight into what Steve had in mind and he could feel the anticipation in the ex-soldier sitting beside him. But then another more disturbing image came to him. Everything was not as Steve thought it was. Something was wrong.

'Steve,' said Psimon as they closed on the overpass.

'Not now, Psimon,' said Steve distractedly.

'But, Steve...'

'Not now,' snapped Steve.

The Chevy slipped under the overpass and Steve brought them to an abrupt halt on the verge beside the highway. Ahead of them a bright red Hyundai was parked well up on the verge. However, pulled up close behind it was a considerably less shiny pickup truck, the drivers of which seemed to have taken an unhealthy interest in the unoccupied Hyundai.

'Shit!' breathed Steve slumping back in his seat.

'I tried to tell you,' offered Psimon.

Steve paused for a second. He grabbed his overnight bag from the back seat and thrust it into Psimon's lap.

'Take this,' he said. 'And stay in the car.'

Using the pickup to conceal his approach Steve closed quickly on the Hyundai. One guy was sitting in the driver's seat. The other was leaning in through the door. Neither would see him coming. Steve made his move.

'Can I help you gentlemen,' said Steve confidently as he came up beside the bright red rental car that he had parked here just a couple of hours before.

The reaction from the men was startling. The man leaning in the driver's door straightened up suddenly and Steve found himself looking down the barrel of Glock 9mm handgun.

*

'Control to helicopter N27484, come in please.'

'2-7 here, control. Go ahead.'

'Car 1 is now mobile. ETA on your position four minutes.'

'Roger that, control. Target has stopped under the overpass at West Sunrise Boule...'

'One minute, 2-7...' cut in the female voice.

There was a pause of several seconds before the voice of control returned.

'Be advised 2-7… authorisation has been granted. I repeat… authorisation to detain subjects has been granted. Car 1 will be at West Sunrise overpass in four minutes…'

*

Steve sighed as the barrel of the gun came to a halt just inches from his face. But his sigh was one of annoyance and not fear. He should have anticipated that even a city as shiny as Fort Lauderdale had its seedier side.

The individual holding the gun had the hard, gaunt face of a man who was no stranger to Florida's judicial system. White, unshaven and grubby-looking he was of slight build and a good deal shorter than Steve, while the man in the driver's seat cast an altogether larger shadow.

For a moment the man seemed unnerved by the lack of reaction from Steve. He looked into Steve's eyes and the gun's barrel wavered slightly.

Behind him Steve heard the door of the Chevy open as Psimon disobeyed his command to stay in the car. The car-jacker's eyes flicked past Steve's shoulder and in that instant Steve's hands lashed out with blinding speed. In the blink of an eye he had disarmed the car-jacker and turned the gun on its owner.

'Easy now, man,' beseeched the car-jacker quailing before the gun that was now pointed at his head.

The gun was rock-steady in Steve's hand.

'You, out of the car,' said Steve to the man in the driver's seat and out climbed a great hulk of a man in torn overalls that were thick with oil and grime.

'Over by the truck,' Steve ordered the two men, and over his shoulder… 'Psimon, get in the car,' he called.

Psimon moved quickly round to the far side of the Hyundai but he hesitated to get inside. His heart was pounding, not because of the scene being played out before him but because he could feel their pursuers getting closer.

'Steve, they're coming,' he said.

'I know, Psimon. Now get in the car.'

The two car-jackers hovered edgily near their pickup still no more ten feet from Steve. Anger had replaced fear in their mean, reckless minds and Steve could see that they were beginning to doubt whether he would actually use the gun. He knew he would not but he could not take it with him and he was damned if he was going to leave it for them. Quickly he grabbed the barrel of the gun popped the round out of the chamber, ejected the magazine and disassembled the gun. Then he threw the parts into a nearby storm drain.

The car-jackers were less than pleased.

'That was a mistake, friend,' said the small wiry man producing a knife from nowhere and starting towards Steve. Meanwhile the big guy reached into the pickup's cab and pulled out a large pick-axe handle.

'Get in the car Psimon,' said Steve as the smaller of the two men closed on him.

Psimon did not move as the violence began and time slowed to a crawl…

As the knife flashed towards Steve he blocked the attack with his left hand and slapped the skinny man in the throat with his right. The slap appeared ineffectual but the man's body tightened with a spasm and he fell, twitching, to the floor.

Steve took a step forward to meet the downward blow of the axe handle as the big fellow launched a mighty overhead swing. He caught the descending club; his hands closing over those of the heavier man and with a savage twist Steve flipped him onto his back.

There was a grunt and the sound of something snapping.

Then, before the big man could regain his feet, Steve crouched down behind him, one arm going round his neck the other round the back of his head. His left hand was clasped firmly in the crook of his right arm. The headlock was secure, and then he began to squeeze. The big man was strong but Steve held him down and did not let go.

'Steve...' protested Psimon when he saw what was happening.

But still Steve did not release his hold. He just squeezed... and squeezed until suddenly the big man went limp in his grasp and Steve dropped him in the dirt. Then without a backward glance...

'Psimon, get in the fucking car!'

Finally seeing the truth of what had just happened Psimon jumped in the car and barely had chance to close the door before the wheels spun noisily in the verge.

'You didn't kill him,' stated Psimon as he reached back to pull on his seatbelt.

Steve kept his foot to the floor looking for a gap in the traffic.

'Of course I didn't kill him,' he said, sounding somewhat insulted. He pulled back onto the main road and by the time the Hyundai emerged from the overpass it was moving at the same speed as the rest of the traffic on the highway.

'Believe me,' added Steve, checking his rear-view mirror. 'It takes a lot longer than thirty seconds to strangle a man. I just cut off the blood supply to his brain. He'll come round soon feeling happy as Larry.'

Steve remained in the inside lane and took the exit immediately after the overpass.

'But you did break his wrist?' insisted Psimon.

'Well, he shouldn't have been so fat,' said Steve.

The slip-road curved round a small circular lake, bringing them up onto West Sunrise Boulevard and passing directly over the Chevy that now lay abandoned under the bridge.

'And what about the other guy?'

'Jiu-jitsu move,' said Steve. 'A Japanese master gave us a demonstration in the Regiment. Don't ask me how it works but if you get it right they're out for a few minutes, wake up with a headache.'

'And you got it right...'

'Didn't I just,' said Steve with an immodest grin.

Psimon smiled at this flash of bravado. Steve had earned it. He had done enough to secure their escape, enough and no more. Psimon settled back in his seat. Their excursion to America was over. He had done what he came to do. Now it was time to leave the bright sunshine and return to the UK where the shadows waited to engulf him. The novelty and adrenaline of the day had proved a useful distraction but now it was time to go back and Psimon could feel the fear lurking on the edge of perception threatening to poison his resolve and crush his will in its merciless jaws.

With a weary sigh Psimon turned his face to the window.

Steve noticed the sudden change in Psimon's mood. He felt a surge of concern but he sensed that this was a personal battle that Psimon needed to face and he remained silent. He manoeuvred across the lanes of traffic, heading for the left-hand filter lane that would bring them back onto highway 95 going south. Meanwhile, a thousand feet above them, a helicopter circled the overpass waiting for a blue Chevy Cobalt to emerge and, as a silver Volvo disappeared beneath the overpass, a bright red Hyundai cruised south heading for the airport.

CHAPTER 16

Friday March 4th

Lucifer felt cheated.

The delusions of normal life had kept him too long from the accused. Now the heretic was close to death and had not yet been cleansed. He hung from the wall still. His torn hands encrusted with blood, his naked body pale and slack, his head hanging forward in oblivious stupor. Only the faint, rasping grate of his breathing and the occasional delirious moan suggested that he was anything more than a corpse.

No, this would not do at all. Those in dominion would not be appeased. The inquisition must be consummated. The heretic must meet his end with open eyes, must confess his sins as the breath of life was taken from him.

The heretic must wake, before he is allowed to die.

*

The late evening skies over England were a world away from the wide sunlit blue of Florida; the low dark clouds illuminated with a lurid orange glow from the lights of the city.

Steve could not say that he was pleased to be back. The only message waiting on his mobile was from his bank manager. A deposit of fifteen thousand pounds should be enough to prevent the bank from foreclosing on the house immediately but they might still insist on the sale of the property to repay the remainder of the outstanding debt. No, their Virgin Atlantic 747 was not the only thing to have come down to earth with a bump and Steve turned moodily to see if Psimon had finished the call he was making.

'Your girlfriend?' he asked when Psimon finally joined him outside Terminal 2 of Manchester Airport.

'No,' replied Psimon putting away his mobile phone, the smile on his face still lingering from the call. 'Actually it was a woman I've not spoken to before.'

'Well you seemed to be getting on well enough,' said Steve sourly.

'Turns out we've got a lot in common,' said Psimon.

Steve snorted and Psimon's smile softened. He knew that Steve was only feeling bitter because he had not heard from Christine and could not bring himself to phone her. Being away from his family, even for a few days, felt like an eternity to Steve but he did not want to call until he had something to offer, something to tell Christine that might make a difference to their awful predicament. And that meant seeing this job with Psimon through.

'Just a few more days,' thought Steve. *'Just a few more days and life can return to normal... Bollocks!'* Steve chided himself. *'We're going to lose the house, maybe the cottage too. And on top of that my wife and daughter think I'm some kind of violent monster. Life is never going to be normal again.'*

'Here's our bus,' said Psimon, breaking Steve's despairing train of thought and regarding him with his penetrating grey eyes. Psimon had his own reasons for dreading their return to the UK. He knew that there was no escaping destiny, not unless you were willing to let someone else pay the price.

The bus ferried them quickly to the long stay car park and Steve disembarked first, his eyes scanning the deserted rows of vehicles before Psimon stepped off the bus. Despite the anxieties tumbling through his mind Steve's senses remained alert for any potential threat to Psimon. For his part Psimon enjoyed the sense of security, even though he knew it was just an illusion.

In the eerie brightness of the towering lamps they made their way to Steve's BMW. They did not see it at first, hidden as it was by a large white transit van parked beside it.

'Where next?' asked Steve as he made his way round to the driver's side.

'My flat,' replied Psimon hovering by the passenger's door. 'Seventy-four, Freshfield Road, Altrincham…' his words trailed off as his chest felt suddenly strained. His shoulders burned with a rending pain and he struggled to draw a breath as the fear seeped like black oil into his mind.

Once again the heretic was waking up.

*

Lucifer took a fistful of the heretic's hair, lifted his head and drew back his arm to strike a waking blow. Then he paused, glancing from the heretic's form up to the inverted image of Christ the Deceiver. The symmetry was pleasing but one detail was missing.

Lucifer walked over to the altar, opened an inlaid wooden box and took out a small, short-bladed dagger. The dagger was not of a conventional design. The stubby handle was designed to sit in the palm of the hand with the blade extending between the fingers. Such blades were known as fist-daggers or push knives. Protruding from Lucifer's massive fist the short three-inch blade looked insignificant but it would be more than sufficient to wake the heretic.

Lucifer returned to the dying man, glanced up at the inverted crucifix for reference then stabbed the heretic between the ribs of his right side. Then as the heretic gasped and choked his way back into consciousness Lucifer stepped back to admire the scene.

Yes, he thought, *there is poetry in life.*

*

The BMW gave a familiar 'beep-beep' as Steve thumbed his key ring. He opened the driver's door and threw his travel bag onto the back seat.

'It's open,' he said when Psimon did not move to get in.

'I said its open,' repeated Steve glancing across at Psimon who just stood there silhouetted against the side of the white transit van. He did not appear to have heard Steve. He just stood there, shoulders slumped, head bowed forward.

'Psimon!' said Steve raising his voice. 'The car's op...'

Steve's words died in his throat as Psimon's arms slowly rose up on either side of his body until he stood there like a scarecrow. Then, with a suddenness that made Steve take an involuntary step backwards, Psimon was slammed back against the side of the transit. His arms stretched out to either side, suspending his body by invisible means, invisible wires... or nails...

Steve felt as if his feet had been welded to the floor. For several seconds he stood there aghast. Then Psimon drew in a sudden, stifled gasp that sent a chill down Steve's spine. It was the sound that someone makes when they are stabbed, a shocked intake of breath. Then slowly and painfully Psimon raised his head but he did not see Steve. Whatever it was that his eyes beheld was terrifying. Psimon's eyes stared straight ahead. The ugly bruising round his left eye, which had faded, now returned; so too the haemorrhaging in the palms of his hands.

And all before Steve's horrified gaze.

Suddenly Psimon's eyes locked onto something in the nether world of his perception. Something that terrified him further still. His lips mouthed pitiful objections then he opened his mouth and let out a horrible scream that reverberated round the empty car park.

*

With an agony of strained tendons the psychiatrist raised his head and looked with abject terror into the black eyes of his tormentor. He watched as the giant in priestly robes donned thick rubber gloves and lifted a small metal bucket and what looked like a holy water sprinkler or aspergillum, the silver head of which was corroded and heavily pitted. A dread sense of foreboding shot through the psychiatrist's mind as the acolyte dipped the head of the aspergillum into the bucket. Drops of clear liquid dripped onto the floor and where they fell the paving flags bubbled and spat as the vitriolic fluid burnt into the stone.

The acolyte raised his hand and, even before the first droplets had landed in his flesh, the psychiatrist was screaming.

Lucifer was placated.

The cleansing had begun.

*

Steve watched in horror as the screams of fear turned to screams of agony and small, dark blisters began to appear on Psimon's face and hands.

This sudden manifestation of pain broke the spell that held Steve in its grasp and he dashed round the car to Psimon's side. He hesitated for a second as if Psimon were afflicted by some deadly contagion then he reached up and put his hands under Psimon's arms. For a moment it seemed as if some force was resisting his efforts to help Psimon down. Then suddenly he collapsed into Steve's arms.

'Psimon,' said Steve desperately. 'God, Psimon. Are you okay? Can you hear me?'

In response Psimon could only moan incoherently.

'I'm sorry,' he sobbed. 'Yes, I confess… I confess…'

'Come on,' said Steve. 'I'm taking you to hospital.'

With that he leaned over to open the car door. Then he gathered Psimon up, lifted him bodily from the floor and manoeuvred him as gently as he could into the passenger seat.

'Hang on Psimon,' he said gently. 'We're going to get you some help.'

Steve slammed the door shut and sprinted round to the driver's side. He jumped into the car, fired up the engine and sped towards the car park's exit before skidding to a halt at the security barrier. He fumbled in his jacket pocket for the ticket he had paid for in the terminal.

'No!' sobbed Psimon suddenly from the seat beside him. 'No…' he said again cringing into the grey upholstery of the car.

*

Lucifer dragged the heretic to the foot of the altar and tied his feet and bloody hands with plastic ties. He offered a short submissive prayer before pulling the shroud over the heretic's head and down the length of his tortured body. He inserted the hose before securing the shroud with another tie around the heretic's ankles. Then he genuflected before crossing to the side of the chapel. Bending down he checked that the other end of the hose was properly connected. Then, with the solemnity of a religious rite, he flicked the switch on the pump and the chapel was filled with a loud unpleasant whining.

Lucifer returned to stand over the condemned as the breath of life was taken from him, the breath of life that had been so heinously abused.

*

Psimon's sobbing was growing quieter. His eyes began to close and he seemed to be losing consciousness.

Steve leaned across the car, grabbed Psimon's chin, and turned his face to look at him.

'Psimon!' he said in an authoritative voice. 'Psimon, look at me,' he ordered.

Slowly Psimon's eyes began to focus on Steve's.

'Good,' said Steve. 'Keep looking at me.' Steve willed Psimon to focus on the here and now. 'There's no one here Psimon. You're in the car, with Steve. You're safe… there's no one here.'

A kind of fearful lucidity returned to Psimon's gaze and he looked up at Steve as if he could not quite believe it was true.

'That's it, Psimon. That's it... look at me… only at me.' Steve was unbelievably relieved that Psimon was coming round and, seeing the recognition in his eyes, he let Psimon relax back into his seat.

Quickly Steve lowered his window and inserted the ticket into the barrier.

'I'm taking you to a hospital,' Steve repeated now that Psimon was more comprehensible. He had no idea what had just happened to Psimon or what to do about it. Bullets, knives, bombs... people trying to kill him. These were things that Steve could handle, things that he could understand. But an invisible enemy that can strike at you without even being present. No warning, no defence... How can you live with that and still retain your sanity.

'No,' said Psimon in a tremulous voice.

'What?' Steve glanced across as he drove through the airport complex heading for the motorway.

'No hospital,' said Psimon more firmly.

'But you're hurt,' protested Steve. 'You need help.'

'They can't help me,' said Psimon.

Steve looked across once more. He was filled with uncertainty. He was not equipped to deal with this, no one was. The only person who seemed to have any understanding of what was going on was Psimon. He was the one who was suffering. It was for him to decide his fate.

Psimon gave a small affirmative nod. 'Seventy-four, Freshfield Road, Altrincham,' he said. 'Flat number two.'

Despite his misgivings and his feelings of inadequacy Steve approached the motorway but instead of taking the exit for Wythenshaw Hospital he veered left, heading away from Manchester and towards the suburb of Altrincham.

CHAPTER 17

Steve pulled up outside Psimon's flat. The street was wide and lined with mature trees. It was after ten now and raining; the bare branches of the trees forming spidery halos round the widely spaced street lamps. Except for a single car, parked some way back on the other side of the street, the road was quiet; there was no one about. Steve turned to Psimon who had been dozing in his seat.

'Nice area,' he said, the idle small talk helping to diffuse the tension that persisted from the incident in the airport car park.

Psimon straightened up in his seat, wincing at the sudden pain in his hands and in his side. 'Yes,' he replied, waving Steve's hands away when he tried to help.

Steve watched Psimon's face anxiously as he unbuckled his seatbelt and reached for his bag. He was clearly still in pain but the crisis had passed. 'I had you in a bedsit,' he said looking up at the handsome Victorian villa.

Psimon managed a weak laugh and reached to open the door but a sharp intake of breath spoke of the pain in his ribs.

'Let me get that,' said Steve jumping out of the car and moving quickly round to open the door for Psimon.

With an effort Psimon managed to get out on his own but his legs felt numb and unsteady and he was grateful for Steve's help when he tried to stand.

'Where are we heading?' asked Steve, supporting Psimon as they made their way towards the driveway.

'Main door,' said Psimon. 'Then up the stairs.'

'Right you are,' said Steve, pointing his key ring behind them to lock the car. And as he glanced back something caught his eye; a tiny glint of light from the car across the street. Light reflecting from a pair of spectacles…

There was someone in the car.

'What is it?' asked Psimon, his voice heavy with fatigue.

'Just a minute,' replied Steve, trying to pierce the shadowed interior of the car with his gaze. He turned to look directly at the car but just at that moment it started its engine and pulled off down the road. Steve's gaze followed the car as it passed them but the light was not sufficient for him to see inside. He caught a quick glimpse of the driver, a woman in a dark suit, nothing more.

'Steve?' queried Psimon.

'It's nothing,' said Steve. 'Come on,' he said. 'Let's get you inside.'

Steve did not know what he had been expecting but he felt surprised that Psimon's flat was so normal. It was a nice flat with large rooms and high corniced ceilings, a good conversion of the original house. Whatever Psimon did for a living he was doing well to be able to afford this. But all that aside it was the home of a normal young man; untidy, with clothes lying about the floor, music CDs, empty glasses, stacks of DVDs piled on the floor, rather than back on the shelves where they belonged.

Steve helped Psimon through to the living room and lowered him into a big comfy armchair. There was a large 'home cinema' unit in the corner, several sweaters and a thick fleecy blanket strewn across the sofa opposite. There were two games consoles set up beside the TV and beside them the obligatory pizza delivery box and an empty bottle of wine.

'Normal,' thought Steve incongruously as he glanced down at Psimon.

Psimon relaxed into the chair with a bone-weary sigh and Steve crossed to the deep bay window. He moved from one side to the other pushing the curtains back so that he could see as much of the road below as possible.

Nothing... the road was clear. There was no sign of the car that had tweaked his suspicions.

With an unconvinced grunt Steve drew the curtains and switched on a couple of table lamps before turning out the main light, which was altogether too bright.

'Coffee?' suggested Steve. 'Brandy?'

'A cup of tea would be great,' replied Psimon without opening his eyes.

Steve looked down at this remarkable young man; his face, which had been almost back to normal, was once again swollen and bruised and now dotted with painful looking blisters; and his hands, trembling slightly as they rested on the arms of the chair, each centred with a blood-black sore.

'Fourteen times...' thought Steve. *'Fourteen times this has happened before. And who was there to help you back to your flat then?'*

Psimon seemed almost asleep and Steve went through to the kitchen to get them some drinks. When he returned a few minutes later with two mugs of tea Psimon was not asleep but staring wistfully across the room, his eyes glistening with tears.

They drank their tea in silence. When Steve saw that Psimon had finished he went over to take the empty mug from him.

'Let's have a look at you then,' he said, putting the mugs aside and drawing a reluctant Psimon gently forward in his chair.

'I'm all right,' said Psimon. 'It'll pass... All this will fade... It always does.'

Steve was having none of it. 'Let me see,' he said taking one of Psimon's hands carefully and holding it closer to the light.

The skin remained unbroken but the trauma to the underlying tissue looked painfully real.

'So how does this happen,' asked Steve as he turned Psimon's hand over, gently testing his fingers to make sure he still had movement and sensation.

'I don't know,' replied Psimon, looking at his hand as if he too were puzzled by it. 'I tend to think of it as a kind of stigmata.'

'You mean the wounds of Christ,' said Steve, 'magically appearing on the bodies of devout followers.'

'That's right,' said Psimon.

'Stigmata's for real then?' asked Steve, glancing up at Psimon.

'No,' said Psimon. 'But that's the way I think of it.'

Steve nodded as he laid Psimon's hand down and leaned forward to inspect his bruised face.

'Besides,' Psimon went on. 'These aren't the wounds of Christ and I'm not a devout follower.'

'Me neither,' said Steve. 'Sorry,' he added when Psimon winced as he checked that his nose was not actually broken.

'But it is true,' Psimon continued as if he were pleased at having someone to discuss it with, '…that the mind can effect physical changes in the body. I just think that with me it's more pronounced.'

'You can say that again,' said Steve, directing Psimon to raise his top so that he could take a look at the injury in his side.

'When these attacks occur,' explained Psimon. 'It's as if they're happening to me. They feel so real… I think my body believes it and makes it so.'

'Doesn't sound very scientific,' said Steve bending forward to look more closely at the livid red weal in Psimon's side.

'That's cos I'm not a scientist,' said Psimon.

'Well it sure as hell looks like someone gave you a good whack here,' said Steve.

'He didn't hit me, he stabbed me.'

'Yes,' thought Steve, *'That's what it sounded like.'*

'Or at least,' Psimon corrected himself. 'He stabbed whoever it was he'd taken.'

Steve glanced up at Psimon. He still found it difficult to believe that someone, somewhere had been murdered tonight and that Psimon was displaying the marks of the killing.

'And has it always been like this?' asked Steve. 'With all the others?'

'No,' said Psimon reflectively. 'At first they were more like nightmares. Terrible nightmares that a young boy couldn't know enough of the world to have.'

Steve paused as he unravelled this awkward sentence, then he shuddered as the meaning of it struck home.

'But they've been growing more powerful over the last few years,' said Psimon. 'More real… the distance between us is closing.'

'What does that mean?' asked Steve, moving back to sit on the arm of the nearby sofa.

'That the time when we meet is getting nearer.'

'How do you know?' asked Steve.

'I just do,' said Psimon somewhat defensively.

'And that's all?' pressed Steve. 'You don't know where or when?'

'Only that it's soon,' said Psimon ominously. 'And close.'

'Close?' asked Steve.

'Manchester,' clarified Psimon. 'We meet somewhere in the city.'

'Oh, well that narrows it down,' said Steve sarcastically.

Psimon turned his bruised face away. It was obvious that this 'encounter' was not something he was eager to talk about. But Steve was finally convinced about the validity of Psimon's fears and he was not willing to let it drop.

'You must know more than that?' he insisted. 'From what I can see you seem to know just about anything you want to know.'

Psimon refused to look at him.

'Come on Psimon,' said Steve. 'You must be able to give me something… a description, a location, a time of day… anything. Why don't you just try?'

'You think I haven't tried,' snapped Psimon, turning to look directly at Steve. 'You think I've felt those people die and never tried to see the face of the man who did it.'

'So what's stopping you,' challenged Steve.

'The fear, Steve! I can't see past the fear.'

The frustration was painfully clear both in Psimon's tone and the bitter regret shining in his eyes.

'There comes a time when we have to face our fears,' said Steve more gently.

'I've tried,' said Psimon and now he just sounded exhausted. 'God knows I've tried. But it's like a black wall in my mind; a shadow that I can't see beyond.'

'But surely if you…' began Steve but Psimon cut him off.

'Steve, you can't even take a piss if someone's standing next to you at the urinal. And believe me, trying to confront the murdering psycho who's terrorised you from childhood is just a tad more difficult.'

This statement had the desired effect and Steve sat up straight on the arm of the sofa, chastened.

'This isn't some kind of trivial phobia,' said Psimon in a kinder tone. 'It's not an irrational fear. Nothing I see beyond the next few days has any substance to it. There's nothing to suggest that it's anything more than wishful thinking. I have dreams that seem more real.'

Psimon's despondency was painfully apparent.

'But if you could see something,' ventured Steve. 'Anything,' he added. 'Any small detail that might help me save you.'

'You can't save me,' stated Psimon. 'All you can do is decide how I die.'

'Don't fucking patronise me!' thought Steve angrily but letting out a deep breath he reigned in his temper.

'I may not be psychic,' he said tightly. 'But I simply refuse to accept that!'

'You have no choice,' said Psimon. 'I have seen it.'

'Okay,' said Steve turning Psimon's gift back on himself. 'What exactly have you seen?'

Psimon looked suddenly small and fearful.

'Why Manchester?' asked Steve. 'What makes you think you meet the killer in Manchester?'

'Because I see nowhere apart from Manchester between now and the time that I die,' replied Psimon. 'I do not leave the city.'

'Useful!' thought Steve, sarcastically.

He thought for a minute.

'And what about meeting the killer?' he said. 'That can't be down to simple deduction… What's he like? And when do you first know he's there?'

Psimon's eyes narrowed as he focussed on the interior images of his mind. He had grown quite pale and Steve could see the sheen of sweat on his upper lip. For a while Steve did not think he was going to answer.

'It's just the presence,' said Psimon distantly.

'Shit!' thought Steve with growing frustration.

'He's big…' added Psimon in a voice that was barely more than a whisper. '…Like a giant.'

Steve rolled his eyes.

Like a giant…' he thought. *'Great!'*

This was not exactly the detailed description he was hoping for. More like the exaggerated image that a child would form of an adult who had frightened them.

'And the eyes…' Psimon went on in the same dreamlike voice. 'So dark they're almost black. And flat,' he added. 'No expression, no feeling at all.'

Steve sat forward. Psimon had never mentioned seeing the man's eyes before.

'Anything else?' he asked.

'No,' said Psimon as if he were in some kind of trance. 'Just the presence, and the eyes, and then he's gone and all I see are the letters **T, I, X**, and the number **3**.'

Steve had been leaning forward in anticipation, now he settled back and sighed. Dark eyes probably meant dark hair. And T, I, X and the number three…

'What the hell did that mean?'

Not much to go on, that was for certain but not nothing either. He raised his hands to his face and then a thought occurred to him.

'What do you mean, he's gone?' he asked.

'Sorry?' said Psimon.

'You said, "…and then he's gone",' repeated Steve. 'I thought this guy is supposed to kill you. But now you're saying he turns up then disappears.'

'Yes,' said Psimon as if he had never seen it that way. 'The killing comes later.'

Steve gasped with exasperation. He leaned forward with his elbows on his knees. 'Okay,' he said. 'So tell me about the killing.'

Psimon was not looking at Steve. He seemed to be pondering on why he had not made this differentiation before.

'Where does it happen?' asked Steve.

'What?' replied Psimon distractedly.

'Your death,' said Steve, finding it distasteful to keep to Psimon's script.

'I don't know,' said Psimon. 'I think it's a church but if it is then it must be an old one.'

'Why's that?' asked Steve.

'Because the walls are bare stone and circular.' Psimon's gaze was focussed on a point some distance beyond where Steve was sitting. 'It's a grim place,' he went on. 'Cold and grim.'

'But you're sure that's where it takes place?' clarified Steve. 'The killing?'

'Yes,' said Psimon in a sinister whisper. 'That's where all the confessions take place.'

Steve felt a shiver run down his spine and he hesitated before asking the next question.

'And you're sure I'm there?' he asked quietly. 'In this place… You are sure it's me?'

'Oh yes,' said Psimon as his gaze suddenly focussed on Steve. 'I'm sure.'

Steve's heart was suddenly beating faster. He felt a strange kind of light-headedness and Psimon seemed to shrink away into the corner of the room. Part of him did not want to ask the next question but he knew he must.

'…if he kills me then it's over,' Psimon had said. *'But if you kill me then everything will be all right.'*

Steve asked the question.

'And what makes you think I kill you?'

'Because I have seen it,' said Psimon, his stone grey eyes boring into Steve's down a long and echoing tunnel. 'I have felt it,' Psimon went on. 'I feel the blade stabbing into my face, slicing through flesh and bone.'

Steve was transfixed.

'I feel a moment's pain,' said Psimon. 'A flash of elation, and then… nothing.'

Steve could feel himself growing faint and he tried to slow his breathing.

Could he do it? Could he actually kill someone he cared about to save them from an otherwise long and agonising death? The prospect terrified Steve. It terrified him because he knew that the answer to the question was yes.

Silence embraced the two men and for some time they just sat there looking at each other until finally Psimon spoke again. 'Does that answer your question?' he said.

'Yes it does,' said Steve shortly, rising from the arm of the couch. 'Now where do you keep the fucking brandy?'

It was after midnight before the brandy had dulled the trepidation in their minds sufficiently for them to think of sleep. Finally jetlag and the disrupted sleep of long hours travelling began to take its toll.

Psimon went first, declining Steve's help as he made his way to the bathroom.

This gave Steve the opportunity to check Psimon's flat for any security issues. He went through to the large bedroom overlooking the garden at the back of the flat. This was obviously Psimon's room. There were locks on the windows and they were on the first floor; no particular problems there. Steve went over to the window shielding his eyes against the glass so that he could see the large suburban garden in the darkness. The property backed onto a series of tennis courts and the smooth expanse of what looked like a bowling green. The green was partly illuminated by a series of small street lamps marking the line of a footpath that linked Psimon's road to the road running parallel to it. The passage seemed to emerge on the far side of the house adjacent to Psimon's.

As Steve's eyes followed the line of the footpath he caught sight of a cast iron fire escape rising up the back wall of Psimon's flat. *'That needs checking out,'* he thought as Psimon entered the room behind him.

'I can barely keep my eyes open,' said Psimon as he shuffled barefoot towards his bed.

'Where does the fire escape come into the building?' asked Steve.

'Just before the loo,' replied Psimon groggily. 'The landing goes off to the left… there's a door at the end.'

Steve moved to leave the room.

'Night,' said Psimon.

Steve paused at the door. 'Goodnight,' he said. And as Psimon pulled his shirt over his head Steve could see the angry red line of the injury in his side.

'Christ!' he thought for the umpteenth time. *'How the hell does he live with this?'*

Steve shook his head as he ducked out of the room. He pulled the door to but he left it open by three or four inches as if he had just said goodnight to a child and wanted to make sure he would be able to hear them if they cried. Then he went to finish checking the flat.

The fire escape door was half timber, half glass. Not the most substantial of doors but the lock was solid; no one was getting through there without making one hell of a racket. That would be warning enough.

Steve found a second bedroom to the rear of the building. Then he went to the bathroom before checking the final room in the flat, a third bedroom opposite the phone in the hall.

Feeling like he could fall asleep on his feet Steve flicked on the light in the room. Despite his exhaustion the vision that greeted him brought him back to startled wakefulness.

*

Lying in his bed, his head resting on the deep feather pillow, Psimon opened his eyes.

*

Steve stared in disbelief at the far wall of Psimon's 'spare room'. It was like the scene from a serial killer movie. Only in this case the obsessive psycho was in fact an obsessive psychic. The wall was covered with information: newspaper cuttings, photographs, diagrams, maps, computer-printed sheets and hand-written notes on small pieces of fluorescent paper; the whole thing haphazardly tied together with interconnecting lines of masking tape and permanent black marker. Some of the lines had been scribbled out or redirected and many of them pointed to nothing at all, or in other cases to a frenzied hatching of frustrated marks. And behind it all, like some kind of macabre wallpaper, were newspaper cuttings chronicling horrific murders going back more than a decade.

Captivated, Steve moved closer to the wall.

Far to the left, where the wall was almost clear, was a photograph of what he took to be Psimon's parents. There was something of each of them in Psimon's pleasant features. From this unassuming photograph the lines expanded, the continuum unfolding to cover the entire wall. And then it struck Steve. This was not the depiction of a mind in turmoil; this was a planning wall. The army used the same kind of thing when planning an operation; simplified, more efficient and far, far neater but essentially the same.

There were hundreds of names; most of them crossed out. There were maps of Manchester, of Fort Lauderdale in Florida and even an Ordnance Survey map of Alderley Edge, where he and Psimon had met for the first time. There were flight schedules, and receipts for tickets. There were articles on the James Randi Foundation and the million-dollar challenge. And, more alarming to Steve's mind, there were articles on the structure of MI5 with tables of hierarchy showing the names of employees. Leaning in more closely Steve saw one name outlined in red…

Richard Chatham, International Liaison for National Security

Beneath this name was pinned a return ticket to London and beside it a large, assertive tick.

As Steve's eyes continued to scan the wall he came to pages on nuclear submarines from Jane's Defence Weekly, a publication produced by the renowned authority on the armed forces of the world. There were more detailed articles taken from subscriptions to Jane's exclusive information packs, information that governments used to plan their defence strategies. Subscription to such material cost thousands of pounds. And then there were obscure technical diagrams of electrical circuits, ballast systems and even the nuclear reactors at the heart of the subs; diagrams of such detail that they were way beyond the reach of even Jane's much vaunted analysts. And within these diagrams several discreet components had been circled in red; inlet valves, temperature gauges and electrical circuits.

Steve traced his finger outwards from these diagrams to promotional photographs of nuclear submarines cutting through anonymous swathes of ocean. Two submarines were featured. The USS Virginia, a US Navy attack sub, and the HMS Vigilant, a Vanguard class ballistic missile submarine from the British Royal Navy. Beside the subs were small photographs of men in naval uniform and beneath each was a name, location, date and time.

Commander Douglas Scott, Manchester Airport, Wednesday March 2nd, 6 - 7.00pm

Captain Philip Kern, Orlando International Airport, Thursday March 3rd, 7.45 for 8.00am EST (cutting it fine).

'Huh,' exclaimed Steve quietly, recognising the two men and seeing that the dates and times coincided with their flights to Florida. And then he realised; meeting up with these two submarine captains was the real reason for their transatlantic jaunt. Could it be that taking the challenge at the Randi Foundation had been nothing more than a side-show, something to do while they were there? But what was the significance? Why was it so important to make contact with these two men?

He followed the lines radiating from these pictures to a small, intense knot of information. "Bootle Street," one of the notes read, and beneath it a list of names:

Chief Constable David McCormack
Admiral Joseph Grant (watch this tosser!)
Vice Admiral Edwin T. Fallon
Mr Chatham

The lines radiating from here were fewer. Only one thread seemed to have a coherent endpoint; it lead to an advertisement cut from a newspaper…

'CHALLENGE THE PSYCHICS… An open debate'

And from here there was nothing… lines leading to empty patches of wall. Masking tape hanging in crumpled ringlets. Dense scribbled blocks of permanent marker and other areas where any writing had been scratched from the wall with such force that the wallpaper was torn and the scrape marks gouged deep into the underlying plaster. Steve looked more closely at one of these obliterated scribblings where the same sentence seemed to have been written over and over before being scrawled out.

S##v# ##st k### m#
Ste#e #ust #il# me
###ve mu## ki## ##

With a growing sense of dread Steve saw what had been written there.

Steve must kill me
Steve must kill me
Steve must kill me

Feeling nauseous and light-headed Steve stumbled back from the wall. This was all becoming too much for him. He felt that he was living through someone else's nightmare and he could no longer distinguish what was real from what was not. How long had it taken to compile this information? What did it mean? What was it for? What did any of it have to do with him?

Standing with his back against the doorframe he fumbled for the light switch as stark newspaper headlines stared back at him from across the empty room.

Torture... Missing... Mutilated... Psychiatrist found Dead... Torture... Missing...

Steve felt an unpleasant sensation of panic crawling in his guts and he steeled his mind against it. Finally he stared defiantly at the wall before turning off the light with a decisive flick of the switch. He was about to leave the room when he noticed a small square of fluorescent orange paper lying on the table beside the door. With a deep sense of apprehension Steve reached down and turned the piece of paper over...

Steve Brennus
Mobile - 0774 0673394

Steve's fist closed around the note. He crushed it to a small tight ball and tossed it aside. Then, feeling more confused and frightened than he ever had in his life, he went to find the half-finished bottle of brandy.

*

Lying in his bed, his head resting on the deep feather pillow, Psimon closed his eyes and went to sleep.

CHAPTER 18

Saturday March 5th

Chancellor of the Exchequer, John Shackleton, poured himself a second cup of coffee and finished off the last of his croissant. With a relieved sigh he pushed the pile of newspapers aside. There was nothing in today's headlines that would require his presence in the office today. In fact he was free until his meeting with the French President tomorrow afternoon. It was Saturday morning, his wife had taken the boys to their respective rugby matches and the Chancellor was enjoying a rare moment's peace.

He opened up his laptop and logged on to the LSE website, idly scrolling through the pages of financial data and business news from around the world. He went to the Investor Centre and before clicking on 'Market News' his attention was drawn to the tables showing the top ten risers and fallers of the day.

'Huh,' he exclaimed with mild interest when he noticed that the top three performers had all risen by the same 13.39%.

'That happened just recently,' he seemed to remember but, as his eyes moved down the list, it suddenly struck him. This had not happened before but he *had* seen this before; seen these figures before…

	Price	+/-	%+/-
YULE CATTO	158.75	+18.75	13.39
STD LIFE	248.00	+29.29	13.39
COSTAIN GRP	22.39	+2.64	13.39
KAZAKHMYS	1720.00	+185.00	12.05
MICRO FOCUS	204.00	+18.25	9.83

The list went on but the Chancellor had risen suddenly from the table and was rifling through the mass of notes, telephone numbers and 'to do' lists on the family's notice board beside the kitchen door. His wife had stuck it up here, he was certain of it. But where the hell was it now?

There it was…

There, under a damned rugby newsletter… a folded piece of A4 paper with the words, A bit of forecasting fun!, written on the front. Please keep until Saturday 5th of March.

The Chancellor recalled being given the piece of paper at a charity function in Manchester almost five weeks ago. He remembered the young man with his shy, pleasant smile and piercing grey eyes.

'I will donate a thousand pounds if you will keep this to hand for the next five weeks,' the young man had said.

The Chancellor had glanced down at what was written on the paper. It was a list of companies and their share prices, a forecaster's guess at the top ten risers and fallers.

'You have a deal,' the Chancellor said with a manufactured smile. But…

'No,' the young man said as if he knew that the Chancellor had not taken him seriously. 'I want your word that you will do as you say.'

The Chancellor looked more closely at the sincere young man and nodded.

'Five weeks,' he said.

The young man smiled. He produced a cheque from his inside pocket and handed it to one of the nearby volunteers who was only too happy to take his cash.

'What's this?' the Chancellor's wife had asked the following morning when she was hanging up his jacket.

'Just something I was given at the dinner last night.'

'Can I bin it?'

'Yes,' the Chancellor had said. Then, 'No!' he amended.

His wife had raised her eyebrows and stood there hovering.

'Just stick it on the pin-board... I'll hang on to it for a while.'

The Chancellor brought the piece of paper back to the table and held it up beside his computer screen.

	Price	+/-	%+/-
YULE CATTO	158.75	+18.75	13.39
STD LIFE	248.00	+29.29	13.39
COSTAIN GRP	22.39	+2.64	13.39
KAZAKHMYS	1720.00	+185.00	12.05
MICRO FOCUS	204.00	+18.25	9.83

There were twenty companies listed; ten risers and ten fallers, and by the time the Chancellor reached the end of the list his hand was shaking so much that he struggled to read the rest of what was written there.

Figures for Saturday March 5th, 9.30am.

For more information contact Richard Chatham, MI5

Yours truly...

The Chancellor reached for his mobile phone. 'Kirsty?' he said when his call was finally answered.

'Yes, sir? I didn't ex...' began the Chancellor's chief personal aid.

'Kirsty,' the Chancellor said, an audible tremor in his voice. 'Get me the number for MI5. And find out if there's someone there by the name of Richard Chatham. Then contact Lesley Stevens in Camp David. Tell him I need to speak with the Prime Minister immediately.'

CHAPTER 19

Richard Chatham had just arrived in the office when the phone rang.

'Hello Mr Chatham,' said the voice on the line with familiar courtesy. 'Working the weekend again?'

'Hello Psimon,' said Chatham. 'How was Florida?'

'Sunny,' replied Psimon. The smile in his voice acknowledging Chatham's awareness of his movements.

'A welcome change from the grey skies of Manchester I would have thought,' said Chatham.

'Quite so,' replied Psimon.

'A successful trip?'

'I think so.'

'Business or pleasure?'

'You don't know?' asked Psimon with mock surprise.

'I didn't think it necessary to follow you abroad,' said Chatham.

'Oh?'

'You initiated contact,' explained Chatham. 'Logic suggested that you were unlikely to disappear.'

'Very trusting for someone in your position,' said Psimon.

Chatham gave a small laugh.

'And if you did vanish…' he asked, 'would we find you?'

'No,' said Psimon with simple honesty.

'As I thought,' said Chatham.

There was a pause in the conversation before Chatham spoke again.

'I'm sorry about your mother,' he said with gentle sincerity.

'Thank you,' said Psimon and Chatham could hear the emotion in his voice. But even with that aside there was a difference in Psimon's tone. He sounded flatter, more subdued than he had during their previous conversations.

'Is Mr Brennus still with you?' asked Chatham.

'He is.'

Chatham nodded. He had been more than a little surprised to hear that Psimon had been travelling with a former member of the SAS. A soldier, now retired but with a distinguished service record. It cast Psimon in an altogether different light. It suggested that he might be more than a maverick individual acting alone; he might be part of a larger network. Chatham did not believe this to be the case but all possible scenarios had to be considered.

'And what about the immunity that we discussed?' asked Psimon. 'Is it in place?'

'I have prepared the necessary paperwork,' said Chatham looking at the black leather folder on his desk. 'But ratifying it is an altogether different matter. I don't think you understand…'

'Just make sure you have it with you for the meeting,' interrupted Psimon.

'The meeting…' echoed Chatham warily.

'Yes, Mr Chatham. I would like you there in person. In fact,' Psimon went on, 'I insist on it.'

'So, you're coming in?' asked Chatham sitting up suddenly in his chair.

'Not exactly,' replied Psimon. 'Let's just say I'm setting the ground rules for reasonable dialogue.'

'I don't understand,' protested Chatham, the frustration of always feeling one step behind was beginning to get to him.

'You will, Mr Chatham,' replied Psimon. 'I promise… you will.'

'But when?' pressed Chatham, sensing that the conversation was drawing to a close.

'Soon,' said Psimon. 'Very soon.'

Chatham sighed with frustration

'For now,' Psimon added in a conciliatory tone, 'I think you have another call coming through.'

Chatham glanced at the phone on his desk. The incoming call light had just started to flash urgently.

'Until our meeting then…' said Psimon. 'Goodbye Mr Chatham.'

And the line went dead.

CHAPTER 20

Steve became aware of daylight and the smell of coffee. He opened his eyes. A bright wedge of sunlight cut across the room, angling in through the deep bay window. He straightened himself up in the chair, pushed away the duvet and tucked in the extending leg support that had allowed him to recline in reasonable comfort. In fact, he had slept pretty damned well and pretty damned long, judging by the height of the sun.

'Who are you phoning now?' he asked, trying to assuage the dryness in his mouth.

'Just a friend.'

Psimon was sitting across the room on the window seat that ran round the inside of the bay.

'It's Saturday morning…' said Steve, leaning forward and running his hands vigorously through his hair. 'Thought you might be calling in your apologies to the psychic's coffee morning.'

Psimon laughed.

'Did that earlier,' he said. 'But they said I needn't have bothered. They already…'

'Knew,' finished Steve. 'Yeh… it was my joke.' His fingers ceased their tousling and began to focus on his temples, soothing a familiar and unwelcome ache.

'God, I could do with a coffee.'

Psimon nodded towards the corner of Steve's chair.

Steve glanced down to see a mug of coffee sitting on the carpet beside him. He reached down. It was still hot.

'Thanks,' he said.

Steve took a long mouth-burning gulp and let out a satisfied sigh. His mind suddenly flashed back to the unsettling events of the previous night and a shudder ran through his body. But things always look different in the morning. Few demons can tolerate the bright reality of morning sunlight. He looked over at Psimon who had put away his mobile phone and retrieved his own cup from the windowsill. Once again the bruising on his face and hands had faded remarkably quickly and Psimon showed little sign of the trauma that he had suffered. There was just an intangible fragility and a certain nervousness that Steve would never have picked up on had he not lived with Psimon for the last few days.

'There *is* a spare bed,' said Psimon, looking at Steve's sleep-rumpled clothes. He had been touched when he saw that Steve had pulled the reclining armchair over to the door, where he could sleep within sight of Psimon's room just across the hall.

'Didn't want to sleep *too* well,' said Steve rising from the chair.

He clasped his hands behind his head and stretched his arms up high, his shoulders making unpleasant popping sounds as he eased the stiffness from his body.

'So what improbable delights do you have planned for us today?' he asked.

The sudden seriousness of Psimon's expression made Steve fear the worst, and yet…

'I thought we might start with an early lunch,' Psimon said.

'Sounds perfect,' said Steve warily. 'Do I have time for a shower?'

'Certainly.'

'Good,' said Steve. 'I'm starting to feel like a hobo in these clothes.' Steve nudged the chair away from the door. 'I've got more clothes in the car,' he said. 'Is it all right if I…'

'Of course,' said Psimon.

'I'll only be a minute.'

'I'm fine,' insisted Psimon.

'Just want to make sure you're not going to be strung up by some sadistic poltergeist while I'm gone.'

'The latest victim is dead,' said Psimon, his tone in sober contrast to Steve's attempt at gallows humour. 'He will be hunting again now…'

'I'll get my clothes,' said Steve awkwardly.

He went into the hall, turned left towards the stairs, and nearly fell over three black plastic bin-bags, each one stuffed full of paper. Steve could see bits of twisted masking tape poking out of the tie-handle tops. He glanced back in the direction of the spare room where he had discovered the bizarre planning wall. It would seem that Psimon had had a busy morning.

A shower, a shave, another cup of coffee and Steve felt pretty good. He picked up his jacket from the back of the couch and checked his phone for messages, nothing from Christine. Steve's good mood evaporated.

'So where's the nearest café?' he asked.

'I thought we'd head into town,' replied Psimon. 'There's a place I know by the canal. And…' he added, holding out a fat brown envelope to Steve. 'I thought you could deposit this on the way.'

Steve frowned.

'Job's not over yet,' he said.

'Just want to make sure you get paid,' said Psimon. 'I might be a little distracted later.'

Still Steve hesitated.

'Your bank's only half a mile from the restaurant and they're open Saturday mornings…'

Steve could see that this was important to Psimon but it felt a bit too much like tying up loose ends to him; setting one's estate in order.

'Lunch is on me then,' said Steve, taking the envelope and tucking it into the inside pocket of his jacket.

*

Steve folded over his last piece of pizza and mopped up the sweet chilli sauce from his plate.

'That,' he said with his mouth still full, 'was the best pizza I've ever had.'

Psimon smiled at Steve's indulgence. His own meal had been barely touched.

Both men reached for their water.

'So, what's so special about this place?' asked Steve as he sat back from the table.

Albert's Shed was a popular restaurant. It was converted from a large brick tool shed and took its name from the old builder who used to keep his tools there. It sat at a junction on the canal, part of the recent regeneration of the heart of Manchester.

'Well, the food's excellent,' said Psimon. 'And I like the view out of these big windows.'

'That's not what I meant,' said Steve.

He knew now that Psimon did precious little without careful planning and, more often than not, an ulterior motive.

'Why this place in particular?'

'Like I said,' said Psimon. 'It's good food, it's close to your bank…'

'And…' pressed Steve.

'And it's handy for our meeting.'

'What meeting?' asked Steve. He should have known that this pleasant lunch was too good to last.

'Our meeting with the British and American governments,' said Psimon calmly.

Steve suddenly found himself wishing that he had not eaten so much pizza.

*

'They're not coming,' said Steve for about the fifth time in two minutes.

They were outside the restaurant now, loitering on the cobbled forecourt. Psimon sat on the edge of a raised brick flowerbed while Steve paced back and forth in front of him, his eyes scanning the small approach road for any sign of the country's top brass.

Psimon watched him, wishing he would just sit down and wait.

'What do they want with you?' asked Steve. 'How do they know you're here?'

He stopped suddenly and looked at Psimon.

'Last night,' he said. 'That car outside your flat.' He raised an accusing finger. 'They were casing your flat... watching for your return. Did you know you were under surveillance?'

Steve had resumed his pacing but Psimon was no longer watching. It was time for him to concentrate. He cast his thoughts back over the last forty-eight hours to two encounters in airport departure lounges and two men briefly met...

Commander Douglas Scott

and

Captain Philip Kern

He pictured their faces, remembered how it felt to stand in their presence, and opened his mind...

Psimon could still see Steve, he was still aware of his surroundings but his mind was focussed on a different location, on two different locations to be precise... dark, confined, and filled with strange noises like those one might hear in the womb. He could hear voices around him; voices speaking in clear, efficient tones. He heard the answers made, the orders given.

He was there and present.

Psimon allowed his mind to explore these alien environs, just enough to reassure himself that the details he had worked so hard to procure were accurate and accessible. They were. Complex systems, exactly as the blueprints had depicted but in the end they were just switches and valves; electrical switches... mechanical valves... sensitive dials... circled in red.

It was time to act.

No one would be killed; no one would be hurt. There would be confusion; there would be fear. But no one would be hurt.

It was time to act.

Psimon flicked the switches, opened the valves and saw the dials swing into the red.

There was confusion. There was fear.

And Psimon withdrew.

'I said, they're not coming,' repeated Steve, bending forwards and raising his voice as if Psimon were hard of hearing. 'The UK Government is not interested in some spoon bender from Altrincham. You'd be better off speaking to the producers of daytime telly. Least that way you could make some decent money.'

Psimon looked up at Steve and the expression in his eyes made the former SAS man feel sick.

'What is it?' he asked. 'What have you done?'

'What I had to,' said Psimon.

Steve stepped back from Psimon as if he did not recognise him. For the first time since meeting him he felt like leaving. He felt like running. Then, out of the corner of his eye he saw them coming. Three dark, unmarked cars, driving with unmistakable purpose.

Steve felt cornered, trapped.

As the cars surrounded the restaurant's forecourt Steve cast an accusing glance at Psimon who looked back at him with an expression of guilt, sympathy and unflinching determination.

Several men stepped out of the cars. They had a hard, no nonsense look about them.

'Special Branch,' thought Steve. *'Christ, what kind of shit have I got myself into?'*

One of the henchmen approached Psimon and Steve.

'This way gentlemen,' he said in a tone that might have seemed polite had it not been so menacing.

Psimon got up from the wall and walked towards the middle car. With a heavy sigh Steve started to follow him but the henchman blocked his path.

'The other car, Mr Brennus. If you please,' he said nodding towards the car at the rear of the convoy.

Steve groaned out another sigh. He recognised the procedure. Divide and conquer, separate the subjects, question them in isolation, play them off against each other, do not allow them the opportunity to corroborate their stories.

Ruing the fact of ever having met Psimon Steve made his way to the rear car. Another henchman held the door open for him and Steve glanced up towards the middle car where Psimon was being similarly apprehended. Steve saw Psimon nod his thanks to the henchman but before he disappeared inside the car he cast a look back at Steve.

Steve gave a soft snort of surprise and found his despairing mood somewhat lifted. There was a fire burning in Psimon's stone grey eyes, and something close to a smile on his face, and Steve found himself feeling suddenly sorry for the people taking them into custody, the people who would soon be interrogating Psimon.

'They haven't a clue of what they're up against,' he thought. *'Not a fucking clue.'*

CHAPTER 21

Richard Chatham had only been to Manchester twice before, both times as a visiting student from King's College Cambridge. The city had changed a good deal since then. It was busier for a start. It had taken them almost as long to get from the airport to the city centre as it had for them to fly from London.

Chatham was still reeling from the speed with which the morning's events had unfolded. After speaking to Psimon he had put down one phone only to pick up another immediately afterwards.

'I think you have another call coming through…' Psimon had said.

Chatham knew it would not be good news even before he recognised the voice of the Chancellor of the Exchequer.

'Chatham?' the Chancellor had demanded. 'Richard Chatham?'

'Yes, sir,' Chatham had replied. 'What can I do for you?'

'Do you know someone by the name of Psimon?'

Chatham had closed his eyes, let out a long heavy sigh, and his feet had barely touched the ground since.

Now he looked out of the tinted window as the car drove past the neo-classical façade of Bootle Street Police Station; a large three-storey, redbrick building in the heart of Manchester. The car turned onto Bootle Street where a high archway allowed cars through to the internal courtyard at the centre of the building.

Chatham felt an oppressive sense of finality as the car passed under the imposing arch and he wondered just how many criminals had been driven in the same way, seeing their liberty come to an end as the building closed around them.

Beside him in the back of the car the Chancellor of the Exchequer was speaking quietly into his mobile phone. Indeed he had hardly been off it since he had picked Chatham up from his office earlier that morning… the Prime Minister, who was on a state visit to the US, the Governor of the Bank of England, the Attorney General, to get provisional authorisation for Mr Brennus' Immunity. Then it was the Foreign Secretary and the Chief of the Defence Staff, Admiral Joseph Grant, who was currently hosting his American counterpart, Vice Admiral Edwin T. Fallon.

'We've just arrived,' said the Chancellor, speaking once more to the Foreign Secretary. 'Yes, they're already in custody,' he added after a pause.

Chatham glanced across discreetly, trying to keep the regret and contempt from his face. It seemed that in the space of just a few hours Psimon had gone from intriguing goldmine of useful information to public enemy number one and threat to the world's economy.

'That's right,' the Chancellor went on. 'It's not just the markets. There are defence implications too. The PM wants the military involved.'

The Chancellor paused, listening…

'No,' he said. 'It's just the Americans for now. Fallon will be speaking for the White House. Admiral Grant is bringing him down from Glasgow. It seems the FBI had already flagged this guy as a possible risk to national security.'

A frown of disapproval creased Chatham's brow. They knew next to nothing about Psimon and yet they were already prepared to cast him in the worst possible light.

The car came to a halt and Chatham took hold of his briefcase as a police officer came to escort them into the building where they were met by Chief Constable David McCormack, the commanding officer of Greater Manchester Police.

'Chancellor,' the Chief Constable said by way of a greeting. 'Mr Chatham.'

'Where is he?' asked the Chancellor as the Chief Constable led them through to an empty office.

Chatham noticed the eyes of the people watching them as they passed. It was clearly no secret that something unusual was going on.

'We've got him in one of our secure interview rooms,' said the Chief Constable closing the door.

'And his accomplice?'

'Likewise,' said the Chief Constable.

'Accomplice... oh please!' thought Chatham with distaste.

Both Chatham and the Chancellor refused the offer of tea or coffee, and neither felt inclined to take a seat when it was offered.

'Forgive me Chancellor,' the Chief Constable began. 'But what exactly are we looking at here? My briefing was somewhat lacking in detail. Just what is it this guy is supposed to have done?'

The Chancellor seemed momentarily at a loss.

'Mr Chatham,' he said.

Chatham was put on the spot. He felt himself flush with indignation.

'Well,' he began. 'He breached MI5 security and compromised a diplomatic clean line... He is in possession of passwords to highly sensitive information,' he added, struggling to think of anything specific that Psimon had done wrong. Breaching security and obtaining passwords were not crimes in themselves. True, a crime might have been committed in achieving these things but as yet they had no evidence of such.

The Chancellor seemed unsatisfied with Chatham's summary of Psimon's misdemeanours.

'With the help of his accomplice, Mr Brennus,' he cut in, 'he evaded federal authorities in America, who wanted to detain him for questioning. 'And,' the Chancellor added with a stern glance in Mr Chatham's direction. 'He is suspected of manipulating stock market figures, which could have unimaginable consequences for the international trading community.'

'So what is he?' asked the Chief Constable. 'A hacker... some kind of computer whiz kid.'

'We don't know,' said Chatham.

'It's not computers,' said the Chancellor reflectively. 'No system for predicting figures could be that accurate. It's impossible.'

The Chancellor sounded like a man whose faith; whose entire worldview had been undermined. Chatham knew exactly how he felt.

There was a sudden knock on the door.

'Yes,' shouted the Chief Constable.

A young officer poked his head round the door.

'Excuse me sir,' he said. 'There are some men in navy uniform to see you.'

'Well don't just stand there,' snapped the Chief Constable. 'Show them in.'

*

The secure interview room was grey and windowless. One of the Special Branch henchmen stood near the door, unmoving, unsmiling. The plastic cup of coffee on the table in front of Steve was cold and untouched. He watched the greyish brown surface ripple with minute concentric rings as heavy traffic rumbled past the building; the only evidence that the world outside existed.

Steve tried to marshal his thoughts. He had no idea what Psimon had done, no idea why Special Branch would be interested in him at all. But whatever it was, Steve was now caught up in it. He had trusted Psimon from the beginning, even when he had no reason to do so. It was a gut feeling and Steve trusted his instincts but now, after what must be an hour of sitting in this room, he was beginning to have his doubts. Psimon had not told him everything; that was clear. And now Steve was paying the price for his trust.

He was not worried about the questioning. His SAS training had prepared him for far worse than this. Besides, he had done nothing wrong. Okay, he had beaten up a couple of American lowlifes and failed to return a rental car to the depot. But one was self-defence and the other was hardly the crime of the century.

No, the thoughts that bedevilled his mind were closer to home.

All Steve could think about was his wife and his little girl. Being apart from them, even for a few short days, had been a torment in itself, not to mention the guilt and regret he felt over what had happened. The practical, financial problems that had befallen them were of nothing compared to that. All right, so they were bankrupt and homeless. But they would get through this, rebuild their lives.

'Two more days,' thought Steve bitterly.

Two more days and this job was over. Steve could forget about Psimon and all this psychic nonsense. Two more days and he could go back to his family; phone call from Christine or not. A few days in the sin bin was the least that he deserved but what he had done had not been deliberate. It was a foolish outburst, understandable in the heat of the moment. Surely Christine would be able to see that. And surely Sally would be able to forgive him… to trust him again… in time, surely…

Steve's eyes pricked with tears. He raised a hand to brush them away. He wished they would come for him and get this started. He wished the questions would begin. He wished he had never met Psimon.

*

Chatham felt strangely nervous. Not about being in the company of such powerful men. He dealt with people of power on a daily basis. No, Chatham felt nervous for an altogether different reason.

He was about to meet Psimon.

A wave of furtive looks followed the procession of dour-looking men as they made their way through the police station. First came the Chief Constable of Greater Manchester Police, followed by the Chancellor of the Exchequer, two admirals in full navy uniform, each with a uniformed aid in tow, and finally Mr Richard Chatham of MI5, International Liaison for National Security. In their wake they left a murmur of excited whispers as people speculated on who the mysterious detainees might be. The group descended the steps to the secure interview rooms. They passed one door with an officer standing outside and moved on to the door at the far end of the corridor.

At a nod from the Chief Constable the officer standing guard produced a key and unlocked the door. The procession moved inside. The door was closed and locked from the outside.

Psimon looked up as they entered the room.

In the centre of the room was a large table. Psimon was seated on the far side, while on the near side there were chairs for the five prominent men. The two naval aids went to stand discreetly against the wall behind their respective admirals. Four of the men moved to take their seats but Chatham remained standing as Psimon rose suddenly from his chair and walked round the table to meet him.

The Special Branch henchman moved to intercept Psimon but he was too far away and had not been expecting the suspect to move.

'Mr Chatham,' said Psimon, smiling warmly. 'It's a pleasure to meet you.'

'And you, Psimon,' said Chatham, smiling in turn despite the disapproving glares from the other men at the table.

The two men shook hands until the henchman directed Psimon back to his chair.

Psimon returned to his seat and Chatham too sat down. He could not take his eyes off Psimon. He was younger than he had been expecting but apart from that he looked just as he sounded on the phone; a pleasant young man, with a knowing smile in his eyes. Considering the predicament he was in he did not seem particularly concerned, although Chatham *could* see signs of tension and nervousness in his body.

Strangely, Chatham found that he was not disappointed.

'Yes,' said the Chief Constable in an attempt to take control of the situation. 'I believe you are acquainted with Mr Chatham.'

'We have spoken on the phone,' said Psimon, giving Chatham a nod of acknowledgement.

'Quite,' said the Chief Constable who seemed to think, that for someone in his position, Psimon was altogether too relaxed. Maybe some introductions would instil a more fitting sense of propriety.

'My name…' he began but, to everybody's astonishment, Psimon cut him off.

'I think introductions should wait until Mr Brennus can join us,' said Psimon.

Chatham almost choked at Psimon's front. Did he have no idea of how serious his situation was?

The Chief Constable reddened and the Chancellor muttered something under his breath, while Admiral Grant's eyes fixed on Psimon like two unforgiving stones. As far as first impressions go, Psimon was not doing very well at all. But he did not appear to be intimidated. He faced them all down.

'I will answer none of your questions,' he said looking at each of them in turn. 'Not a single one, until Mr Brennus is sitting here beside me.'

The Chief Constable practically steamed in his chair but he seemed to realise that this intransigent young man was telling the truth. Drawing his fingers firmly across his broad brow he nodded to the Special Branch henchman in the corner of the room. The man left the room and what descended was about as awkward a silence as it was possible to get.

A minute or so passed and Psimon turned to Vice Admiral Fallon as the door opened and Steve was escorted into the room. Another chair was found and Steve was invited to take a seat next to Psimon.

'Vice Admiral,' said Psimon suddenly, as Steve sat down beside him. 'I wonder if I might ask you a question?'

The Vice Admiral glanced at the men sitting beside him before giving Psimon a curt nod.

'Imagine if you will,' said Psimon, 'that someone was going to kidnap you and hold you against your will.'

The Vice Admiral's eyes focussed sharply on Psimon as he spoke.

'They will hold you captive and never let you go. To your friends and family, to everything you hold dear in life, you will be as good as dead.'

The Vice Admiral's eyes narrowed threateningly.

'Tell me,' said Psimon. 'What would you do to prevent this from happening?'

'Anything,' said the Vice Admiral.

'Anything?' asked Psimon.

'Whatever it took… I would not let it happen.'

Psimon slid a sideways glance in Steve's direction. 'Thank you,' he said

'All right,' said the Chief Constable in an angry, sarcastic tone. 'Now that we're *all* together.'

Psimon gave an acquiescent nod.

'My name is Chief Constable David McCormack. The Chancellor of the Exchequer I'm sure you recognise. And this is Richard Chatham from MI5.'

He turned to the two naval officers.

'This is Admiral Grant of Her Majesty's Royal Navy, and Vice Admiral Fallon, Commander of U.S. Fleet Forces Command, and former Chief of U.S. Naval Intelligence. He speaks on behalf of the American Government.'

Steve looked at Vice Admiral Fallon. Fleet Forces Command was the name given to that part of the US Navy responsible for operations in and around the Atlantic Ocean. It was one of the most powerful military bodies in the world.

'And now, if you please, *we* will be asking the questions.'

Psimon met the Chief Constable's hard, unpleasant gaze but in his mind he heard his mother's voice…

'They will fear you,' she had said.

'I will help them understand.'

'They will try to control you,' she had warned.

'Yes,' Psimon had said. 'They will try…'

'Do what you have to do,' she had told him.

And he would.

CHAPTER 22

HMS Vigilant (S30)

North Atlantic Ocean

Commander Douglas Scott was embarrassed, angry and deeply concerned. It was over an hour now since the monitors had shown an unprecedented spike in the reactor's primary cooling system and the chief of the watch had been forced to activate the emergency blow, bringing the submarine to the surface with explosive force. Over an hour and the engineers still had no idea as to what had caused the problem. And now it appeared that there was also a problem with the submarine's ballast system. The inlet valves were letting in water and the compressed air cylinders, used to purge the tanks, appeared to have seized.

The sub was slowly sinking.

'Was it the emergency blow?' asked Commander Scott, clearly exasperated by the lack of progress.

'I wouldn't have thought so,' replied the chief engineer. 'But surfacing like that puts a good deal of strain on the systems.'

Commander Scott rolled his eyes and put a hand to his forehead.

'And the reactor?'

'Seems okay now. But that heat spike was like nothing I've ever seen.'

The chief engineer sounded distinctly defensive.

'There's no way we could ignore it, Captain,' he said.

'No, Geoff. Of course not.' The captain's tone was mollifying. 'Everyone has acted just as they should. It's just so damned embarrassing. We're barely a day into this exercise… The Yanks will think we're a bunch of incompetents.'

Commander Scott straightened up and cast his eye over the attack centre. The anxiety in the air was palpable and everyone looked to the captain to see what they should do next.

'Suggestions!' he said, turning back to the senior members of his engineering crew.

'We can replace the valves on the air cylinders. Put divers in the water to examine the inlet valves.'

'And the cooling problem?'

'We've run the diagnostics,' said the chief engineer.

'And?'

'Inconclusive. We'd need to wait for it to happen again… see if we can lock it down then.'

'Great,' said Commander Scott sarcastically. 'Wait for the reactor to hit meltdown and we can identify the problem.'

The sense of failure in his crewmen's eyes was not an easy thing to behold, and the thought of losing the sub to a mere technical problem was almost impossible to comprehend.

'Can we make port?'

'Not if we keep taking on water at this rate.'

'How long do we have?'

'An hour… maybe two.'

Commander Scott pushed his hands through his hair.

'Send out a team,' he said. 'Tell them to weld the inlet valves shut. Seal them up with anything they can get their hands on.'

He felt like he was taking part in some 'scrap yard challenge' for a low budget television channel, not commanding one of the most sophisticated ocean going vessels in the world.

'And comms,' he said turning to the communications officer. 'Contact Force Command. Tell them we have a DISSUB emergency and request contingency plans for evacuation of the entire crew.'

'Aye, sir,' said the young communications officer, trying to work some moisture into his dry mouth.

Commander Scott listened while the unthinkable message was relayed. Then he watched as the young man at comms queried something that Force Command had told him.

'What is it?'

The young officer turned towards him and slid the earphones back from his head.

'Message received and understood, sir,' he said.

'And…' asked Commander Scott.

'It's not just us, sir,' the officer said. 'It seems there's another sub experiencing similar problems.'

'Good God,' said the Commander. 'Which one?'

'The USS Carolina, sir. It's one of the Americans' Virginia Class attack subs.'

'The Carolina,' thought Commander Scott. *'That's Philip Kern's boat.'*

CHAPTER 23

The mood in the secure interview room was charged with disbelief.

'And you expect us to believe that?' said the Chief Constable with contempt.

'You have no choice,' said Psimon. 'It's the truth.'

'Psychic,' thought Chatham incredulously. *'Nonsense! And yet...'* he mused. *'It would certainly explain a great many things.'* And strangely, if it were true, it would make him feel a good deal happier about the security of MI5. *'Then again...'* he reflected, his thoughts racing ahead. If it were true then nothing would be safe; not a secret, not a password, not a personal private thought... *'Christ,'* he thought. *'That would be terrifying...'*

'Yes, Mr Chatham,' said Psimon, fixing Chatham with his stone-grey eyes. 'It would be terrifying.'

Chatham's blood turned to ice.

'And frightened people do frightening things,' Psimon added.

The rest of the 'inquisition' looked at Chatham who had turned markedly pale.

Psimon's gaze moved down the line from one scornful face to the next.

'Dangerous? Vice Admiral Fallon,' said Psimon. 'Not unless you give me cause.'

The Vice Admiral raised a menacing eyebrow.

Psimon continued down the line.

'No, Chancellor. You could not use it to your advantage.'

'*Bullshit* is not what I would call an intelligent response, Admiral Grant.'

'And, Chief Constable McCormack, if you think this is a 'waste of time' then I wonder that you are bothering to hold me at all.'

The room echoed with a stunned silence.

'Take that, you tossers!' thought Steve with just the hint of a smile on his stern face.

Psimon allowed the impact of his impossible insight to sink in. He saw the fear and insecurity in their eyes; the crumbling of their conviction that this could not be true. These men were not accustomed to the sensation of vulnerability. It was not a feeling they found comfortable, although some dealt with it better than others. Mr Chatham, for instance, seemed as much fascinated as he did threatened. As for the others... shock and surprise quickly gave way to fear and paranoia.

Psimon knew what was coming next.

'Are you trying to intimidate us, young man,' said Admiral Grant suddenly. His voice, like his face, had a gravelly quality to it.

Psimon held the admiral's implacable gaze.

'Do you think you can impress us with Victorian parlour tricks; a quick display of pocket-book psychology.'

Psimon said nothing. Despite having known what to expect, he looked disappointed.

'Just who the hell do you think you are talking to?' the admiral ground on.

With the exception of Chatham, those seated on that side of the table seemed to sit up straighter as the admiral took the helm.

'You seem to have no comprehension, whatsoever, of your situation.'

'You are in a great deal of trouble,' added Chief Constable McCormack. 'The best thing you can do is tell us exactly how you breached MI5 security, why you did it, and the names of anyone else involved.'

Psimon looked from one to the next. They wanted answers; something they could understand. He could not give them that.

'You have to understand the implications of what you did,' said the Chancellor in a more conciliatory tone. 'The figures you gave me were accurate to the last detail. No one makes forecasts with that level of certainty. Forecasts work on trends, patterns, complex mathematical algorithms but never with such precision.'

The Chancellor's face effectively portrayed the dismay that he was feeling inside and Psimon almost felt sorry for him.

'Do you have any idea of the consequences of predictions like that?'

His wide eyes appealed to Psimon.

'It would be disastrous!' he stated. 'Trust and co-operation between nations would collapse. The normal flow of international trade would be devastated.'

He threw up his arms as he voiced the fears that had struck him like a thunderbolt over breakfast this morning. Now his eyes beseeched Psimon.

'I'm not talking about a blip on the stock exchange,' he said with quiet forcefulness. 'World recession, depression… that would be the least of it.'

'I know,' said Psimon so quietly that only Steve heard him.

'Wars have been started over much, much less,' the Chancellor concluded as if he could not believe how irresponsible Psimon was being.

'I know,' said Psimon.

He spoke louder now, and to Steve's surprise there was something like contrition in his voice.

'That's why you were the first person to know about it. That's why I have asked Mr Chatham to arrange a multinational symposium to examine the ramifications.'

All eyes turned to Richard Chatham.

'Err, yes,' said Chatham recovering quickly from being put on the spot. 'Twenty-seven specialists from thirteen different countries. They have been invited to attend the convention to err…' His words petered out.

Psimon came to his aid.

'I possess abilities that I do not understand.' He looked up at the wall of rapt faces. 'I am the first person to possess such abilities,' he went on. 'I am the only person to possess such abilities… but I may not be the last.'

Psimon's grey eyes were as fathomless as the sea.

'The world needs an opportunity to understand these things. To see what consequences they might have.'

There was no need to try and speculate on what these 'consequences' might be. The fears raised by the Chancellor had been but the tip of the iceberg.

Despite the varying degrees of disbelief, indignation and outright hostility emanating from the questioning panel, Psimon certainly had their undivided attention. He took a deep breath.

'That is why I have decided to put myself forward for study… to donate my body to science.'

As Psimon said this he pointedly refused to look at Steve.

The line of questioners were suitably stunned.

'All I need from you is your assurance that I will not be followed, detained or in any way constrained until the commencement of the symposium in four days time.'

Psimon looked at the Chancellor of the Exchequer.

'But first, Chancellor,' he said, 'I need your signature on the immunity for Mr Brennus. I understand that you have been authorised to endorse it in the absence of the Prime Minister.'

Chatham quickly flipped open his briefcase and slid the immunity documents in front of the Chancellor. He turned to the last page, indicated the blank space that awaited his signature, and laid a pen across the page.

Steve turned in his seat to look directly at Psimon. He certainly knew nothing about this!

The Chancellor stared at the documents before him. This was not the way he had expected this meeting to go. He had expected to encounter a frightened young man, thoroughly intimidated by the weight of power ranged against him.

And yet... If what this 'Psimon' was telling them was true, then they needed to know more. They needed to know everything. And if granting Mr Brennus immunity was the way to ensure full co-operation then it was surely a small price to pay.

The Chancellor's hand twitched as he considered signing the form. Then he caught himself. What if this was all a load of nonsense? What if this was a smoke screen for something else; something more plausible, something unlawful. Surely that was more likely; surely genuine psychic ability did not really exist.

Psimon watched as the Chancellor talked himself back from the brink of the believing. Even after all these years, he could still understand people's doubts. It was just that now he could no longer afford them.

Psimon looked down at the pen.

The Chancellor had come to his senses. This young man should not be calling the shots. He represented the British Government for God's sake. Admiral Grant was right; this was all just bullshi…

The pen rose up from the table and the Chancellor's burgeoning assertions were scattered to the winds.

The pen hung in mid air, point down and rotating slowly as if it were hanging from an invisible thread. But there was no thread, only incontrovertible proof that Psimon was telling the truth. The pen angled itself to suit the Chancellor's hand, poised to write.

Almost unconsciously the Chancellor reached out to take the pen. His fingers closed around it and he felt the vaguest sensation of having taken it from another's hand. The point hovered over the dotted line. Then the Chancellor made to write…

'That's enough for me,' said Vice Admiral Fallon suddenly.

He turned to Admiral Grant who gave him a small nod of concurrence. Then he looked at Chief Constable McCormack who raised a hand to one of the Special Branch officers. The henchman gave a stiff nod and immediately left the room.

Both the Chancellor and Mr Chatham looked concerned and surprised at this development. It was clear that some prearranged agreement had been put into action. The Vice Admiral glanced at them both before he spoke again.

'The detainees are to be transferred to a high security military facility without delay,' he said by way of explanation. 'They will be kept in isolation until we convene a specialist team to question them properly.'

'On whose authority?' asked the Chancellor.

'On the authority of the American President,' said Vice Admiral Fallon. 'And that of your own Prime Minister.'

The words echoed in Psimon's ears but he did not really hear them. Once again he was absented from this place; the light of his mind casting shadows of himself, shadows that were present elsewhere.

'The Prime Minister said nothing of this to me,' the Chancellor objected.

'The final decision was given to us,' explained Admiral Grant. 'If we considered this matter to have defence implications we were to respond accordingly.'

The situation had taken a serious turn for the worse. Steve could keep silent no longer.

'You can't do this,' he said. 'Psimon's no threat to you. He's done nothing wrong.'

'You misunderstand, Mr Brennus,' said Vice Admiral Fallon. 'This is not about the threat, nor is it a matter of wrongdoing. This is about control.'

The Vice Admiral looked at Steve as if he, of all people, should understand this.

'Psimon represents a new entity,' the Vice Admiral went on. 'A new capability if you will. Governments have been looking for years at the possibility of ESP and its applications, both military and otherwise. But there has not been a single breakthrough, anywhere in the world. The conclusion has always been that extra sensory powers did not exist. But now…'

Here he looked again at Psimon, and somewhere in the background a mobile phone began to ring.

'…Now we know they do. And we must make certain that it is we, and not our enemies, who control this new capability.' Then… 'Will someone answer that damned phone,' he barked.

'But what will happen to Psimon?' asked Mr Chatham as the American aid rummaged in his attaché case for source of the insistent ringing.

'Psimon will be detained and studied,' explained the Vice Admiral. 'He will be treated well and housed in comfort.'

'But he will not be free?' persisted Chatham.

Vice Admiral Fallon seemed to have no problem with the scruples of this action.

'We cannot afford to have Psimon falling under the influence of other parties who might take an interest in his abilities. I can assure you,' he added smugly, 'the Russians or the Chinese would not treat him so well as we intend to.'

'And what if he refuses to co-operate?' asked Steve.

'He has no choice,' said Vice Admiral Fallon. 'In time he will see that.'

'And how long will you detain him?' asked the Chancellor, who clearly had considerable doubts of his own.

'Oh, we cannot let him go,' said the Vice Admiral. 'The world can never know that he exists.'

There was silence in the room as the implications of what he was saying began to sink in.

'No one will speak of what happened here today,' the threat in the Vice Admiral's voice was deadly serious. 'No one will even acknowledge that Psimon ever exists. You will forget you ever…'

'Vice Admiral Fallon, sir,' interrupted the aid who had answered the phone and was now clutching it anxiously as he approached his commanding officer.

'Not now, damn it!' snapped the Vice Admiral.

The Vice Admiral turned back to look at Psimon to see if he showed any sign of understanding that his life, as he knew it, was over. He felt no sympathy for the young man. As far as he was concerned Psimon had brought this upon himself. Did he expect them to ignore someone who could break their codes, read their secrets and tamper with their technology.

'Hell, no!'

But if the Vice Admiral was looking for signs of regret and humility in Psimon's face then he was sorely disappointed. Indeed, Psimon's eyes burned with an intensity that was decidedly unnerving.

'Vice Admiral,' said the American aid more urgently.

'I told you…' said the Vice Admiral, rounding on his subordinate. 'Not…'

'I think you should take this call,' said Psimon in a voice which, for all its softness, was utterly chilling.

The Vice Admiral shot a blazing look at Psimon.

'Who the hell is it?' he demanded, thrusting out his hand to take the phone.

'It's Force Command,' said the aid, leaning in to convey his message more quietly. 'Two of the subs on Operation Tsunami have broken radio silence.'

'Nonsense,' dismissed Fallon in a fierce hiss. 'Nuclear submarines do not break radio silence.'

'They do if there's a DISSUB emergency,' said Steve who had overheard the whispered words.

Fallon's eyes fixed on Steve like the barrels of a gun. DISSUB was the code word used to designate a submarine in distress.

Fallon put the phone to his ear.

The room hung on his words, and watched the storm clouds gather on his brow.

'You're joking,' said Vice Admiral Fallon in a tone that could not have been more devoid of humour. 'When?'

'What is it?' asked Admiral Grant. He moved closer to his American counterpart, speaking in a hushed tone of concern.

Vice Admiral Fallon held up a hand as he concentrated on what the Force Commander was telling him. Then he leaned in close to speak to Admiral Grant.

'Operation Tsunami,' he said quietly. 'Two of the subs are in trouble.'

'Yours or ours?' hissed Grant.

'One of each,' said Psimon, and suddenly all eyes were back on him. 'The HMS Vigilant under Commander Douglas Scott, and the USS Carolina under the command of Captain Philip Kern.'

They looked at him as if he were an alien from another world.

'They will sink within the hour unless you do as I say,' said Psimon, his eyes holding the horrified gaze of Vice Admiral Edwin T. Fallon.

'This is impossible,' breathed Admiral Grant. 'There's no way on God's earth you can affect something hundreds of miles away…'

'Tell that to the Prime Minister,' interrupted Psimon. 'Tell it to the American President.'

'What is it you want?' asked Vice Admiral Fallon, in a tone that suggested he would consider just about anything to prevent six billion dollars worth of military hardware from falling to the bottom of the Atlantic Ocean.

'As I said,' intoned Psimon. 'I want your assurance that I will not be followed, detained or in any way constrained until such time as I choose to put myself forward for study. And…' Psimon added, nodding towards the Chancellor who was still holding the pen in his hand. 'I want a signature on that Class A Transactional Immunity.'

'And if we refuse to do as you ask?' demanded the Vice Admiral in a final gesture of defiance.

Psimon smiled but it was someone else who spoke.

'Then we sink your fucking boats!' said Steve.

CHAPTER 24

Lucifer surveyed the interior of the black transit van. Not a trace of the heretic remained. He locked the van and closed up the barn, lowering the steel bar across the heavy doors before securing it with the padlock. Then he turned his back on the unsavoury requirements of the delusional world and crossed the yard to the chapel. In the sacristy he donned his cassock and cotta before entering the chapel itself.

The stench of confession assaulted his nostrils.

He breathed it in.

It was confirmation that his calling was being fulfilled; that the prophets of mendacity were being systematically removed from the world, those who claimed to know the minds of men; those who spoke of ailments, conditions, insanity.

They knew nothing.

They did not know the rapture of attending the chorus in one's mind, the ecstasy of obedience and the supreme agony of non-compliance.

How *could* they know, those empty vessels of flesh?

Lucifer coiled up the corrugated hose and stowed it against the wall of the chapel. The aspergillum and silver bucket he had washed out earlier. A few small spots of the acid had landed on his arm, just above the gloves, and he had clenched his teeth against the pain; silent, not crying out as the heretics would during the cleansing. Their screams spoke of weakness; his silence spoke of strength.

He approached the altar and picked up the fist-dagger from where he had left it. The blood had left a crimson slick across the short blade. It shimmered attractively in the light. He would not clean it off. He would leave it to dry like that… put it away another time. Then he crossed over to the lectern to see where his vocation would lead him next.

Lucifer gathered up the massive bible and stood it on its spine. Then, with a quick prayer for guidance, he let the book fall open. On the page that revealed itself two lines of text were underlined…

'…I hate pride and arrogance,
evil behaviour and perverse speech.' (Proverbs 8:13)

And, tucked in the crease of the page, a cutting from a medical journal…

The role of anti-psychotics in treating audio hallucinations
A Lecture by Professor Christian Thomas
Saturday March 12th

Lucifer looked at the cutting. He noted the date and the time and heard the rising clamour for action. But no… The latest heretic's body would be found soon, the medically debauched would be alert and wary. The choir agreed… the clamour subsided.

Lucifer would be prudent. He flipped the pages back to a leaflet that lay in Psalms…

'His mouth is full of curses and lies and threats;
trouble and evil are under his tongue.'
Psalms 10:7

He lifted the leaflet…

INTERNATIONAL PSYCHIC CONVENTION

He opened it and scanned through the programme of events for the following day…

Sunday 6th of March

Morning

10 – 11.00am Beyond the Veil with Jonathon Fry, Clairvoyant:

11 – 12.00am Sixth Sense & Sensibility with Colleen Edwards, Medium:

Afternoon

1.00 – 2.00pm A Winning Mind with Sam Delaney, Sports Psychic:

2.30 – 3.30pm Challenge the Psychics: An open debate

4.00 – 5.00pm Be Thine Master with Suzie Murkoff, Psychic Healer (treating everything from shingles to schizophrenia)

Lucifer looked at the name of the psychic healer, Suzie Murkoff,. The name had been circled in black. People like her should not be given a platform for their deceit. She obviously had no comprehension of what true authority was.

Be Thine Master!

Perhaps she should be the one to attend a lecture…

Know thy place!

Heresy comes in many guises.

Lucifer would go.

CHAPTER 25

Psimon's flat was filled with the smell of Chinese food. The mood of the two men stuffing their faces was buoyant, triumphant. It felt like a victory feast

'…we sink your fucking boats!' said Psimon, doing his best to mimic Steve's voice but there was no way he could match the savage certainty of Steve's tone.

'Well that's what you were going to say, wasn't it?' asked Steve, laughing and scraping together the last of his Kung Po Chicken with his chopsticks.

'No,' said Psimon, failing miserably to keep a straight face. 'Actually I was ready to tow the line.'

'Yeah, right,' said Steve, spinning a prawn cracker in Psimon's direction.

Psimon looked across the room at Steve. This was the first time he had seen him smile; really smile, as if he were happy. Despite everything, the relief that they would not be 'disappeared' to some secret military base was intoxicating. It put everything else into perspective.

'Well, almost everything…' thought Psimon.

Steve put his plate to one side and took a swig from the cold bottle of beer.

'So just how long have you been planning this whole 'coming out thing'?' he asked.

'A while,' said Psimon, taking a sip of his own beer.

It was a typically understated answer.

'And the rest,' thought Steve, casting his mind back to Psimon's planning wall and thinking how efficiently Psimon had humbled those in power; those who had thought to confine him.

'So tell me about this business venture of yours,' said Psimon suddenly.

'You mean you don't already know,' teased Steve.

'I'd rather hear it from you.'

Steve quirked his head. It seemed a lifetime ago since he had been wrangling with bank managers, negotiating with suppliers and paying a fortune in research costs to companies across the globe.

'It was all about power generation for the domestic user,' said Steve wistfully. 'Self sufficiency for the home.'

Psimon noted the use of the past tense.

'Wind turbines on chimney stacks,' he said.

'Exactly,' said Steve with a smile.

'I thought you could get those from B&Q nowadays.'

'Yeah, you can,' said Steve. 'But we were working on a more integrated approach.'

He sat forward in his chair and it was clear that, despite everything, his enthusiasm for the project had not been extinguished.

'Super efficient turbines, designed in Sweden... solar panels from Germany... and a new generation of photo-electric cells developed here in the UK.'

'Sounds expensive.'

'Not as bad as you might think,' said Steve. 'Thanks to a charming wife who haggles like a Moroccan carpet seller.'

Psimon smiled at the pride in Steve's voice.

'We'd also managed to secure enough orders to bring down the unit costs. We'd designed a system that would pay for itself in five to ten years; not the fifteen to twenty that the market was currently offering.'

'Impressive,' said Psimon. 'I'll take one.'

'Sorry, sir,' said Steve regretfully. 'There's a small problem with supply on account of the business being completely screwed.'

Steve looked down at his hands. Then he clapped them together and grabbed his bottle of beer.

'Well, enough about my woes,' he said. 'There's just one more day of our agreement to go. And I can't wait to see how you plan to top today.'

Again Psimon smiled.

'Nothing quite so dramatic,' he said.

He reached down the side of his chair, pulled out a leaflet and tossed it to Steve. Steve caught it against his thigh. He turned it over. He recognised the title. He had seen it on Psimon's planning wall.

INTERNATIONAL PSYCHIC CONVENTION

'Oh, you've got to be kidding,' said Steve, opening it up and glancing through the articles that trailed the various speakers. 'I used to know a Sam Delaney,' he said, reading the article about the 'Sports Psychic', who was apparently having great success with one of the premier league rugby teams.

He read down the list of sessions scheduled for the Sunday, smiling at the ridiculous names that the speakers had given them. Then, just as it had been on the planning wall, there was one session circled in red.

2.30 – 3.30pm Challenge the Psychics: An open debate

It was in between the Sports Psychic and the Psychic Healer.

'Should be an easy crowd, at least,' said Steve.

'How do you work that one out?'

'Well, they already believe in psychics,' he said. 'Then again…' he added with feigned gravitas. 'They say a prophet is never recognised in his time.'

Psimon failed to respond to Steve's cautionarytone. He seemed pensive and subdued.

'I was only joking,' said Steve, seeing that Psimon looked uncomfortable. Surely you must know how it goes.'

Psimon lowered his eyes.

'Things get a little hazy from here,' he said quietly.

Steve was suddenly concerned. Was this the same man who had faced down the head of Fleet Force Command? Who had manoeuvred the British and American governments into abiding by his will?

'This is the fear you mentioned?'

Psimon gave an almost imperceptible nod.

'And you can't see through it?'

The shake of the head was just as slight.

'Well, are you sure you want to go then?' asked Steve.

'I must,' said Psimon.

'Why?' demanded Steve, feeling suddenly annoyed at Psimon's irrationality. 'In fact,' he said. 'Why didn't you just let the Americans take you?'

Psimon looked up but Steve refused to be unnerved by the dark expression in his eyes.

'I mean it,' he went on. 'You say you are going to die soon… *tomorrow*, by the sounds of it.' Steve's anger and frustration were coming to a head.

Psimon averted his eyes.

'So why not let Vice Admiral Fallon take you?' he beseeched. 'You'd live a comfortable life on a secure military base. No one could get to you. And, if you co-operated, who knows what they'd allow you. You might not be free… but at least you'd be alive.'

Steve sat back as if he had made a pretty convincing case.

Psimon said nothing for a while. His posture was closed, withdrawn… his eyes downcast. Then finally he spoke, in that quiet arresting tone.

'Could you do that?' he said.

'Do what?' asked Steve.

'The killer won't stop,' said Psimon, seeking out Steve's eyes with his own.

Steve felt a familiar and unpleasant chill run down his spine.

'In sixteen years they haven't caught him,' said Psimon. 'Who's to say they'll catch him at all.'

Steve stared into Psimon's stone grey eyes.

'If he doesn't take *me*,' said Psimon. 'He will take another…'

And suddenly Steve understood.

'So I will ask you again…' said Psimon. 'Could you live in safety, while another took your place in death?'

'No,' said Steve, speaking as a man who had faced a similar dilemma more than once in his military life.

'No,' repeated Psimon, 'and neither could I.'

Steve looked at Psimon. He had an appealing face, the face of a nice young man, as Steve had thought from the first. But his eyes were those of an older soul. They were the eyes of someone who had known pain and fear. They were more like the eyes of a seasoned combat veteran than those of twenty-something lad from the suburbs of Manchester.

'For fourteen years,' Psimon went on. 'I have shared the pain and deaths of people who have died at his hand.'

'I know.'

'Steve,' said Psimon, his voice breaking with tears. 'I see what happens in the future… I can read the thoughts of people standing half a mile away… I can know places I've never been to!'

'I know,' repeated Steve as Psimon's despair climbed higher and higher.

'I have led the police to finding twenty-one killers; helped them with countless other crimes. I've stopped children running out in traffic, grounded planes that I knew would crash…'

'Psimon, please,' said Steve.

'But not him!' said Psimon, his voice rising close to a scream. 'Why can't I stop him?'

Steve could think of nothing to say. He had only recently come to believe in Psimon, much less understand him. He was in no position to advise him on how to use his powers.

'He kills us Steve,' said Psimon desolately. 'He kills us in the most horrible ways.'

Steve did not want to hear this. He had just started to relish the fact that all this was coming to an end. Now it seemed like it was only the beginning.

'And he does not see it as a crime,' Psimon went on. 'He sees it as a duty, a divine vocation.'

'We'll stop him,' said Steve.

'No. We won't!' cried Psimon. 'He takes me Steve… I have seen it. The only question is whether I die slowly at his hand, or quickly at yours.'

'I refuse to accept that,' said Steve stubbornly.

'You have no choice,' said Psimon.

'We always have a choice,' said Steve, rising angrily from his chair and going over to stand beside the window. 'It's just that we don't always like the ones we're given.'

Psimon watched him walk away, an enigmatic expression on his face.

Steve stared out of the window, thinking that Monday could not come quick enough. Bankruptcy, homelessness, marital strife… These were manageable things, unpleasant, unwelcome but manageable. Things he could understand. Things he could confront. Visions of death and a psychopathic bogeyman were something else altogether.

With a sigh of weariness Steve reached out to close the curtains. He paused as the growl of an approaching motorbike rattled the window. A Harley Davidson surged into view, closely followed by a large Suzuki and a second Harley. The bikes turned in to the house next door coming dangerously close to Steve's BMW, which was parked between the two driveways.

'My new neighbours,' said Psimon from his chair. 'Their mate moved in a few months ago after a spot of good fortune.'

'Lottery?' said Steve, relieved that the dour mood had lifted.

'Littlewoods.'

Steve snorted his acknowledgement.

‘Things have been a bit rowdy since then,’ said Psimon.

Steve hesitated at the window; it was years now since he had owned a bike. He had sold his last one shortly after meeting Christine. She had not asked him to but Steve knew she did not like them. She worried about him. That had been enough.

Still, he missed it.

Steve took hold of the curtains just as two massive trikes thrummed down the street. One of them made for the drive but the turning circle was too sharp and he ended up on the grass verge running down the side of the pavement. The second one made an even worse hash of it, coming too close to Steve’s car and finding himself unable to manoeuvre either forwards or backwards.

‘Idiot,’ thought Steve, tugging the curtains closed. ‘I need to move my car,’ he said.

‘Sure,’ said Psimon as Steve crossed the room.

‘I’ll just be a minute,’ said Steve but just as he was about to leave the room Psimon sat bolt upright in his chair.

‘NO!’ he shouted in a shrill voice of fear.

‘Why not?’ asked Steve coming to an abrupt halt in the doorway.

For all the weird ways he had seen Psimon behave over the last few days, he had never heard him panic like that.

‘What’s the problem?’ asked Steve impatiently. The last thing he needed was more hassle over a damaged car.

‘I don’t…’ began Psimon, looking scared and apologetic at the same time. Then he got up from the chair and stood there anxiously wringing his hands.

‘No… sorry. I think it’s ok,’ he said.

‘Well make up your mind,’ said Steve. He could almost hear the squeal of chrome on paintwork.

‘Go,’ said Psimon. ‘I’ll be fine.’

Steve sighed and shook his head despairingly. Then he trotted down the stairs and out onto the street.

Psimon was left alone.

‘Hang on there mate,’ said Steve as the BMW gave the familiar ‘beep-beep’ of being unlocked.

‘You didn’t leave us much space to get in,’ said a gruff voice from further up the drive.

Steve looked up as several of the bikers ambled back onto the footpath, helmets in hand. They had a grizzled, unwashed look. These were not your fair-weather weekend bikers; these were the real thing.

‘I know,’ said Steve. ‘Hang on I’ll move it back for you.’

Just then the rider of the marooned trike tried to reverse out of trouble grinding the side of his engine up against the wing of Steve’s car.

‘I was just going to move it,’ said Steve with rising annoyance but the rider of the trike just stared at him from his open-faced helmet.

‘Two wheels good, four wheels bad,’ he said in a voice that led Steve to think he was stoned.

‘You’re on three wheels you fucking idiot,’ said Steve, having finally lost patience with these jokers.

He snatched open the door of his car, slumped inside and reversed his car back to the far side of Psimon’s drive. Then he got out, locked the car and ignored the hostile stares that followed him back to the house.

Steve was gone.

The doorway yawned.

Psimon could not breathe.

He could not move; he could but barely think.

He had seen this before; seen it through the shadows and the fear. Now he waited for the hulking figure to fill the doorway and eclipse all hope. The rushing of his blood echoed loudly in his ears and yet his heartbeat pulsed to a sluggish, swollen beat as time slowed and stretched before him. He lost all feeling of his physical self. Psimon was locked inside his mind, and his mind was filled with fear. A fear that was validated as ***He*** appeared in the doorway.

Steve rushed forward as Psimon collapsed to the floor. He knelt down beside him, checked his pulse and breathing. He seemed all right but for some reason he had passed out. The look of abject terror on his face, when Steve entered the room, had given Steve such a fright that he had felt compelled to look back at the doorway to check that Satan himself was not standing there. As Steve drew him into a more comfortable position Psimon began to come round.

His eyes stared, unseeing, and he clutched at Steve like a child caught in the wake of some horrific nightmare.

'He was here,' cried Psimon. 'He came for me.'

'No one's here, Psimon,' said Steve firmly. 'You are all right… you just fainted.'

'No… I saw him,' insisted Psimon. 'I saw him there in the doorway.'

Psimon pointed at the doorway.

A chink of fear opened up in Steve's mind as he followed the line of Psimon's trembling finger. Steve clenched his jaw and slammed the door shut on the fear.

'You saw me,' he said almost angrily.

Psimon started to object but Steve grabbed his chin and turned Psimon's frightened grey eyes to meet his own solid brown.

'You saw *me*!' he stated with a finality that got through to Psimon.

'I saw you?'

'Yes,' said Steve. 'You saw me… there is no one else here.'

For a while Psimon's wide eyes just looked up at Steve.

'Then I was wrong,' he said at last and there was something like relief in his voice.

'I guess so,' said Steve.

'But I'm never wrong,' said Psimon sounding puzzled.

'Yeah, well join the club,' said Steve hauling Psimon up and guiding him back to his chair. 'Most of us spend half our lives getting shit wrong.'

Psimon sank into the chair, the beginnings of a smile on his face.

'I was wrong,' he said again in a wondering tone as if he were entirely happy about the fact.

'So you said,' said Steve reaching for his unfinished bottle of beer. 'I'm sure you'll get over it,' he added, taking a much-needed swig.

'But don't you see,' said Psimon, sitting forward excitedly in his chair. 'If I'm wrong about this, then I might be wrong about other things.'

Some of the colour had returned to Psimon's cheeks and there was a brightness in his eyes. But the brightness had a manic quality to it and Steve did not trust it. It was not like the many other shades and moods that he had seen in Psimon's gaze. This emotion was an impostor. This was not the Psimon that Steve knew. The brightness was dishonest.

'Everything could be all right, Steve,' said Psimon wonderingly, his gaze turning inwards as he tried to think things through in the light of this new experience.

'Yeah, of course it will be,' said Steve, although he did not truly believe it.

Steve felt suddenly flushed by a deep sense of weariness. Despite the eventual outcome it had been a stressful day, a stressful week in fact. He bent down and began collecting together the bags, cartons and plates of their takeaway supper.

'What do you say we call it a day?' he said.

'It's still early yet,' said Psimon but Steve could see the fatigue behind Psimon's new-found optimism.

'It's dark outside,' said Steve. 'That's late enough for me.'

Psimon smiled.

'You might be right,' he said.

He stood up and started towards the bathroom. Then he stopped and turned round, looking at Steve with that strangely intense gaze of his.

'That's more like the Psimon I know,' thought Steve.

'Thank you,' said Psimon.

'For what?' asked Steve.

'You said *we*.'

'We what?' puzzled Steve.

'You said… *We* sink your fucking boats.'

And Steve understood.

'Figured I'd chose the winning side,' he said.

'Right,' said Psimon with a smile. 'Goodnight.'

'Night, Psimon,' said Steve.

And with that Psimon left the room, leaving Steve to finish clearing up.

Steve scraped the uneaten food into the bin in Psimon's kitchen.

'One more day,' thought Steve. *'Just one more day.'*

He felt incredibly tired now but he would be sleeping in the chair again tonight. The fear on Psimon's face had been far more convincing than the relief of his new-born hopefulness. Steve went round the flat, checking once again that everything was secure. Then before he retired he stopped by the kitchen once more, taking a glass of cold water from the tap. Their victory feast now felt more like the last meal of a condemned man and the euphoria of outwitting the 'powers that be' seemed like a distant memory. A new image loomed large in Steve's mind, the image of a deranged serial killer who murdered his victims in the most horrible of ways.

'He's big,' Psimon had said. *'Like a giant.'*

Steve put down his glass and his eyes moved to the Sabatier knife block next to the cooker. Maybe tonight he would sleep with a little reassurance close to hand.

'You stab me in the face with a short-bladed knife,' Psimon had told him.

Steve chose the longest knife in the block and went to get some sleep.

CHAPTER 26

International Psychic Convention: Manchester

Lucifer felt sullied.

To be surrounded by so many feeble, vacuous minds was sickening. He had listened to this self-glorifying fool expounding the effects of the mind over the body and how he, with his powers, could unlock their true potential. He had watched in scornful disbelief as the congregation lapped up his drivel. Only a handful of those listening showed any discernment, laughing at his pretensions and mocking his claims. These men, at least, showed some measure of will. They were big men, physically strong, some of them almost as big as he. He was pleased to see that they were not so easily duped.

But no…

Lucifer was not interested in anodyne frauds, no matter how ridiculous their claims might be.

Those in dominion concurred.

The chorus was silent.

Lucifer waited until the hall had begun to empty before he left his seat. A man and woman stepped into his path, talking excitedly about what they had just heard. They looked up and apologised for their discourtesy. Lucifer graced them with a smile and they went quickly on their way. He had a good smile, although he found it an odious task to use it. But over the years he had come to acknowledge the benefits of conforming to the conventions of the inconsequential world.

A face of wrath was long remembered; a smile was soon forgot.

Lucifer continued up the aisle towards the exit.

*

'Aren't you nervous?' asked Steve as they crossed the quadrangle and approached the entrance to the lecture hall.

'Nope,' said Psimon, taking hold of the door and holding it open for Steve.

Psimon's optimism had persisted through the night. He had greeted Steve that morning with a cheerful air that Steve found more than a little uncomfortable. He preferred the old Psimon, the unsettling Psimon, the always slightly melancholy Psimon.

Steve gave Psimon a sideways look as he went through into the lecture hall's foyer.

'Two?' enquired a man sitting behind a long wooden counter.

'Just one,' said Psimon, before Steve had a chance to speak. 'I'll be taking the stand.'

'Jolly good,' said the man, reaching for a nearby clipboard. 'Have you registered?' asked the man eagerly.

'Yes,' said Psimon.

'Name?' asked the man.

'Psimon,' said Psimon.

The man glanced down the short list of names.

'Ah yes,' he said, ticking off Psimon's name. 'You're sixth on the list.'

The man handed Psimon a small card.

'Give this to Natasha,' he said, pointing through the door into the hall. 'She will show you where to sit and invite you onto the stage if you get a chance to speak.'

'If he gets a chance?' queried Steve.

'Depends how quickly we get through the speakers,' the man explained. 'Each speaker has the opportunity to introduce themselves before facing the audience and the panel of experts. They can speak for as long as they like or until the audience votes them off.'

'And why would the audience vote them off?' asked Steve.

'If they are not impressed by their performance,' said the man as if this were common knowledge.

Psimon met Steve's raised eyebrow with a bright, unapologetic smile.

They had arrived early for the debate. Sam Delaney, 'Sports Psychic', had just finished his talk and the hall was slowly emptying of people. They stood to one side as a group of people emerged from the exit and passed through the foyer. Then Psimon and Steve went through into the hall.

They passed through a small anteroom, the walls of which were lined with mirrors, and on into the main lecture hall where the seats rose up in a broad semicircle around the stage.

Natasha met them as they entered the hall. Psimon gave her a dazzling smile and held out his ticket. Steve rolled his eyes as he noticed the affect this had on the young woman.

'This way,' she said, blushing and smiling in return as she led Psimon away towards the left-hand aisle.

Steve stood there, feeling somewhat at a loss, until Psimon looked back and nodded at him to take a seat. Steve glanced down the aisle looking for somewhere to sit. People were still leaving their seats. Most were talking quietly as they left but one group was laughing and noisily carrying on. They were all big, solid men.

'Rugby players,' thought Steve. *'Probably Sam Delaney's own team, come to give their 'psychic coach' a hard time.'*

Steve looked across the hall at Psimon. Even in these innocuous surroundings he felt uncomfortable being separated from Psimon. This was the final day of their contract and despite Psimon's positive transformation Steve still believed there was something of substance behind his fears. As he descended the shallow steps down the middle of the hall Steve's eyes followed Psimon as Natasha led him down the left-hand aisle to a bank of chairs to one side of the stage.

'Sorry,' said Steve, distractedly as he almost collided with a man and woman who seemed to be talking excitedly about the validity of Mr Delaney's ideas.

'Sorry,' Steve said again as he bumped hard into another member of the departing audience.

Steve glanced up at the figure who had stopped him in his tracks.

The guy was massive, several inches taller than Steve and, even in his smart blue suit, Steve could see that he was built like the proverbial 'brick shit-house'.

'Sorry,' Steve repeated as he stepped round the man.

The big guy said nothing. He didn't seem the least bit inclined to move out of Steve's way but he smiled as Steve edged round him. It was the smile of a charming man; a man with obvious, if somewhat 'Neanderthal', good looks. But Steve was not reassured, for the smile never came near the man's eyes, eyes that were so dark they were almost black.

'Fucking rugby players,' cursed Steve as he squeezed past.

He looked up to check on Psimon who had just put a hand to his head as if to ease a headache or a moment's dizziness. Natasha helped him to a chair and put a hand on his knee. Steve worked his way into a row of chairs near the front of the auditorium. He shook his head at Psimon's dramatics.

'She's already interested,' he thought. *'No need to play the sympathy card.'*

But when Psimon raised his head, Steve grew more concerned. There was a familiar haunted look in his eyes. It seemed the fleeting levity of Psimon's rosy outlook had come to an end.

'Are you all right?' Steve mouthed the words.

For a few seconds Psimon just looked at him uncertainly. Steve was about to rise from his seat when Psimon waved him down.

'I'm okay,' he mouthed back.

The shadow had passed.

Lucifer had left the building.

*

Steve was actually enjoying this. The panel consisted of a clergyman, a scientist, a magician-come-illusionist and a psychologist who had spent many years researching the way 'psychics' performed their so-called supernatural feats. They were all intelligent and well informed and none of them had that unpleasant edge of superciliousness that often plagued the detractors of the psychic world.

And up against them came the psychics, the clairvoyants, the mediums and the rest…

The first guy had been more comedian than psychic and had been hugely entertaining until the clergyman had caught him out with a clever piece of logic.

The clergyman had led the applause as the comedian left the stage.

Next came a man who claimed to be able to speak to the dead. But when the psychologist gave a more impressive performance than the would-be medium, the poor man had nothing else to say.

The clairvoyant made some impressive claims and dire prophecies for the future but as there was no way to prove or disprove what she was saying, the audience lost patience and sent her packing.

The fourth pretender was a spoon bender and clock mender, firmly in the mould of the great Uri Geller but the illusionist showed the audience how such trickery was accomplished and Uri had only one place to go.

Another medium then, who claimed to be able to speak not just to the spirits of the dead but also to animals and babies who had passed away without ever being able to talk. Despite her impressive list of satisfied clients she had been unable to pass a simple challenge set her by the psychologist.

'Only those who want to come through will do,' she had protested as the audience invited her to leave.

And then it was Psimon's turn.

Steve shifted anxiously in his seat as Psimon crossed to the lectern in the middle of the stage. He looked at Steve and gave him the smallest of smiles as if to settle the former-soldier's nerves. Then Psimon lifted his eyes to the expectant faces.

'Hello,' he said in a quiet steady voice. 'My name is Psimon… and I am psychic.'

Steve looked up at Psimon with a mixture of pride and embarrassment. It was like watching a psychic version of Alcoholics Anonymous.

'Hello Psimon,' said the clergyman. 'Can you tell us what makes you think that you are psychic?'

'The fact that I am,' replied Psimon to a ripple of soft laughter.

'But what abilities do you possess?' asked the scientist.

'Many,' said Psimon. 'Chose one and I'll tell you if I can do it.'

The scientist sat back in his chair raising a contemplative hand to his chin. This softly spoken young man displayed none of the ego and self-aggrandisement that most of the other speakers had. But it was clear that he had already captured the attention of the audience.

'Can you talk to the dead?' asked the scientist.

'No,' said Psimon.

'Why not?'

'I don't know,' replied Psimon. 'But I believe it's because the dead no longer exist, other than as corpses in the ground, and in the memories of those left behind.'

The scientist seemed entirely satisfied with this answer but there were mutterings of disapproval from amongst the audience.

'Can you read people's minds?' asked the psychologist.

'Yes,' said Psimon.

'Can you read my mind?'

'Yes,' said Psimon.

The psychologist raised his eyebrows at this bold claim and the murmurs from the audience grew louder as they began to realise that there was something different going on here.

The psychologist bent down and retrieved a large brown envelope from the briefcase beside his chair.

'In this envelope is a picture,' the psychologist announced to the audience holding up the envelope with more than a touch of showmanship. 'Not a picture of a cross or a moon or a boat sailing across a wavy sea.'

He looked meaningfully at the audience. They knew exactly what he was talking about. They had all seen such feats repeated by countless clairvoyants.

'This is a picture that it would be almost impossible to guess.'

Here he looked directly at Psimon.

'Now,' he went on. 'I'm going to hold an image of this picture in my mind and you can either have a stab at guessing what it is… or you can leave the stage now and save yourself the embarrass…'

'It's a picture of Leonardo da Vinci's giant crossbow firing an arrow at the world,' said Psimon, cutting across the psychologist. 'Only the arrow is a pen and the world is actually a human skull with the countries cut away to reveal the brain inside.'

The psychologist almost dropped the envelope. His mouth sagged open and he could only stare at Psimon. The audience waited with baited breath for him to open the envelope which, with trembling hands, he duly did.

'Child's play,' thought Steve as the auditorium echoed to the sound of astonished gasps and enthusiastic applause. *'Give him a real challenge.'*

'How did you *do* that?' asked the psychologist in a breathless whisper.

'I have no idea,' said Psimon as the noise in the hall subsided. 'All I know is it's as clear in my mind as it is in yours.'

'Can you read anyone's mind?' shouted someone from the audience.

'Just about,' said Psimon with a quick glance at Steve.

'What about mine?' someone else called out… 'And mine,' said another.

'Wait, wait… just a minute,' said the scientist, rising from his seat and appealing to everyone to calm down. 'How do we know you didn't set this up with Martin?' he gestured towards the psychologist who was still quite obviously stunned by Psimon's performance.

'A true scientist,' said Psimon with a small smile on his lips. 'Do you always demand proof?'

'Not when it's a matter of opinion or belief,' replied the scientist. 'But when it's a matter of fact, yes... I do.'

Psimon acknowledged this answer with a respectful nod. Then his eyes suddenly fixed on the man and the audience watched as the scientist first gaped in surprise then blushed to the roots of his thinning blonde hair.

'Is that proof enough?' asked Psimon reining in his gaze.

'Yes,' gasped the scientist. He sat down heavily in his chair and looked up into the audience, to an attractive woman sitting near the back of the hall; his face a picture of anxiety.

'Don't worry about impressing her,' said Psimon gently. 'She's already fallen in love with you.'

The audience laughed as the scientist blushed all over again but the beginnings of an astonished smile showed that no damage had been done.

Psimon turned back to the entranced faces of the audience. There were a few moments of bewildered silence and then the avalanche of questions began.

*

Lucifer was waiting beneath the vaulted skeleton of a willow tree. Waiting for the ridiculous debate to be over and for the heretic healer to begin her sermon and seal her fate. He had seen her arrive, this bride of speciousness; seen the fawns and the sycophants vying for her favour. He had seen her enter the hall by the door reserved for the privileged few. He would see her soon and watch with constraint as she condemned herself and left him no choice but to take her.

Lucifer looked ahead to her confession, to the humbling, the question, the cleansing and the end… the end of all her lies. He would take his time with her. The last one had not followed the rightful order of the mass ordained by the chorus. He would make sure she knew the glory of pain before he took the breath of life from her sobbing lungs.

Lucifer's spirits lifted in anticipation of the rite to come but his expectancy was interrupted by a growing hubbub from people milling around in the quadrangle between the various rooms and halls.

Lucifer widened his perception and listened to what was being said.

'That's what they're saying.'

'Bullshit!'

'Straight up… This guy's the real thing.'

'…The scientist called his bluff.'

'Yeah but he shot him down… spoke directly into his mind.'

'A genuine psychic.'

'Let's go and see.'

'Can we still get in?'

'It's this one over here… the psychic debate.'

'Come on, let's go.'

Despite his contempt, Lucifer was intrigued. He fell in with the swelling crowd and returned to the hall of lies.

*

Steve was getting more than a little concerned. The atmosphere had changed from shock and astonishment and was rising towards a kind of hysteria. And still more people were coming into the hall. The word had obviously got around that something extraordinary was going on. He looked up at the rows of seats behind him. They were all full now and people were sitting and standing in the aisles.

Back on stage Psimon was fielding one question after another.

'So you're saying that *none* of the other people speaking here today are actually psychic. That none of them have supernatural powers of any kind.'

‘That’s right,’ said Psimon and Steve found himself wishing that Psimon could be a little less honest and a little more diplomatic.

‘Don’t you think that’s incredibly arrogant?’

‘It would be, if it weren’t true,’ replied Psimon.

‘So they are all liars and con-artists.’

‘No,’ said Psimon. ‘Only three of them are guilty of wilful deception. The others believe their powers to be real.’

‘But they’re not.’

‘No.’

‘Then what are they?’

‘Yeah, what are they?’

Psimon bowed his head. How quickly the brightness of wonderment fades to the dull flames of hostility.

‘People seek explanations for things they do not understand,’ Psimon said. ‘Some turn to science, because logic and reason prevail and endure.’

Here he turned to the scientist on the panel.

‘Some turn to God, and find their answers there.’

The clergyman inclined his head.

‘While others turn their gaze within, to the mysteries of the mind.’

Psimon’s hand gestured towards the psychologist but he raised his eyes to the audience.

‘People believe in the supernatural because they do not understand. They do not understand the amazing complexity of the human brain and the influence of the subconscious mind. They believe in the supernatural because they do not appreciate just how unendingly wonderful nature truly is.’

‘And you do?’ came the unpleasant challenge.

‘No,’ said Psimon. ‘No one fully does. But we can try. And when we reach the limits of our understanding we must have the courage to say, I don’t know.’

‘So what about us?’

‘Yeah, are we all deluded?’

‘No,’ said Psimon, much to Steve’s relief. ‘You have simply believed in something that is not true.’

The audience was silent.

'But we can believe in you,' said a woman from the back of the hall.

'If you like,' said Psimon with a smile.

Silence again and Steve wondered whether Psimon had succeeded in calming the mob or if it was just taking a breath before going for his throat.

Then once more from the back of the hall.

'My husband hears the voice of our dead son,' the woman went on in a small, tremulous voice. 'But it brings him no comfort,' she said. 'It only makes him weep.'

Psimon looked up at the woman. His eyes glittered with tears. The lecture hall was full but he spoke only to her.

'Liam is gone,' he told her. 'He exists only in your hearts.'

The woman put a hand to her mouth. The tears spilled down her cheeks.

'The voices are not real,' said Psimon. 'Your husband is suffering from a mental disorder. He is grieving and he is ill. He will find no peace in chasing after ghosts.'

The woman was too upset to answer. She could only nod her thanks.

*

Lucifer was inflamed.

Who was this blasphemer to doubt the voice of this woman's son, to dismiss what he had never heard?

'His mouth is full of curses and lies and threats;

trouble and evil are under his tongue.'

He had been right to follow the chattering crowds. This man was dangerous. He spoke his lies with authority. He spoke with the power of the damned.

*

Silence claimed the crowded hall once more. The aching clarity of the woman's grief had sobered the volatile mood. Then an old man from the front row raised himself up on a walking stick that was carved in the likeness of a Jack Russell terrier.

'I once knew a priest who told me he knew a real and genuine psychic,' the old man said. 'A child truly gifted from God,' he said.

Psimon held the old man's eyes, which, for all their years, were still clear and bright and had not changed.

'Was he lying?' the old man asked.

For the longest time Psimon said nothing. Then he smiled at the memory of a kind old Priest; a memory that still warmed his soul.

'No, he was not lying,' said Psimon. 'He spoke of me... I knew Father Kavanagh well.'

The old man nodded his understanding.

'I loved him,' said Psimon. 'I was with him when he died,'

*

Lucifer's mind erupted in a conflagration of hate.

And the chorus roared in fury.

'It is the witness! The witness in the house of Jehovah!'

He reeled with the force of revelation. He put out a hand, crushing the shoulder of the man standing in front of him at the back of the hall.

'Hey! What the hell,' protested the man.

But Lucifer did not hear him. The chorus was deafening, the pain unendurable.

'No one must know...'

Lucifer opened his burning eyes and sought out the blasphemer at the front of the hall.

'Silence the witness.'

The rage was too great. It was all he could do not to rush down the steps and tear the heretic's face off there and then. The chorus was rising, the blackness encroaching on Lucifer's sight.

'Cut out his tongue.'

'Fill his mouth with dirt.'

He could not bear to be in the presence of such profanity and suffer it to live.

Lucifer turned and fled.

*

Steve was out of his seat.

The look of absolute terror on Psimon's face left him in no doubt. Any vestige of hope in Psimon's mind was gone. The fear in all its fury had returned.

He called out to Psimon but the rising clamour drowned out his words as people began to realise that something was wrong. Steve shouted louder but Psimon would not even look at him. He just kept staring up towards the back of the hall as if he had seen the killer himself.

Steve turned to follow the line of Psimon's gaze and as he did so he saw the shape of a huge man in a blue suit pushing his way out of the hall. The great figure moved on through the small anti-chamber and disappeared. Steve looked back at Psimon but as he did so an image froze in his mind. It was the image of the exit sign reflected in the mirrored walls of the anti-chamber. The ubiquitous metal box; the green sign, lit up from within. The bright letters shining clearly for all to see…

T I X and the number **Ǝ**

TIXƎ

EXIT

CHAPTER 27

Steve felt torn and tormented. Torn because he did not know whether to go and help Psimon or go after the 'giant' who had just left the hall. And tormented because he had come face to face with the killer and failed to recognise what was standing before him; what was smiling down at him, smiling down with those dead black eyes.

The indecision lasted less than a second. Steve went to Psimon's aid.

'Psimon,' called out Steve as he leapt up onto the low stage.

The members of the panel were gathered hesitantly round Psimon who had collapsed to the floor and was clinging to the base of the lectern like a man caught in a flood, fearful of being swept away.

'It's all right,' said Steve as the scientist moved to block his approach. 'He's a friend of mine.'

'That's right. He is,' said the young woman called Natasha when the scientist looked doubtfully at Steve.

'He just collapsed,' said the scientist as Steve knelt down beside Psimon.

'Is it some kind of seizure?' asked the psychologist. 'Is there anything we can do?'

'He gets these attacks,' said Steve vaguely, then... 'Psimon... it's Steve. Can you hear me?'

But Psimon just clung to the lectern his face pressed against the hard edges of wood.

'He's here... he's here... he's here,' Psimon whispered over and over, his eyes staring blindly ahead of him, his brow beaded with sweat.

'Is he all right?' asked Natasha crouching down next to Steve, a glass of water in her hand.

'He'll be fine,' said Steve although he did not really believe it. 'Let's get him to a chair.'

A chair was brought from across the stage but it took all Steve's strength to pry Psimon's hands free from the lectern.

'He's here… he's here… he's here…'

Steve half carried Psimon to the chair.

'What's wrong with him?' asked Natasha.

'He'll be all right,' said Steve with more annoyance than he intended.

Psimon just sat there gripping his knees rocking backwards and forwards, whispering over and over. Steve took his head in his hands, gripped him firmly and turned his face to look up at him.

'Psimon,' said Steve. 'Psimon, look at me.'

It was several long moments before Psimon's eyes focussed on Steve and then the tension melted from his face and Psimon began to weep.

'Steve,' he said in a voice that was so forlorn that Steve felt the tears standing in his own eyes. 'He's here.'

'I know,' said Steve. 'I know.'

Still clasping Psimon's head Steve looked into his sad grey eyes. That chink of fear had opened up in his mind once more. Not fear for himself but for Psimon. He could not bear the thought that he might be hurt, that he might be killed. Psimon had hired Steve to protect him. '…keep me safe,' Psimon had said but for the first time Steve truly doubted that he could.

If Psimon had seen it, how could he possibly stop it?

'You saw him,' said Psimon suddenly.

Steve nodded. 'I actually apologised to the bastard,' he said.

'You saw him,' repeated Psimon as if he had not heard Steve. 'Did you see the hatred and the pain? Did you hear the chorus of angels in his mind?'

Steve shook his head, frowning at the strangeness of Psimon's words.

'They are not angels...' hissed Psimon ominously. 'They are demons. They hold him in thrall. He is the vessel of their torment, the instrument of their wrath.'

The small crowd of people gathered round Psimon drew back at the alarming change in the tone of his voice. Concern changed to discomfort and awkwardness.

'Come on,' said Steve angrily. 'Let's get you out of here.'

He drew Psimon's arm across his shoulders and hauled him to his feet.

'Then we're calling the police.'

'No,' cried Psimon. 'No, Steve, you mustn't.'

'Police?' enquired the psychologist anxiously as Psimon seemed to become increasingly debilitated. 'Why would we need to call the police?'

Steve groaned. He was not about to tell them that a serial murderer had just vacated the building and might, even now, be prowling around outside. With Psimon hanging deliriously from his shoulder Steve turned about looking for the quickest way out of the building. He spotted a fire exit at the back of the stage and forged a path towards it, the people parting nervously before him.

'Can I help?' came a quiet voice beside him.

It was Natasha.

'You could get that door,' said Steve, nodding towards the exit.

Natasha moved ahead to the set of double doors.

'It's closed,' she said apologetically as Steve approached the door.

The bar across the doors was sealed by a small plastic security tie. Natasha held it up between her fingers.

Steve looked down at the tie then nodded Natasha to stand aside. Then he raised his foot and gave the doors a hefty kick. The plastic tie flicked away as the doors slammed open. There were gasps of shock and disapproval from the stage behind them but Steve could not have cared less. Hitching Psimon higher on his shoulder he started through the doors.

'Will he be all right?' asked Natasha as he passed.

'I hope so,' said Steve, pausing in the doorway to look at her. 'Thanks,' he said.

'He's special isn't he,' said Natasha, her hand starting to reach out to Psimon.

'Yes,' said Steve. 'He is.'

And with that he marched Psimon quickly back to their car before the campus security, or anyone else, could stop them.

*

Lucifer would not have seen them if he had been waiting with the crowds but the closeness of so many people had been more than he could bear. He had retired to a quieter vantage point where he could watch the entrance to the hall of lies and calm the din of righteous ire that raged in his mind.

And then he had seen them.

Seen them slinking from the back of the building, the accursed witness and his guardian angel. He watched them as they moved between the cars. He followed closer now, watchful, wary. The guardian angel was not a man like other men. Lucifer could see that.

He knew a predator when he saw one.

He would take care with that one.

They stopped at a car and the angel propped up the witness while he opened the door. Lucifer crossed quickly to his van. He must move with care, with guile, lest the angel mark his presence. He slipped inside, started the engine and waited for them to leave.

*

Steve bundled Psimon in through the passenger door and watched as he curled into a foetal position making it impossible for Steve to fasten his seatbelt.

'Sod it!' thought Steve, closing the door and moving quickly round to the driver's side. He jumped in, started the car and drove quickly out of the car park heading away from the

psychic convention and away from the man who would do Psimon harm. Beside him Psimon cowered in his seat muttering incoherently.

'Hang on, Psimon,' said Steve. 'We're going to get you home. Then I'm phoning the damn police.'

Psimon could manage nothing more than a stifled protest. He was lost in a life's worth of fear.

*

Lucifer was careful not to get too close but still he dare not lose them. Those in dominion would not be forgiving if he were to let the witness go a second time. It was fourteen years since his first killing; fourteen years since the priest had failed to stop him, and died for his sins, for his shame. But the witness had heard him. The witness knew what he had done.

The witness must be silenced.

Lucifer was calmer now. The pain had lessened; the tumult subsided. But the chorus had not retreated; it hovered over the deep, waiting to see that he would not fail.

*

Steve was having difficulty concentrating on the road. Psimon kept twisting in his seat making it difficult to move the gear stick. He was sweating and mumbling like a man caught in the grip of a nightmare.

'Pain and death,' he muttered. 'All is pain and death.'

'It's all right, Psimon,' said Steve, reaching out a hand to calm him. 'We're almost there.'

Steve kept glancing down at Psimon, growing more concerned by the minute, and when Psimon slipped down into the foot well beneath his seat Steve just let him lie there. He was driving on auto-pilot, navigating the traffic with one eye always on his tormented passenger. He barely glanced in his rear-view mirror. He did not notice the stealthy shadow that matched their every turn; the black van that followed them like a hearse.

*

Lucifer hung well back. He drew the van in to the kerb. The car had stopped; stopped outside a house, a row of large motorcycles lined up on the road ahead of it. He waited to see if this were the place, the place where the witness lived.

Yes. There... The angel climbing out of the car. Moving round to get the witness; dragging him out, heaving him up the driveway like a boneless cripple.

'Where are your bold words now?' thought Lucifer. *'Your boasts and your certainty? Has your courage failed in the presence of the chorus?'*

Lucifer's gaze burned as he pulled back out into the road, coasting slowly down the tree-lined street. He wanted to see where they went. Knowledge was power. The more he knew the easier it would be to overcome them.

*

'Oh, great,' thought Steve as he pulled up outside Psimon's flat. *'A bikers' rally on our own fucking doorstep.'*

There was a row of five or six bikes parked up on the road outside the neighbour's house, many more packed onto the driveway. And, strung up between the trees on either side of the drive, a crude banner fashioned from a white bed sheet.

'**WELCOME HOME SPIKE**,' the banner read.

Steve shook his head and climbed out of the car. He went round to the passenger's side and manhandled Psimon out of the car. Then with Psimon barely able to walk he shuffled awkwardly towards the flat. Holding him up against the door he felt in Psimon's pockets for the key.

'That's it, Psimon,' he said. 'We're back at the flat.'

'He's here... he's here,' moaned Psimon looking at Steve through his watery eyes.

'I know,' said Steve. 'It's okay, you're home now.'

'No,' said Psimon but all assertiveness had gone from his voice and Steve took little notice of his objection.

'Let's get you upstairs,' he said.

And as he closed the door a black van cruised slowly past the house.

Had he not been so distracted Steve would surely have noted the slow speed of the van. Had he not been so distracted he would have recognised the unusually large shape of the van's driver. But as it was, he did not. The van just grazed his peripheral vision and was gone. Then without a second thought Steve closed the door and turned to face the stairs.

*

It wasn't until he had driven past a second time that Lucifer made sense of the house. It was split into two. Two flats, one up and one down. The lights in the upper flat had come on and he caught a fleeting glimpse of the angel through the large bay window.

'We have you now,' he thought, turning off the road to check the area and to see how he would come at the house.

He had seen a small pedestrian footpath leading off down the side of a neighbour's house. He would head round the block to see where it led. Perhaps it would offer a less conspicuous approach.

Lucifer surveyed the terrain and laid his plans.

He would wait till dark and then, chorus willing, he would take the witness.

CHAPTER 28

Steve ceased his pacing and crossed once more to the window.

'Where the hell are they?' he cursed.

It was over three hours since he had first called the police, more than thirty minutes since they had last assured him that someone would be with them directly. It was dark now and Steve peered up the street hoping to see the lights of an approaching police car. If they did not come soon he would pack Psimon into the car and take him down to the police station himself.

Steve glanced in the other direction, to the house next door, where Psimon's rowdy neighbours seemed to be warming up for the evening. The noise from the biker's 'homecoming party' was getting louder by the minute. With an irritated snort Steve stepped back from the window and went over to check on Psimon.

Psimon sat hunched in the armchair as he had for hours, knees drawn up against his chest, head tilted to one side, staring into space. He was traumatised, insensible. Steve had not been able to get a coherent sentence out of him since they got back to the flat. He had tried gentle reasoning and stern commands but all to no avail. Now he knelt once more beside his chair and lifted the fourth mug of tea with which he had tried to coax Psimon out of himself.

'Why don't you just try and drink something,' he suggested, although he knew that it was less for Psimon's benefit than for his own reassurance.

If Psimon would just take a drink, do something normal; at least that would give Steve something to work with, some way of breaking through this wall of fear. But Psimon did not even register the tea. His gaze simply passed through the cloud of steam as it did through Steve.

Steve put the mug of tea down beside Psimon's chair. He sat back on the sofa, a twisted knot of frustration in his guts. If there were ever a time that he needed Psimon's special abilities it was now. But Psimon was lost to him, locked away in the fearful mind of an eight-year-old boy, a little boy waiting to feel the cool touch of his mother's soothing hand, a touch that would never come.

*

Lucifer kept to the shadows.

The fates were smiling upon him. The footpath had led to the perfect place to leave the van; a small car park beside some tennis courts, dark, unused, surrounded by trees, perfect. He had left the van in the corner of the car park, reversed it close to the footpath while staying clear of the dim pool of light cast by the first of the small street lamps. He had swapped his suit jacket for one of dark leather that absorbed the light. He had donned his black leather gloves then reached into the back of the van to take what he would need.

A small crowbar to gain entry… a gag… some black plastic ties… a telescopic security baton and of course his pistol; a handful of lightening that made it all so easy.

Lightening for the angel.

Baton for the witness.

That would be more than enough.

Now he padded down the path, keeping to the side where the widely spaced lamps did not reach. A vast shadow moving through the lesser shadows of night; moving with stealth and purpose, doing what he had done a dozen times and more, doing what he had been called to do, to seek out those who spoke untruths.

And to silence them.

*

‘Psychic?’ said Detective Inspector Hunt.

‘Yes,’ said Steve with a deep sigh of annoyance.

‘Like Uri Geller?’ asked Detective Inspector Regan.

‘No,’ said Steve trying to retain his composure. ‘Not like Uri Geller. Psimon is the real thing… a genuine psychic.’

The two plainclothes CID officers had arrived a few minutes earlier and it was clear that neither of them considered this a worthwhile use of their time. Now they stood in Psimon’s living room looking down at him and even Steve could read their minds…

‘So what makes you think it was the killer?’ asked DI Hunt.

‘It was Psimon’s reaction,’ said Steve. ‘And the exit sign, TIX and the number three.’

Steve raised a hand to his forehead. He knew how this sounded. He wished that Psimon were coherent. He could convince them in a second.

‘And he fitted Psimon’s description,’ Steve added futilely.

‘So Psimon had seen him before?’ asked DI Hunt.

‘Not exactly,’ replied Steve, the sinking feeling getting stronger as he spoke. ‘Psimon has visions,’ he said wearily. ‘Glimpses of the future, of other places.’

The inspectors looked as if they had heard enough.

‘He had an impression of this guy; a big guy, like a giant… with eyes so dark they are almost black.’

‘And that’s the best description you can give us?’ asked DI Regan.

‘No,’ said Steve with more excitement in his voice. ‘I’ve seen him. I can tell you what he looks like.’

The inspectors continued to look at him but Steve noticed that neither of them had so much as reached for a notebook.

‘He’s big,’ said Steve. ‘I mean really big… six-seven, six-eight. And well built; must be nineteen or twenty stone.’

They looked at him now as if he were exaggerating and DI Regan actually started moving towards the door.

'He's good looking too, in a scary kind of way…' persisted Steve. 'Strong jaw, dark eyes, heavy forehead.'

DI Hunt lowered his eyes.

'Dark hair,' said Steve, doggedly refusing to let them write him off as a crank. 'Long,' he added. 'But he had it smoothed back with grease or wax. And he wore a suit,' he concluded. 'A smart blue suit.'

'I'm sorry, Mr Brennus,' said DI Hunt. 'But in the absence of any actual *evidence* to suggest that this man might be the killer, there's really nothing we can do.'

Steve ground his teeth against the frustration. He looked down at Psimon but Psimon had started to rock slightly in his chair.

'He's coming… he's coming… he's coming…' he whispered over and over.

'That's not helping our case,' thought Steve bitterly.

'Your friend really does seem to be in some distress,' said DI Hunt and it was the first time that Steve had heard anything like sympathy in his voice. 'Maybe you should call a doctor.'

'So that's it,' said Steve, ignoring the inspector's well-meaning advice. 'You are not going to do anything.'

'As I said,' said DI Hunt. 'There's nothing we can do.'

'You could call Chief Constable McCormack at Bootle Street police station,' said Steve. 'You can bet your ass he'll take Psimon seriously.'

'It's Sunday night,' said DI Regan from the doorway. 'What do you want us to do, call him at home?'

'Damn right,' said Steve, his voice rising to a shout.

DI Hunt raised a calming hand.

'We'll call him in the morning,' he said. 'If he supports what you're saying then we'll call back tomorrow.'

'Tomorrow might be too late,' said Steve.

'That's the best we can do.'

'So you're just going to let the killer go free?' challenged Steve.

The inspectors gave him an unpleasant look.

'Let him go free to kill again.' Steve followed them out of the room as they headed for the stairs. 'Well you won't have to wait long,' he called after them. 'In fact you should be finding another body soon.'

The inspectors started down the stairs.

'That's right,' Steve went on. 'Another tortured body... Only this poor bastard has been crucified.'

The inspectors stopped. They turned. They looked back up at Steve with an intensity that had been sadly lacking till now.

'What did you say?'

*

Lucifer had seen them arrive, the pawns of so-called justice. One big, one small. He had ventured round the house to watch them enter, to make sure. But the guardian angel had opened the door and let them in. There was no doubt, this complicated things. Three was an awkward number to handle. He would consult the chorus, ask for guidance, find a way.

Should he wait?

No, the pawns might remove the witness to a more secure place.

Should he leave?

The chorus would not hear of it.

He must take the witness tonight.

He must take the witness now.

Lucifer crouched in the shadows but the noise coming from the house next door made it difficult to think, the sounds of debauchery flooding out into the street. He looked across at the bikes packed onto the drive and lined up along the kerb. A row of bikes and then the angel's car.

A row of bikes and then the angel's car.

That might just do it. Yes, that should be enough.

Lucifer checked to see that the road was clear. Then, leaving the shadows, he approached the bikes.

*

'How did you know the latest victim had been crucified?' asked DI Hunt. 'No one knows about that.'

They were back in Psimon's living room, only now the mood had changed. Where before there had been apathy and impatience now there was heightened interest and something that Steve should have anticipated… suspicion.

'I've already told you,' he said, nodding towards Psimon. 'It's Psimon. He sees things.'

Still the inspectors hesitated.

'He experiences the deaths.'

'What do you mean?' asked DI Hunt.

'He feels what the victims are feeling,' said Steve, thinking back to those harrowing attacks. 'He has done for sixteen years.'

The inspectors looked back at Psimon's huddled form.

'He's coming… he's coming… he's coming…' Psimon continued to whisper over and over.

Steve could see that they were struggling to accept what he was telling them, who would not. But they no longer gave him the impression that he was wasting police time.

They turned back to Steve.

'Where were you on the night of Wednesday the 2nd of March?' asked DI Regan.

'Oh for fuck's sake,' thought Steve putting his head in his hands.

'Last Wednesday night,' said DI Hunt. 'Where were you?'

'Flying out to Florida,' growled Steve with growing annoyance. 'With him!' He stabbed his finger at Psimon as he got to his feet.

'There's no reason to get angry, Mr Brennus,' said DI Regan.

'There is every reason to get angry, you pompous twat,' stormed Steve. 'I called you guys for help; to help you catch a psychopathic serial killer. And all you can do is…'

Steve reigned in his temper and turned away from the inspectors.

'Do you really think I would call the police if I had anything to do with these murders,' he said.

'Wouldn't be the first time,' said DI Regan.

Steve rounded on the annoying police officer but before he could say anything else he was interrupted by the sound of a car alarm; a very familiar car alarm.

DI Hunt moved to the window.

'Is that your BMW?' he asked.

'Yes,' said Steve crossing quickly to the window.

DI Hunt nodded down to the car and the row of bikes that had fallen like dominoes towards it.

'Aw, shit!' cursed Steve.

The last bike in the row had fallen heavily against his car, the handlebars wedged firmly in the BMW's radiator grill.

'I think you'd better move it before your neighbours hear the alarm,' said DI Hunt. 'Unless you want to knock on their door and ask for their insurance details.'

'It's not my sodding fault,' protested Steve but he knew the inspector was right.

A hoard of drunken bikers might not be the most rational of folk, especially when their beloved bikes had just been trashed. He strode towards the stairs but stopped when the two inspectors made to follow him.

'Someone needs to stay with Psimon,' he said.

'I'll stay,' said DI Regan but Steve was not happy about that.

'No offence,' he said. 'But this guy is twice your size. I'd rather you stayed.'

Steve looked at DI Hunt, who was a heavy-set man a fraction taller than Steve's six-foot two, a far more formidable prospect than the diminutive DI Regan.

DI Hunt gave Regan a nod to send him on his way and Steve ran down the stairs.

Back in Psimon's living room DI Hunt looked down through the large bay window, a mobile phone held to his ear.

'Control, this is DI Hunt, at seventy-four, Freshfield Road, Altrincham.'

There was a pause.

'Do you have any uniforms in the area? I've got a feeling we're going to need them.'

Another pause.

'Good,' said DI Hunt. 'Quick as you can, control.'

He hung up.

*

Lucifer watched as the angel appeared with one of the pawns. That would do. That left just one of the pawns between him and the witness. It was the bigger one of the two, although still far smaller than he, and besides, he held the lightning in his fist.

*

Steve killed the alarm while he was still on the driveway and after the briefest examination of the damage to his car he went straight for the driver's door. The radiator grill was smashed but the bike should pull free easily enough. He climbed into the car but as he did so the sound of music and raucous laughter from the house next-door grew suddenly louder as the front door opened. One of the revellers stumbled outside, fumbling with his flies and heading towards a row of bushes. Steve started the car and put it into reverse.

*

Lucifer moved quickly round to the rear of the house; to the fire escape that climbed up the back of the building. He took the metal steps three at a time until he stood at the fire exit door. He tried his crowbar between the door and the frame but the lock was solid. He would need to give it some force; the glass would probably break. It could not be helped. Besides, the racket from the bacchanals next door might be enough to cover the sound.

Lucifer set the point of his crowbar and leaned his weight against it. The door resisted, he gave it a wrench. There was the sound of breaking glass and Lucifer passed within.

*

Standing on the pavement, DI Regan winced at the unpleasant sound of screeching metal as the bike was dragged for several feet before coming free.

'What the fuck is going on here?' cried a slurred voice from the driveway next-door.

DI Regan took out his ID and went to intercept the drunken biker who seemed to be sobering up rapidly as he surveyed the row of toppled bikes. He turned back to the house and before DI Regan could stop him he had called out in a night-splitting shout.

'Hey guys… someone's been fucking with the bikes.'

Bodies appeared in the doorway, faces peered out from windows and as Steve got out of the car the din of heavy metal music ceased.

*

DI Hunt turned away from the window.

'Was that the sound of glass breaking?'

He started to cross the room, drawing level with Psimon who was still sitting hunched in the chair.

A spasm of trepidation gripped the inspector's bowels, a sudden feeling of fear not helped by Psimon's chanting…

'He's coming… he's coming… he's coming…'

He stared at the doorway, straining for any further sounds, sounds of an intruder.

Nothing.

Still he had better take a look, just in case.

'I'm just going to…' he turned back to Psimon but Psimon was no longer in his chair.

DI Hunt jumped with fright. Psimon was standing beside him.

'Jesus,' said DI Hunt. 'You frightened the shit out of me.'

But Psimon did not respond. He was looking straight through the inspector to the gaping doorway of his living room. Psimon had stopped his chanting but DI Hunt found the silence even more unnerving. Then Psimon spoke again.

'He's here.'

DI Hunt spun round as a huge shape loomed like a demon in the doorway. He reached for his mobile phone, turned to look for a weapon, another exit, anything…

Too late.

The vast demon ducked into the room, the black sheen of a pistol held level at his waist.

DI Hunt had chance for a single word…

'Police,' he gasped as the lightening struck him down.

*

Everything happened so quickly.

Steve got out of the car and started back towards the house. He did not want to leave Psimon for a moment longer than was necessary. But the bikers had different ideas. The one who had raised the alarm walked round DI Regan to confront Steve just as seven or eight more came striding down the drive.

'What the hell!' came the common response when they saw their bikes sprawling across the road.

'Let's just stay calm,' said DI Regan but his voice lacked any real conviction.

The bikers began to converge on Steve and a police car appeared at the end of the road, its flashing blue lights illuminating the trees as it came quickly towards them.

'Where the fuck do you think you're going?' asked the first biker stepping directly in front of Steve. '

'Back inside,' said Steve making an attempt to move past the biker but the biker would not let him pass.

The biker grabbed his arm and Steve punched him squarely on the nose. He slumped to his knees as the police car pulled up beside the line of fallen bikes. Steve braced himself as the rest of the bikers started towards him. DI Regan did his best to slow the advancing bikers but only succeeded in tackling one of them.

'It's him from yesterday,' the man said as two uniformed officers leapt out of the police car and rushed to intervene. 'The one with the smart mouth.'

A second police car turned into the road.

Fists, feet and angry faces lunged at Steve. He backed away parrying anything that came too close. All the while trying to back away towards the house.

'You trashed our bikes,' one of the bikers said.

'If I'd hit them they would have fallen the other way, brainiac,' said Steve.

The uniformed policemen were trying to get between Steve and the angry bikers. The adrenaline was rising; this was about to descend into a full-scale scrap. One of the bikers succeeded in grabbing hold of Steve. Steve grabbed the man's hand, twisted his wrist and thrust him down to the floor.

'That's enough,' said an authoritative voice and Steve found himself being restrained by one of the new policemen who had just arrived on the scene.

Chaos reigned, the tension mounted.

Steve had to get back to Psimon.

*

Lying on the floor, DI Hunt peered out through the pain in his skull. His entire body ached and he could barely move. His muscles kept twitching with uncontrollable spasms and his heart was racing fit to burst. He turned on his side, peering around the room. But there was no one there; not the man called Psimon nor the demon in the doorway. He fumbled for his mobile phone but could not extricate it from the folds of his jacket. He tried to call out but he could manage little more than a harsh whisper.

Regan was out front with the man, Steve Brennus. He had to warn them, he had to let them know. But the smallest movement was painful and he could feel that he was about to faint. He looked around the floor for some way of alerting them. As his vision started to fade his eyes settled on a mug of tea sitting on the floor beside a nearby seat.

DI Hunt reached out towards it. His trembling fist closed around it, the warm liquid sloshing over his hand. Then with one last desperate act he launched it towards the window.

*

The policeman's forearm was across his throat and Steve's right arm was twisted up behind his back. One of the bikers took advantage of Steve's predicament and punched him in the face. Steve kicked the biker in the groin and the man went down with a grunt.

Scuffles broke out all along the pavement as the uniformed police officers struggled to control the escalating violence. More bikers were emerging from the house and Steve could hear the sound of approaching police sirens as additional units were called in to attend the scene.

Then the sudden sound of breaking glass made everyone look up. Something had smashed into the bay window of Psimon's flat. Steve watched as a large shard of glass fell out of the frame and shattered noisily on the driveway.

'Psimon!'

'Just calm down,' said the policeman holding Steve.

But there was no time for a rational explanation. Steve slammed his head back into the officer's face and as the man relaxed his grip Steve broke away and sprinted up the drive.

DI Regan followed in his wake.

*

Lucifer was elated.

It had been easier than expected. The pawn had dropped into a twitching heap and the witness did not even struggle. He looked too frightened to call out, too frightened even to move. He just stood there, staring at the doorway as if he had been expecting him.

Lucifer had stepped up to him and felled him with a slap, a massive slap with his massive hand. Then he had tied the witness, and gagged the witness, and slung him over his shoulder. He seemed to weigh nothing at all as Lucifer carried him down the fire escape and off into the night.

The chorus was singing in anticipation of a new confession.

The night's devotions had only just begun.

*

Steve charged up the stairs to Psimon's flat and turned in to the living room. DI Hunt was lying unconscious on the floor, two thin wires trailing from his chest.

Steve looked up at Psimon's chair.

But the chair was empty.

Psimon was gone.

CHAPTER 29

Steve raced through to the back of the house, to the door at the head of the fire escape. The door hung open, the frame splintered, the glass broken. He darted through and stood at the top of the fire escape, staring down into the dark expanse of the garden.

Nothing.

'God Psimon, I'm sorry... I'm so sorry.'

Steve was almost paralysed by the sense of guilt and failure.

'*Keep me safe,*' Psimon had said, and he had failed.

The killer had him.

With an effort Steve thrust aside these destructive thoughts. The killer could not have got far. He started down the fire escape and then he stopped. Something had caught his eye; something moving down the footpath leading from this street to the next; a large, bulky, unnatural shape. The shape was keeping to the shadows, moving quickly.

The killer.

Steve's first instinct was to give chase but his military training demanded a rapid assessment before he moved. Steve followed the line of the killer's flight to the car park beside the tennis courts. It was dark and empty but Steve could just make out the shape of a black van tucked away in one corner.

A black van.

Steve's mind flashed back to earlier, when they had arrived back at the flat. A black van had sidled past them on the road. A black van had followed them from the convention.

Steve cursed his carelessness.

The killer was halfway down the passageway; he would be in the van before Steve reached him. Steve had to get back to his car, and quick.

Steve turned round and ran back through the flat. He met DI Regan in the hall.

'What happened?' asked the inspector looking through the doorway into the living room. 'Where's Psimon?'

The inspector made to stop him but Psimon could die at any time and Steve would brook no further delay. He winded the inspector with a punch to the stomach and continued on his way.

Back outside the house the inevitable brawl was in full swing. More police had arrived but still the bikers seemed in no mood to be placated. They scuffled and fought up and down the pavement and no one noticed when Steve emerged.

Steve ran straight to his car and then he cursed again. He had reversed right up to the inspectors' car and now a quarter ton of Harley Davidson was sitting in his way. He was boxed in. He was just resolved to smash his way out when he heard a voice from beyond the inspectors' car.

'What's going on here, man?'

Steve looked up to see another biker sitting astride an old Kawasaki z1300. The biker had pulled up behind the inspectors' car, beyond the press of police cars and the glare of the flashing blue lights.

'The brothers having a spot of bother with the filth?' he asked Steve, turning off his engine and climbing off his bike.

Steve looked at the biker, the wheels of his mind turning.

The biker reached up to unclip the chinstrap of his open-faced helmet, the keys for his bike still clutched in his leather-clad fist. And written across the front of his helmet, in bold white letters, was the biker's name.

SPIKE

Steve slipped his car keys into his pocket and started towards Spike who gave him a sudden wary look. But it was too late. Steve punched Spike hard in the face and as he dropped to the floor he snatched the keys from his limp fingers.

The sudden movement caught the attention of those still wrangling outside Psimon's flat and Spike's prostrate form drew concerned shouts from police and bikers alike. Steve ignored them. He climbed onto Spike's bike, turned the key, flicked out the pedal and kick-started the Kawasaki into life.

Then as bikers and police rushed towards him Steve revved the engine but he did not head off down the road. Going round the block would waste yet more precious time. Instead he spun the back wheel of the massive bike until he faced the pavement. Then he let out the clutch, mounted the pavement and tore off along the pedestrian footpath down which the killer had fled.

The footpath was narrow for such a big bike and Steve was grateful that no one else was using it tonight. He was not driving with the greatest of care. What he needed now was speed. He shot out into the car park and the bike wobbled dangerously as he skidded to a halt. But the car park was empty. There was no sign of the van.

Steve emerged onto the road running parallel with Psimon's. Still nothing to be seen. Turning left would take the killer into a warren of cul-de-sacs and residential back streets. He would be heading for more open roads.

Steve turned right.

The bike growled up the quiet suburban road until Steve reached the T-junction with the high street. This was more brightly lit and there were shops and businesses along the way. He looked to the right where the long straight road headed back into Manchester. There was a fair bit of traffic on the road but still no sign of the van. He turned to the left. More traffic, a couple of black cabs and several buses and there, just disappearing around the distant bend, a single black van.

Steve gunned the bike and sped off in pursuit.

The lazy Sunday evening traffic frustrated Steve's sense of urgency but he maintained a decent speed as he wove his way past the intervening cars. He was closing quickly on the van when a bus pulled right out in front of him. With a heartfelt expletive Steve hit the brakes hard. The bus had pulled out to get past a long row of parked cars and now it stopped in the middle of the road unable to pull into the kerb and the people waiting at the bus stop.

Steve made to go past but there was a pedestrian island in the middle of the road, with two brightly-lit bollards blocking his way, and the flow of oncoming traffic made it impossible to overtake on the other side of the road.

He fumed and swore and had no choice but to wait.

By the time he got past the bus the van was out of sight. The road ahead was clear for a while and Steve accelerated close to seventy in the thirty mile-an-hour zone. When he rounded the bend he could see the van once more. It was way out in front, beyond two sets of traffic lights, heading towards a series of roundabouts where the killer could choose to take the motorway, a dual carriageway or one of several small country roads.

If Steve was going to lose him now that would be the place.

He maintained his reckless speed, weaving dangerously between the slower moving cars. The first set of traffic lights was accommodatingly green but the second turned to red before he reached them. Steve dropped his speed but he did not stop. He manoeuvred past the waiting cars and threaded his way through the contra-flow of traffic at the junction. He ignored the shouts and honking horns of irate drivers and did not notice the police car peeling away from the traffic and turning in pursuit of this dangerously irresponsible biker.

Steve had lost sight of the van again. His eyes streamed from the cold wind in his face and he blinked away the tears as he scanned the road ahead.

Then he saw it.

It was in the left-hand lane, rising up towards the first roundabout, stuck in a line of slow-moving traffic, waiting to turn onto the dual carriageway. This was his chance to close the distance. He opened up the throttle and the Kawasaki gave a throaty roar as it powered down the road.

The wind was loud in his ears but Steve slowly became aware of a police siren behind him. He glanced in his wing mirror to see the police car closing fast, the cars that had slowed him down now moving aside to let it pass.

Steve ignored it.

His thoughts were only for the black van, and for the prisoner within.

He closed rapidly on the van and as he reached the back of the slow-moving line of traffic he pulled onto the gravel verge running down the side of the road. The back wheel of the Kawasaki slid and skidded in the gravel as he advanced on the van but he just needed to get ahead of it. Then he could block its path and tackle the driver.

*

Lucifer was frustrated by the slowness of the traffic but he had learned over the years to master his annoyance at the failings of the immaterial world. Impatience led to errors and errors led to failure and confinement. And so he waited in the line of traffic anticipating the service that would soon commence.

The witness lay in the back of the van, quiet but for the odd snuffle and moan.

Lucifer had been required to strike him a second time when they reached the van. Harder this time. Enough to quieten the witness until the time of his confession.

A sudden flash of blue light in his wing mirror caught his attention.

An agent of false justice.

Lucifer looked to see if it had any bearing on him. It seemed not. It was some way back although it was now driving on the gravel verge at the side of the road, seemingly in pursuit of a motorbike that was coming up fast on the inside.

Lucifer glanced at the bike, and then he looked again and the sudden flash of fury made his skin burn.

It was the angel, the guardian angel of the witness, riding out to save his ward.

But Lucifer would not have it. He let the traffic move away in front of him, opening up a gap. Then he turned the wheel to the left and lifted his great foot until the van's clutch engaged. He waited until the angel was almost level with him and quickly lifted his foot. The van lurched forward into the bike's path and Lucifer felt a satisfying crunch as the bike crashed into the side of the van.

*

Had he been a fraction slower Steve would have slammed right into the back of the van. As it was he glanced off the side and went careering up a grassy bank and straight into a wooden fence. The bike was wedged against the broken fence trapping his leg and Steve tried desperately to free the bike as the black van drew away. The traffic ahead had opened up and the van drove steadily up towards the roundabout. Steve heaved against the bike and was just working his leg free when the police car skidded to a halt on the gravel behind him.

Two policemen jumped out and before Steve could regain his feet they had rushed across to restrain him. Steve found himself sprawled across the front of the police car his face pressed against the warm bonnet and his hands snapped quickly into handcuffs.

'Just take it easy,' said the policeman holding him down when Steve tried to adjust his position.

He was trying to twist round so that he could see the van, see which way it went.

'You don't understand,' said Steve. 'You have to stop that van.'

'You were driving like a maniac long before that van pulled out on you,' said the policeman without relaxing his grip on Steve. 'Now, what's your name?'

*

Glancing in his mirror, Lucifer was gratified to see the angel being apprehended by the police. There was a certain, pleasing irony in that. He watched as they hauled him across the front of the car.

'Farewell, guardian angel,' he thought. *'The witness is mine.'*

The chorus sang victorious.

*

Steve watched despairingly as the van turned left onto the dual carriageway heading east. One of the police still held him down while the other sat half inside the car, the police radio in his hand.

'Relax,' said the policeman holding him. 'We're just checking to see if we've run into you before.'

Steve closed his eyes in the face of utter defeat.

'Psimon,' he thought. *'Oh God, Psimon...'*

The policeman in the car was waiting for a reply.

'That's right,' Steve heard him say. 'Brennus... Steven Brennus, 70, Court Farm Road.'

'What is it?' asked his colleague at the unusual delay.

The policeman in the car did not answer at first. He held up his hand, listening. Then his eyebrows shot up and his mouth fell open. His face flushed visibly as he hung up the radio and stepped out of the car.

'What is it? What's going on?' asked the policeman holding Steve. 'Has he got a record?'

'No,' said the other reaching into his pocket for the key to the handcuffs. 'He's got immunity... Class A Transactional Immunity.'

The policemen's demeanour had changed completely; 'all possible assistance' was the term they had used. Now they quickly helped him manhandle the bike down the grassy bank and back onto the road. It took several attempts to clear the carburettor and get it started but finally it spluttered and coughed its way back into life. Steve revved the engine as it found its feral voice.

‘Is there anything else we can do?’ asked the policemen over the noise.

‘Yes,’ said Steve as he turned the bike in the direction of the roundabout. ‘You can put out an alert for a black Mercedes van.’

The policemen nodded.

‘And then,’ said Steve as the Kawasaki sent a hail of gravel flying against the police car. ‘You can stay the fuck out of my way.’

The massive bike powered away as Steve took up the chase once more. The van had vanished but the dual carriageway was a long straight road and…

If he were quick…

And if he were lucky…

He might yet still find his friend.

CHAPTER 30

'How long had it been?' thought Steve. *'Four minutes... five?'*

It did not sound like much but on a fast road like this that could be four or five miles at least.

'How far to the next junction?'

He was not exactly sure. All he knew was that the junctions were few and far between. The only things he passed were small private side roads leading to big houses, farms and there was one sign for a scrap-metal yard and tip. Some of these smaller roads were to the left and some to the right with short filter-lanes allowing would-be users to cross the other side of the dual carriageway.

Steve flicked glances left and right as he past each driveway but they were dark and unlit and there was no sign of the van. He blazed down the road doing upwards of ninety miles-an-hour. He streaked past the other vehicles, the cold wind tearing at his clothes and hair but he did not feel the cold as he tried to control his mounting anxiety.

'Where are you? Where are you?'

The road climbed a small rise and Steve remembered that the first junction lay a mile or so beyond. If he had not found the van by then which road would he take? How would he decide? He shut away the doubts and screamed up the hill. And when he reached the top his spirits rose.

The traffic had come to a standstill, queuing all the way up to the junction almost a mile ahead. Nothing that had come through here in the last twenty minutes had passed through this jam. The van must still be there.

Steve sped down the long slope and picked his way through the standing traffic, searching all the while for sight of the black Mercedes van.

The first quarter mile… nothing.

Halfway through and still no sign.

Steve's heart felt like a heavy lump of stone as he reached the end of the traffic jam.

The van was not there.

'I've lost him,' thought Steve. *'Oh God, I've lost him.'*

The bike idled impatiently as Steve sat astride it in the middle of the road. Cars honked at him but he did not hear them. He was fighting to keep despair at bay.

'Where did he go? Where the hell did he go?'

Steve had definitely seen the van come onto the dual carriageway. So where was it now?

'He must have turned off?' concluded Steve.

That was the only answer. The killer must have turned down one of the private side roads. But which one? There was no way of knowing and it was foolish to try and guess.

Steve would have to check them all.

*

Lucifer would waste no time with the witness. The light of providence shone upon him. The sudden appearance of the guardian angel proved it so. He had thwarted the angel but still he must act quickly. There would be no mistakes tonight.

He locked the van in the barn, carried the witness into the chapel and laid him at the foot of the altar. He took the short-bladed fist-dagger from the altar and cut off his clothes. Then, leaving the witness naked on the floor he went to change.

When he returned the witness was starting to come round, shivering and moaning round the wire gag in his mouth.

Lucifer stood over him and began to pray.

*

Steve crossed the central reservation through one of the gaps reserved for emergency vehicles. Now heading back the way he had come he pushed the bike as fast as it would go. The first turn-off was just back over the rise, on this side of the road; he would be there in less than a minute.

'Private: No Entry,' the sign read but Steve ignored it. He turned onto the rough track and switched the bike's headlamp to full beam illuminating the twisting way ahead. The potholed track continued for perhaps two hundred metres to an old cottage abandoned long ago. However, enclosing the cottage and the surrounding area was a high chain-link fence. The area inside had been cleared and covered with gravel and was filled with numerous large metal containers.

Steve stopped in a wide puddle outside the heavy gate. A dog started barking and two big Alsatians loped into view barking aggressively through the wire. The sign on the gate read, 'No Tipping / Keep Out' and Steve was not inclined to go any further. The gate did not appear to have been opened recently and there was nowhere else for a van to go. He manoeuvred the bike round and headed back to the road.

*

Psimon opened his eyes to a waking nightmare.

The killer loomed above him, the tall dark youth from his childhood, the stranger from the church, the constant terror of his dreams and waking hours too.

He was here.

He was real.

And Psimon was at his mercy.

*

Lucifer concluded his opening prayer and lowered his upturned hands. The witness had awakened; he could feel his eyes upon him. He looked down and the chorus rose up in fervent harmony. This was what he lived for. To humble such as he.

*

Psimon could not comprehend the lack of humanity in those dead black eyes. His mind was blinded by the dark light of evil before him. Shrinking back against the hard stone floor he tried to cry out but found that he could not.

*

Lucifer smiled at the fear in the witness's eyes.

'So,' he thought. *'Not so formidable after all. Not so strong as we had thought.'*

He turned his back on the witness and crossed to the wall of the chapel, to a wooden stand where he kept the rod and the staff. The witness would be quickly humbled. He would confess his sins, he would be cleansed, and he would die. Lucifer would take the breath of life from his lungs and dump his body in the ground, like so much rancid meat.

*

Psimon tried to squirm away as the killer returned, arching his body like a worm. But the killer grabbed his legs and hooked his ankles over the end of one of the short pews. Psimon was left with just his bare shoulders against the stone; his hands were tied securely behind his back. Naked and freezing he felt horribly vulnerable and exposed. He watched as the killer lifted two long staves. One a brass crosier and one a wooden shaft that might once have held a cross. Both were battered and stained. The killer raised the staves and began to speak.

'Yea, as you walk through the valley of the shadow of death, you will fear my anger. For I am there with the rod and the staff. With the rod and the staff I humble thee.'

The killer's voice was deep and guttural and possessed of a horrible melodic quality. And as he ended his short perversion of scripture he brought the staves down on Psimon's naked form.

Psimon screamed as the thick brass rod smashed into his shins, the wooden shaft whacking down against his unprotected feet. He stared up with utter panic in his eyes. He could not move; he could not twist away. Over the years he had felt the torture again and again but now he was here in the chapel of night, and in reality the pain was far, far worse. The rod and the staff, they rose and fell again… and again... and again.

And Psimon screamed.

*

Steve had checked a farm and a track that led to a disused electricity substation. Now he followed another private road that was sign-posted 'Private: Access Only' but a vehicle had driven down this track recently. The splashes from the puddles along the way were still wet and shining in the Kawasaki's headlamp. Steve wondered if this were the place.

God, he hoped it was!

He followed the track round a broad curve and came upon a large house with two big cars parked upon the gravel drive. One an expensive-looking Audi and the other a Range Rover still wet from its splashing through the puddles on the track.

The front door of the house opened, light spilled out and several well-dressed adults emerged.

'No,' said one of the men. 'No trouble at all.'

'Most people end up at the substation, next turn down,' said a woman coming to help carry the bags from the back of the Range Rover.

Steve ground to a halt in the gravel.

The people turned to look at him, a dour looking man riding a big motorbike, no helmet and a face of fury.

'Can I help you?' asked one of the men taking a step towards Steve.

Steve ground his teeth and let out an animal growl.

'No,' was all he said. And with that he spun the bike round and headed back to the main road.

'Oh, God,' he thought as he pulled back onto the dual carriageway. *'How long has it been?'*

It must be forty minutes now since he had last seen the van, maybe more. The killer could be anywhere. Steve was losing hope. He turned onto another private road with a sign saying Dryden Farm. The track rose up slightly and Steve could see the lights of farm buildings through the trees. It looked homely and peaceful but Steve could not afford to pass it by. He tore up the track, turned into the yard and almost collided with a tractor reversing out of a barn. The bike slid sideways on a slick of mud and slurry and Steve careered into a row of aluminium feeding troughs.

The elderly farmer climbed out of the tractor and hurried over to Steve.

'Are you all right?' he asked. 'I didn't see you there… you came in pretty fast.'

Steve could not hide his disappointment and frustration. He was struggling to keep the bike upright in the slippery yard.

'Easy there,' said the farmer. 'Let me give you a hand.'

Steve felt the bike steady as the farmer grabbed the pillion bars behind the seat. He pulled it backwards allowing Steve to steer the bike away from the feeding troughs.

'You lost?' asked the farmer warily when he saw the expression on Steve's face.

'I'm looking for a friend of mine,' said Steve as he tried to turn the bike around.

'Oh?' said the farmer.

'He's in a black Mercedes van,' said Steve.

The farmer paused for a second, thinking.

Steve drew slowly forward not wanting to accelerate too quickly on such a slippery surface. He was almost back on the road where the bike's tyres could find some purchase and speed him away.

'The Harper boy drives a black van,' said the farmer and Steve came to a lurching halt. 'Though I've never known him have a friend.'

Steve just stared at the farmer, his heart suddenly pounding excitedly in his chest.

'The Harper boy?' he said.

'Aye,' said the farmer. 'Is that who you mean?'

'Big guy,' said Steve. 'Dark hair.'

'Bloody massive, more like,' said the farmer. 'Aye that's the fella.'

'So I've come up the wrong track?' said Steve, trying not to sound too desperate for information.

'Yep,' said the farmer. 'You need to get back on the main road and turn left. Go up to the roundabout and come back down on the other side of the road. It'll be the third turning on your left, big pylon by the drive. The house is set back some way from the road. Grim place now,' he rambled on. 'Not what it was when Mr Harper was around. Mind you he was an odd one too,' he gave Steve a knowing look. 'Bible basher if you know what I mean…'

Steve could only stare at the farmer.

'Do me a favour,' he said. 'Call the police and tell them to get some people round there straight away.'

'Is something wrong?' asked the farmer.

'Please, just do it,' said Steve as he kicked the bike into gear. 'Tell them Steve Brennus told you to call.'

And with that he took off down the track like a man possessed. Indeed he was a man possessed; possessed of new-found hope.

'Hang on Psimon,' he implored. *'Hang on.'*

CHAPTER 31

Lucifer removed the wire gag and waited to see if the witness would wake unaided. He needed to be conscious before he could confess. He looked down at the pathetic figure lying on the flagstones before the altar… the battered flesh, the broken skin, the bright blood flowing from the ghostly whiteness of his body.

There was something of beauty in that at least.

He went over to the font, drew some water in the great bowl of his hands and returned to stand over the witness once more.

'Or don't you know,' he whispered quietly. 'That all who are baptised here are baptised into death?'

The chorus approved of his words, the reference to scripture.

Lucifer basked in the music of it as he let the water fall. It was fitting that he should rouse the witness with an act of aspersion.

*

Psimon gasped with the sudden shock of cold. The pain that had been dulled by stupor now assaulted him once more, streaming in wave after wave from his ravaged nerves. Through swollen eyes he looked up into the face of death as the killer reached down towards him.

*

Lucifer took the witness by his arms and lifted him to his knees. The weakling was too feeble to bear his weight at first but Lucifer took a fistful of his sodden hair and held him up until he found his strength. Then he nodded and went to bring the bucket and the aspergillum.

*

Psimon could not stop shaking, shaking from the cold and the pain but more so from the fear. He knew what was coming next. With desperate eyes he watched the killer, he could not look away. The killer, in his altar clothes, his filthy bloodstained altar clothes, a mockery of service to the church. He watched him and he could not look away. And when the killer turned, the silver bucket and the holy water sprinkler in his hand, Psimon began to weep.

How many times had he felt this before? How many times had he screamed his confession before the acid fell? Screamed it and meant it and believed that he had sinned, and prayed that he would be believed, that he might be spared the pain.

But now that he was here he wept. He wept because he knew he could not do it. He could not willingly confess, he could not lie; not in the face of such abhorrent lies. He could not give them credence. He would not; not while any strength of will remained.

God give him strength, he wished he could.

But he could not.

*

Lucifer returned to stand before the witness, and when he spoke it seemed to be in answer to some unheard question.

'With the sin of heresy,' he said. 'And with questioning the authority of those in dominion…'

He dipped the aspergillum and raised it to one side, the vitriolic fluid falling on the stone and burning it away.

'He has dismissed the sublime rapture of the chorus, and must confess…'

Lucifer looked down at the witness. And the witness met his gaze.

The arrogance remained; there was defiance in him yet. But Lucifer watched as it melted away, running in rivulets from his eyes.

'You will learn humility and you will die,' thought Lucifer as he cleared his mind to pray.

'Do you confess to those in dominion?' he began.

'And to these my brothers and sisters,
That you have sinned,
In your thoughts and in your words,
In what you have done and in what you have failed to do?
And do you ask the blessed chorus, ever present,
And all the angels and saints,
And these my brothers and sisters,
To pray for you to those in dominion.
That the almighty might have mercy on you,
Forgive you your sins,
And bring you to everlasting truth.
Amen.'

The tears flooded down Psimon's face and every fibre of his being screamed at him to confess; to do whatever it took to escape the pain. But man is more than fibre and he found that he could not. He drew a ragged, sobbing breath and…

'No,' he softly said.

The killer frowned and let the cleansing vial fall.

Psimon screamed a sinew-snapping scream, a scream to shred his lungs. The splashes of acid ate away his skin, devoured his flesh and fizzed against his bones. Burning worse than any fire. Pain enough to drive one mad. He collapsed onto his side writhing and thrashing in agony.

'YES!' he screamed. **'YES! I CONFESS!'**

Lucifer smiled.

The cleansing had begun.

*

Steve did not take the farmer's advice. He did not go up to the roundabout. He crossed straight over to the other side of the road hugging the verge as he sped the wrong way down the inside lane of the dual carriageway.

Coming from this direction he was not sure which the 'third turning on the left' would be, so he looked instead for an entrance with a 'big pylon' beside it. And there it was, just a few hundred metres ahead, a big electricity pylon beside yet another private road.

Steve turned into the drive, skidding and bouncing along the poorly maintained driveway. The Kawasaki was not suited to such terrain and he had to fight to keep it upright, finally a deep pothole proved too much and the bike slid out from under him. He was sent sprawling across the road but he scrambled up immediately running back to the bike and heaving it upright. He made several attempts to get it started but the engine would not bite.

'Shit!' thought Steve, letting the bike fall back down.

In the darkness ahead he could make out the shape of buildings. Better just to run.

*

The witness lay moaning in his own filth, his head resting on the flagstones, blood and drool hanging from his mouth and nose.

Lucifer was disgusted.

There was no defiance now, no vanity of self. The witness was broken. A witless corpse too lost in pain to know that it was dead. There remained just one thing left to do, to shroud the witness in his funeral garb and to take from him the breath of life, the breath that had given voice to his lies.

Lucifer went and brought a shroud but when the witness saw it he found the strength to recoil in a final gesture of horror. His eyes stared and he squirmed away like something that lived in the earth. But Lucifer took a step and knelt beside him and placed the shroud over his head pulling it down the length of his body until he was enclosed.

*

Steve slowed as he approached the buildings. There were no lights on in the house, no sign of life at all, and no sign of the black Mercedes van.

Could he have got it wrong?

Could there be more than one house with a large pylon standing beside the drive?

'Please, God,' he thought. *'Please, God.'*

He padded into the yard, house to the left, a large barn straight ahead and several stone-built outhouses to the right. This had once been a working farm.

Steve looked around.

But for the light of a gibbous moon it would have been too dark to see. He approached the barn but it was locked. He tried to peer in through cracks in the side but the moon's light did not extend that far. The sense of despair returned as the fear that he might be at the wrong place took hold.

'This has to be the place,' he told himself. *'It has to be.'*

He started towards the house. But just as he turned away from the barn something caught his attention. The trees surrounding the outhouses seemed to be faintly illuminated by something other than the pale light of the moon. There was another source of light.

Steve started towards the stone buildings to the right. Two of them were simple sheds but one of them looked like an old grain store, a large circular building built from undressed stone. Something in Steve's memory pricked up at this; something that Psimon had said, something about an old stone church with circular walls. Steve's heart rate quickened as he approached the peculiar old building. And when he reached the arched wooden door he knew.

There was a large black cross in the door and a thin crack of light at its base.

Someone was inside.

In the pallid gloom Steve looked to see if there was a lock. There was but he could see, by the way the door was lying, that the lock was not engaged. Steve put his eye to the keyhole… church pews in candlelight, an altar, and wait… someone crouching down before it, a priest or an altar boy dressed in a black robe and filthy white surcoat. But this was no priest or servant of the church. The figure stood and in so doing revealed itself in all its size. Few men cut such a form at such a scale.

Steve had found the killer but was Psimon still alive?

*

Psimon was utterly helpless. Panic fluttered in his mind like the wings of a trapped bird, while his heart beat out the metre of his death.

'No,' he thought. *'Not yet... you can't. Please no...'*

But he had no breath for words only breath for fear; fear in panting gasps that drew the plastic against his face and blew it away in a transparent misty veil.

*

Lucifer stood up from the witness and went to get the hose. He bent to make sure that one end was properly attached to the pump then he grabbed the other and took a plastic tie to secure the shroud.

He did not hear the tiny click of iron as a latch was raised with utmost care.

He returned to the witness and pushed the hose up into the shroud.

He did not hear the slow scrape of wood on stone or the faint complaint of a rusty hinge.

He gathered the shroud together around the witness's ankles and secured it with the plastic tie.

He did not hear the stealthy footfalls on the flagstones of the chapel.

But when he stood he felt the movement in the air.

And when he turned to look he saw the angel standing there.

*

Steve froze as the killer's eyes fell upon him. But he did not shrink in fear. He met the malice in those dead black eyes and when he spoke his voice was calm and steady and weighted with the promise of violence.

'Where is he?' Steve demanded.

By way of an answer the killer looked down at his feet, and when he looked up he raised his arms as if to say 'behold'.

Steve looked down to the shape lying at the killer's feet; a large, clear polythene bag with something pale inside.

At first he did not see it for what it was but then, feeling suddenly sick, he did.

'Psimon!' he cried, taking an involuntary step forwards down the aisle.

The killer stepped over Psimon's body, coming to stand protectively before his prize.

Steve's eyes flicked from the killer to the obscene shape of Psimon's naked body in the bag.

'He's dead...Oh, God he's dead!'

But then the bag moved and Steve heard a quiet, pitiful moan.

'Alive!' Thought Steve, the relief sweeping through his mind. *'He's alive.'*

But for how long?

The bag was tied around his ankles and Steve knew that he could not survive for long on the air that remained inside the bag. He had to get him out and quick. But first he had to get past the killer.

Steve looked up at the killer and saw his eyes shift to the side of the chapel, to what looked like a small generator or pump. There was a black hose connected to the pump and Steve's eyes followed it as it snaked across the floor. The other end had been pushed between Psimon's feet up into the bag. Steve frowned at the killer's depravity then looked up at him once more.

For a second the two men held each other's gaze and then, as if at some unspoken command, they started towards each other. Steve moved in slow measured steps, while the killer came on more quickly enraged that the angel was here in this most sacred place.

Steve let him come, this mountain of a man. And when he reached for him Steve moved with lightening speed. He caught the killer's arm, took a handful of his dirty robes and swivelled at the waist, using the killer's own momentum as he threw him over his hip. The killer's feet crashed into the wooden pews as Steve slammed him down against the hard stone floor. With his left hand he kept hold of the killer's robes holding him down while he punched him in the face. It was like punching a boulder but he did it again and again, searching for that perfect blow that would do some real damage. But the killer was not so easily subdued. He let out an animal growl and grabbed hold of Steve's clothes and Steve witnessed his terrible strength as he was hurled aside.

The killer came quickly to his feet but Steve was quicker. Before the killer had risen fully to his feet Steve launched a scissor-kick and rammed his heel into the killer's jaw. The hefty kick rocked the killer and he swayed on one knee, unable to stand. Steve closed quickly, broke his nose with a solid punch, then hammered his elbow into the killer's face. The killer's arms reached out blindly for Steve, blood pouring from his nose, his mouth and a cut above his eye, then his eyes rolled back and he collapsed heavily to one side.

Steve raced to Psimon's side.

'Not too late!' he prayed. *'Please, not too late!'*

He knelt down beside his friend and paused for just an instant at the awful sight. Psimon's body was covered in blood and bruises, his face misshapen, his eyes flickering as the air in the bag turned bad, poisoned by his own exhalations. Steve went to his ankles, tried to break the plastic tie and tug the plastic free. He could do neither. He grabbed the bag near Psimon's face and tried to tear it with his hands but it was industrial strength polythene and simply would not tear. He pulled out the hose and tugged at the bag, drawing air through the narrow gaps at Psimon's ankles and he saw Psimon gulping down a breath as the small amount of air in the bag was replenished.

'Hang on, Psimon,' he said. 'Hang on. I'll get you out of there.'

Steve looked round for something to cut or tear the heavy plastic.

He did not see the warning look in Psimon's eyes.

He did not see the vast shape of a man rising from the chapel floor.

Steve put his teeth to the polythene but still it proved too strong. Then…

'Car keys,' he thought.

He put his hand in his pocket and pulled out his keys. He had just managed to single out the sharp metal rod of the car key when the killer fell upon him.

Steve felt like he had been hit by a falling tree as the killer brought a massive fist down across his back. He collapsed onto the floor beside Psimon, winded and dazed. Then he was lifted from the stone as the killer kicked him in the side. The kick cracked several of Steve's ribs and he groaned with the pain as he got up on his hands and knees. Then the killer strode up next to him and kicked Steve in the face sending him flailing back against the altar.

Stars and black blotches swam in Steve's vision as he clawed at the great marble altar trying in vain to stand but the killer came up behind him and punched him in the small of his back then hammered a massive fist down at the base of Steve's neck.

This would have been enough to finish most men but Steve Brennus was not 'most men' and he tried again to stand. With a sneer of disdain the killer reached down and took hold of the smaller man. He hooked one of Steve's arms in the crook of his elbow and placed his huge hands behind Steve's head, then he began to squeeze.

Steve grunted as the killer lifted him from the floor. His left arm was pinned and he thought his neck would break with the force of the killer's hold. He flailed about with his free arm but there was no way of reaching back at the killer. Then, looking down, he saw a small push-knife on the altar. The knife was out of reach but not so a large brass candlestick. As his breathing grew ever more constrained Steve reached out and grabbed hold of the candlestick. The thick candle fell away and Steve used the empty stick to try and reach the knife. He got the lip of the candlestick behind it and drew it closer, and closer yet but just as he was about to pull it within reach the killer jerked him up. The knife was sent clattering away to the foot of the altar.

Rage and frustration surged through Steve and with a final effort he lifted his feet, placed them against the altar, and shoved with all his might. The killer stumbled back, taking Steve with him. He lost his footing on the small step at the base of the altar and the two men came crashing down into the pews at the front of the chapel.

The corner of a pew caught Steve squarely on the temple and knocked him out cold.

*

Lucifer rose unsteadily to his feet. He wiped the blood from his shattered nose and looked down at the body of the angel. He was not dead but he soon would be.

They both would.

The angel and the witness.

Lucifer spat a bloody mouthful across his fallen adversary. He bent down over the witness and pushed the hose back into the bag. Then walked somewhat drunkenly to the side of the church. He lifted the thick brass crosier from the stand and moved along to the pump. It was time to take back the breath of life from the witness.

Mindful of the ceremony that was not yet concluded Lucifer offered up the briefest of prayers before he flicked the switch.

*

Steve tried to blink his vision into focus. Psimon lay before him; the polythene bag misted with condensation. He was still alive, just. As if in a dream Steve raised himself up and crawled towards Psimon fumbling at the polythene, trying to work a few more mouthfuls of breathable air into the bag. His senses were dulled, his mind foggy with concussion but when Steve saw the push-knife, lying not three feet away, his body found the strength to make a final lunge.

Steve's fist closed on the handle of the knife and he settled it in his palm. But when he turned back to look at Psimon he was horrified to see the polythene bag shrinking in against him, the slick material drawing tight around his body as all the air was sucked from it.

Steve crawled towards Psimon but before he could reach him the killer struck him down.

*

Lucifer struck the angel with the rod. Then he hooked it under his chin and across his throat.

'Let him watch as the witness dies. Let him watch as the breath of life is taken back. Let him watch and let them die together.'

The chorus rose up in glorious exultation. Lucifer had prevailed against the witness and against the angel, against providence itself. Those in dominion were pleased; he was the vessel of their righteousness, the instrument of their wrath. He was their servant and they his gods.

*

Steve watched as Psimon suffocated before his eyes, right there in front of him, just out of arm's reach. He watched but he could not move. The killer held the bar across his throat. He had managed to get his left hand under the bar but despite this the killer was slowly throttling the life out of him. Psimon looked up at him, his grey eyes bulging with fear, his mouth gaping wide for the breath it could not take, the plastic stretched tight across his bluing lips.

Steve reached forward with the knife in his hand. If he could just make a few more inches and pierce the membrane over Psimon's mouth. But he could not reach. He strained and strained but he could not reach. Then in one last gesture of aggression he stabbed the knife into the killer's hand. And then, as the killer relaxed his grip, Steve lunged forward stabbing out with the knife but just as he did so the killer snatched him aside and Steve's aim went astray. Instead of stabbing the knife into the gaping hole of Psimon's mouth Steve stabbed him in the face.

'NO!' cried Steve as he felt the blade slice through flesh and bone.

'You stab me in the face with a short-bladed knife.'

'NO! Psimon, NO!' he cried as the killer struck the knife from his hand and hauled him back, dragging him away from Psimon so that he could no longer see his friend, the friend that he had killed.

The killer pulled harder on the bar across Steve's throat, his wrist was the only thing preventing his windpipe from being crushed. But, even with the killer squeezing the life out of him, Steve thought not of himself but of the young man dying behind him.

'I'm sorry, Psimon,' he thought as the darkness claimed him.

'I'm sorry.'

CHAPTER 32

There was an eternal moment of nothingness, in which nothing existed and nothing did. And then Psimon took a breath and the universe exploded into life.

He woke into a world of pain.

He woke into a world of pain but not of fear. He had passed through the valley, through the shadows of death and now he need fear no evil. The worst of all his fears had come to pass and it had passed. For all the pain that wracked his body Psimon's mind was clear. It shone, it burned and Psimon opened his eyes.

He looked like a bag of pummelled meat, a grizzly horrible sight. Psimon trembled from the cold and the pain but he fought against his tortured body and tried to turn. The plastic bag restricted his movements. His body was beaten and cut and spattered with raw wounds where the acid had eaten away his skin, and inching round was an exercise in agony but still he turned.

He turned to see the man who had saved his life.

The short knife had gouged into his cheek, just below his eye. It had sliced down through his upper lip and taken out a tooth. But it had cut through the suffocating plastic and let the air rush in. Psimon gulped it down and his body tingled with agonising ecstasy as feeling returned to his flesh. With a Herculean effort he pressed his head against the stone and struggled to his knees. He blinked the blood from his eyes and looked out through the slit in the plastic across his face.

There in front of him was the killer, his childhood terror. He stood with his back to Psimon; his massive form hunched over as he slowly strangled Steve. Psimon could hear the coarse decline of Steve's last breaths, and in the background, the insistent whine of the electric pump that sucked in vain at the punctured bag.

Psimon swayed unsteadily, struggling to keep his balance but then he drew a breath and focussed his mind.

*

Lucifer raised his head as the pump cut out, the familiar, discordant noise fading away to silence.

'No matter,' he thought.

The witness should be dead by now. And the infuriating angel was soon to follow. He looked away and bent once more to the task of killing.

'NO!'

The voice echoed loudly in his mind.

Lucifer paused to listen. If this were the chorus speaking then it was louder and clearer than it had ever been before. Maybe those in dominion had deigned to speak to him at last, in recognition of this his greatest conquest.

'NO!'

Lucifer froze. The voice was not in his mind; it was coming from behind him. He felt a strange and unnerving emotion, an alien sense of fear. With uncharacteristic trepidation he relaxed his grip on the angel and turned to look back over his shoulder.

The witness was alive.

He knelt there like an apparition of death. The ghost of all his victims kneeling before the altar, looking up at him with eyes he had never noticed before; grey eyes staring out through the blood smeared plastic. They were the eyes of vengeance, the eyes of wrath and Lucifer was afraid. But his fear quickly turned to fury.

Lucifer let the angel fall.

He turned to face the witness. His lip curled in an animal snarl and he started forward, the rod raised high in the air. He would kill him, he would crush him, he would tear his body apart with his own bare hands. He would rend him asunder and then he would burn his remains until nothing remained but ash.

Lucifer reared up above the witness and the rod began to fall.

'NO!'

The voice was like a thunderclap in Lucifer's mind and the rod went flying from his grasp. It tumbled through the air, clattering and clanging against the wall of the chapel.

What was this new manifestation of evil?

Lucifer looked down at the witness. A fire burned in those stone-grey eyes. He must quench it, snuff it out. He reached out with his massive hands.

Silence the witness

Cut out his tongue

Fill his mouth with dirt

'NO!'

The invisible force struck Lucifer in the chest and sent him reeling back. He stumbled over the body of the angel and almost lost his footing. He looked up at the shrouded form of the witness, hunched and kneeling on the floor. He looked into the face of death, and was afraid, and he faced his fear in the only way that he knew how.

With violence, and with hate.

Lucifer charged forward like a raging bull but the invisible force struck him again. It lifted him from his feet and propelled him through the air. It slammed him back against the wall of the chapel and held him there, his feet flailing six feet from the floor.

'Abomination!' screamed Lucifer, straining to break free of the bonds that held him. 'Spawn of iniquity!'

Psimon looked up at the killer. His eyes bored into him, holding him fast.

'Blasphemer,' shouted Lucifer. 'Child of profanity. Accursed witness. The chorus condemns thee. Thou art abhorrent to those in dominion, a stain upon the land. You must die… confess your sins and die…'

Psimon had heard enough.

His eyes narrowed as he pressed the killer's face against the wall.

'Foul malefactor! You… cannot… be… allowed… to live…'

The killer's words became broken and strained as his great jaw was crushed against the stone. Saliva spilled from the corner of his misshapen mouth as Psimon began to squeeze. The killer's curses turned to stifled moans and his dark eyes rolled back in his head but still Psimon did not stop. He was determined to silence the vitriolic stream of hate.

'Psimon.'

At first Psimon did not hear the soft, croaking voice.

'Psimon.'

Steve crawled across the bloodstained floor until he knelt at Psimon's side.

'Psimon,' he said again, reaching out a shaking hand. 'Psimon, let him go.'

For all that had happened Steve could not bear the thought of Psimon becoming a killer. He would not blame him if he did, no one could. But he knew that if he did Psimon would be forever changed, diminished, tainted… changed.

'Psimon, let him go.'

Finally the fire went out of Psimon's eyes and with a great shuddering sob he lowered his gaze and the killer dropped heavily to the floor.

Steve knelt up beside Psimon and took hold of the bag. He hooked his fingers into the tear that he had made and tore it back from Psimon's head.

Psimon turned his wretched face to Steve, his eyes brimming with tears.

For a moment they just looked at each other. Then, in a voice of terrible sadness, Psimon spoke.

'He was just a man,' he whispered, the blood still running from his severed lip. 'All this time… just a man.'

Steve just nodded, clenching his jaw in the face of Psimon's distress.

'All those people,' said Psimon, the sobs welling up in his chest.

'I know,' said Steve.

'All those people who died here because I...'

'I know,' said Steve. 'I know.'

Steve reached for Psimon. He took his head in his hands and looked at him intently.

'It's not your fault,' he said but Psimon's eyes were unconvinced.

Steve pulled Psimon towards him and held him, like a child, against his chest.

'It's not your fault,' he said, his own voice breaking with emotion. Psimon was still naked, still bleeding and still bound in a grotesque and filthy plastic bag. But there were things of more importance here, and so he held him while he cried.

He was still holding him some minutes later when the distant whine of police sirens sounded in the night. And still yet when the cars skidded to a halt outside.

It did not take them long to find them.

The police entered the 'chapel' cautiously, not knowing what they would find. But whatever they might have anticipated fell well short of what they saw. The members of the armed response team came first, moving with disciplined precision as they secured the room. They identified Psimon and Steve and went to check the body at the base of the wall. One of the officers covered the enormous man with his firearm while the other bent to check him.

Steve turned to watch.

The police officer put two fingers against the killer's neck then jumped back as the hulk of a man let out a moan and made to rise. But nothing of his great strength remained and the officers subdued him with ease.

'You didn't kill him,' said Steve, easing back from Psimon.

Psimon did not look at Steve at first. He just stared across at the large figure dressed in altar clothes and lying prostrate on the floor.

‘I just cut off the blood supply to his brain,’ said Psimon, glancing briefly up at Steve, and damn it all if he did not smile.

Steve looked down at Psimon, a strange sense of pride surging in his chest.

God but if he ever had a son…

*

Sitting in the back door of the ambulance Steve dabbed at his mouth and nose with a wad of sterile gauze while the paramedic strapped up his chest.

Psimon was sleeping in the back of the ambulance.

They had tended him with exquisite care, these people whose job it was to help the injured and the sick. They talked to him as they cleaned the muck and the blood from his body, never once hinting at embarrassment or disgust. They dressed his wounds and wrapped his naked body in soft white blankets and laid him down to sleep. And even then they did not leave him.

Steve looked up as a second ambulance drove off down the track taking the killer away and out of their lives.

‘How did you know?’

DI Regan was standing beside Steve at the back of the ambulance. He handed Steve a plastic cup of water as he too turned to watch the departing ambulance.

‘It’s not me,’ said Steve nodding towards the sleeping figure behind him. ‘It’s him.’

‘What?’ said DI Regan. ‘You mean he really is psychic?’

Steve just nodded his head and sipped his water. He was starting to feel desperately tired. He felt like he could sleep for a week.

‘My wife’s cousin swears she’s psychic,’ DI Regan went on. ‘Makes a living from it and everything.’

Steve was barely listening. The paramedic tied off his bandage and helped him up into the ambulance.

‘We always thought she was just nuts…’ said DI Regan taking the cup of water back from Steve.

'She is,' said Steve as the paramedic ushered the inspector away from the ambulance and helped Steve up so that he could sit across from Psimon.

As Steve settled into the seat in the back of the ambulance he looked down at the person lying opposite him. He still looked a frightful mess but Psimon was sleeping soundly, peacefully. Steve cast his mind back to the day that they had met. A few short days that felt like a lifetime.

'I will pay you three thousand pounds a day if you will accompany me while I go about my business and keep me safe for the next five days.'

Steve wondered…

If he could wind the clock back and, knowing what he knew, would he still take the money and take the job. He truly did not know. But in his mind he heard his father's voice, Geordie accent and all…

'Of course you would, soft lad... of course you would.'

'Not for the money,' thought Steve, as he drifted off to sleep. *'No fucking way!'*

But for the chance of knowing Psimon and doing what he could…

'Perhaps,' he thought as sleep engulfed him.

'Perhaps...'

CHAPTER 33

Monday March 7th

Front Page Headline

KILLER STOPPED AFTER FOURTEEN YEAR REIGN OF TERROR

Richard Chatham put down the phone and sat back in his chair.

'Well,' he thought. *'I wasn't expecting that.'*

But then he had not been expecting much of what had happened over the last few days. He steepled his fingers and tapped them lightly against his lips. Then he raised his eyebrows, blew out his cheeks and smiled.

'Suppose I'd better go and tell the boss,' he said quietly to himself.

He started to rise from his chair. Then…

'No, sod it,' he thought with a new sense of liberation. *'I'll phone my wife first.'*

CHAPTER 34

Tuesday March 8th

'That your girlfriend again,' teased Steve when Psimon put away his mobile phone.

'I told you,' said Psimon with a smile. 'She's not my girlfriend.'

'Well you seem to get on very well,' said Steve. 'Maybe you should ask her out to dinner.'

'No need,' said Psimon. 'She's already asked me.'

Steve raised his eyebrows approvingly. 'There ya go, you see,' he said.

Psimon just shook his head and turned away and Steve laughed at his coyness. *'Him and that mobile phone,'* he thought.

What is more, the sister had told him off for using it. 'They interfere with the equipment,' she had told him. 'And you should be resting,' she had chided. 'You need your sleep.'

'Sorry sister,' Psimon had said like a naughty schoolboy who knew he would do it again the moment the teacher's back was turned.

Steve was amazed at how quickly Psimon had recovered from his ordeal. Not his body… the bruises, the burns, the neatly sown up lip. All that would take weeks to heal. But his mind… After what he had been through Steve would have expected a severe degree of trauma but Psimon seemed almost cheerful. There was just the occasional moment when Steve caught him staring into space, the tears standing in his eyes. Steve knew that he did not cry for himself but for the people who had gone before him, those who had died at the killer's hand.

'It's not your fault,' Steve had told him again.

'I know,' said Psimon. 'But it feels like it is.'

'You should be worried about yourself. After what you've been through...'

Psimon pursed his lips.

'After so many years living with fear,' he said. 'It's a relief to be free of it.'

'So no more visions of death.'

'Oh,' said Psimon. 'I have a new vision of my death.'

Steve looked sharply up at him.

'You know how you die,' he asked him. 'And that doesn't frighten you.'

Psimon shook his head.

'No,' he said. 'It's sad… Not what I might choose... But it's a normal death and I can live with that.'

Steve just looked at him, wondering at what kind of strength it took to live with what he knew.

They had remained in hospital for the rest of the day and a second night. But, for all the unpleasantness, their injuries were largely superficial and there was no reason for them to remain. Now they sat to the side of the BBC studio while people bustled all around them preparing for the press conference that was scheduled to go out just before the evening news.

'You needn't have come,' said Psimon as they sipped their BBC coffee.

Steve did his best to sound insulted.

'And miss your moment of glory,' he said.

'I didn't pay you for an extra day,' said Psimon.

'Let's just say this one's on the house,' said Steve although both men knew that Steve was there because he wanted to be.

He knew that he would soon be passing Psimon over into someone else's care but for now he felt that his duty was not over. Indeed he did not want it to be over, not quite yet. He longed to get back to his family but he had the rest of his life for them. He could spare another day.

They sat in silence for a while watching the journalists fill up the seats in front of the stage. Most of the world's major news networks were present but none of them showed any great enthusiasm at being there. Indeed they seemed puzzled and annoyed that they had been told so little about what to expect. Despite the impressive array of journalists the press conference had not been widely publicised and, with the exception of the senior production staff, no one even knew what it was about.

All that was about to change.

'Oh, ye of little faith,' thought Steve.

He watched them frown and humph as they wondered if it was worth their while being here at all. But Steve suspected that their irritation would not last for long.

Another minute or so and two men were shown into the studio; one a tall man with sandy hair and glasses, the other an older man; bald, glasses and a bushy, stark-white beard. The assistant directed the white-haired man to a chair on the stage. The other man was invited to take a chair to one side where, like Steve, he could watch the proceedings but would play no part in them. However, as the two men looked around the studio they caught sight of Psimon and Steve and came across to speak with them.

'Psimon,' said the white-haired man, waving Psimon down when he made to stand.

'Mr Randi,' said Psimon looking up at the elderly man. 'Thank you for coming.'

James Randi laughed, his sharp eyes sparkling.

'Like you could have kept me away,' he said.

He reached down to shake Psimon's hand warmly.

'Thank you for the invitation,' he said.

'You're welcome,' said Psimon.

Randi looked at Psimon a moment longer. Then he patted his hand and turned to Steve.

'Mr Brennus,' he said extending his hand.

'Mr Randi,' said Steve. 'Jeff,' he added turning to shake the hand of Jeff Wag, the manager from the Randi Foundation.

'I hear you're quite the hero,' said Randi without any hint of cynicism.

Steve blushed and started to object but Randi just smiled. 'I think they're nearly ready for us,' he said as the studio assistants began to look in their direction.

Psimon started to rise from his chair, reaching for the walking stick that lay against it.

'If you'll allow me…' said Randi extending his arm for Psimon to take.

Psimon glanced down at Steve.

'Go get 'em psyche-boy,' said Steve with a smile and Psimon limped onto the stage and into the glare of the studio lights.

As Psimon made his way up onto the stage Steve sighed and took out his mobile phone. He could put it off no longer, indeed he could not bear to put it off any longer. He would call Christine and tell her that he would be home tonight.

'I'm sorry sir.' The studio assistant leaned across to Steve. 'We're about to go on air… You'll have to go outside if you want to make a call.'

Steve raised his eyes and put away his phone.

'Something important, Mr Brennus?'

Steve started at the sudden voice.

'Mr Chatham!' he said as the civil servant sat down beside him. 'Er... no,' he said, referring to the disallowed phone call then… 'Yes,' he amended quickly. 'It can wait another hour,' he concluded feeling flustered.

Chatham just smiled.

'Not started yet then?' he asked.

'No,' said Steve. 'They're just… What are you doing here?' he interrupted himself, feeling a familiar sense of suspicion at such unexpected events.

'I'm here to start my new job,' said Chatham.

Steve looked none the wiser.

'Psimon asked me if I would consider managing his affairs,' said Chatham. 'His life is about to become considerably more complicated.'

'Psimon offered you a job?' Steve felt surprised and strangely piqued.

'He did.'

'And you said yes?'

'I did.'

Steve turned to look at Psimon who was being given some direction as to what was about to happen.

'I hope you know what you're letting yourself in for,' he said.

'I haven't the faintest idea,' said Chatham cheerfully.

Steve was about to speak again when the lights in the studio came up and the shouts rang out that they were ready to go on air.

*

It did not appear to be going well but Steve was not worried because, whenever he looked across at him, Psimon did not appear to be worried. They had introduced him as 'the world's first psychic' and most of the press agencies had reacted with predictable scepticism. Steve had just smiled. He knew they would be convinced. They just had to ask the right questions.

'So what makes you different from the thousands of other psychics in the world,' asked the man from Fox News.

Psimon just smiled and was about to speak when Randi leaned across.

'If I may,' he asked and Psimon responded with a nod.

'What makes Psimon different,' said Randi. 'Is that he can do the things he says he can do. He is a genuine psychic.'

The journalists were paying attention now but they were still far from convinced.

'A few days ago,' Randi went on. 'Psimon came to be tested at the James Randi Educational Foundation.' He paused.

'There Psimon was able to demonstrate his psychic ability under carefully controlled conditions.'

The journalists had begun to frown. It was starting to dawn on them that this might just be for real.

'Are we supposed to take your word for it?' asked one.

'Do you have any proof?' asked another.

'We have video evidence,' said Randi.

'What psychic ability did he demonstrate?'

Randi looked at Psimon who gave him another small nod. He reached into the pocket of his waistcoat and pulled out a small glass tube that Steve instantly recognised. 'This steel rod is sealed inside a glass tube.' He held it up for all to see. 'Psimon was able to bend a similar metal rod in a similar glass tube without touching it.'

'Wouldn't it break the glass if the rod bent?' asked one of the journalists.

Randi nodded. 'Psimon removed the rod from the tube, with his mind, before bending it into shape.'

Eyebrows went up, lips were pursed but still they had no reason to believe.

'What shape did he bend it into?'

Randi smiled and again he looked to Psimon for consent. He reached once more into his pocket only this time he pulled out a steel rod that had been formed into a perfect circle.

Some of the journalists seemed impressed but they would not be doing their job if they had left it there.

'How do we know this isn't just a setup… a publicity stunt?'

Randi inclined his head. In their position he would suspect the same.

'What about a demonstration?'

The suggestion came from the back of the room and was quickly taken up by several others.

The person chairing the press conference sat forward.

'I'm afraid we can't ask Psimon to…'

'It's okay,' said Psimon in that quiet, arresting tone of his. 'If I were them I would expect no less.'

The chairman sat back in his seat, the doubt written large across his face.

'Mr Randi, if I may…' said Psimon coming out from behind the table.

Randi placed the circle of steel in Psimon's palm and smiled as if he were thoroughly enjoying this.

Psimon turned to the room full of journalists.

'Mr Tyler,' he said to the man from Sky News. 'If you could please hold this so that everyone can see it.'

The man from Sky News seemed surprised that Psimon should know his name but he was not about to miss the opportunity to raise the profile of his network. He jumped up and took the circle from Psimon.

'It's okay,' said Psimon. 'You can bring the cameras in.'

It was clear that the floor staff had not expected a close-up demonstration.

'The boy's a natural,' thought Steve with a smile.

Psimon waited until everything was ready and everyone was settled. He smiled slightly at the wall of rapt faces. Then he glanced at the circle of steel.

The room erupted in a collective gasp of astonishment.

The Sky News man had flinched and almost dropped it when the metal began to change its shape. Now his hand shook as he tried to hold it steady for the cameras to get a good clear look.

What had been a perfect circle was now a perfect square.

'Smart arse!' thought Steve at Psimon's use of the ancient metaphor for the impossible.

'Mr Brennus.'

Steve turned at the sudden voice beside him. One of the production staff was leaning down over the back of his chair.

'Your wife and daughter are outside,' the young woman said over the hubbub of excited voices in the room. 'Would you like me to show them in or would you rather speak to them outside.'

'My wife and daughter?' said Steve as if he did not understand what the woman had just said.

'Yes,' she said. 'They're waiting outside. Would you like me to show them in?'

Steve had never felt so flustered, confused and nervous in his entire life.

'I… er… yes… show them in please.'

He rose from his seat and Chatham gave him a reassuring smile as he moved to the side of the room, away from the lights and the intense interest that was now focussed on the stage. He waited near the door while the studio assistant popped outside. His heart was hammering in his chest as he tried to think of what he was going to say but then the door opened and Christine and Sally were there.

Steve glanced down at his little girl; her eyes were still ringed with yellow bruising. He put a hand to his mouth as the tears sprang to his eyes. But then his wife came to him and wrapped her arms around him and nothing else mattered. Not the money, not the business, not the pain in his broken ribs. All that mattered was his wife and his little girl.

Steve crouched down and looked at Sally. He held out his hand to her but still she hesitated. Christine reached back and put an encouraging hand on her shoulder and finally Sally moved. She threw herself at her daddy and melted against his chest. Steve held her, enfolded her in his great strong arms. He buried his face against the soft skin of her neck and breathed in the smell of her hair. He did not speak… he could not speak.

Finally Sally pushed away from him.

'Did someone hurt you, daddy?' she asked reaching out a slender little finger to trace the cuts and bruises on his face.

'Yes they did,' managed Steve through the tightness in his throat.

'Was that because you were naughty?'

Steve looked puzzled. He glanced up at Christine.

'She thinks you hit her because she was naughty,' said Christine, wiping the tears from her cheeks.

'Oh God,' said Steve with a shuddering gulp.

'You shouldn't sneak about and listen to other people's conversations,' said Sally looking down at her shoes.

Steve was lost for words but not for tears. He clasped his daughter to his chest and when he could he whispered to her… 'You were not naughty darling,' he said. 'You did nothing wrong. Daddy was naughty for losing his temper and hitting the door.' He held Sally gently away from him and looked into her big green eyes. 'And I am sorry,' he said. 'I'm very, very sorry.'

Sally looked at him for a moment. 'That's okay, daddy,' she said. 'It doesn't hurt anymore.'

Steve reached out to hold her some more then he stood to kiss his wife. 'I'm sorry,' he said. 'I'm sorry for everything.'

'It's okay,' said Christine putting her palm against his bruised face.

'No it's not,' said Steve. 'I left you with everything, with barely a word.'

Christine seemed puzzled.

'Steve, it's okay,' she said.

'No,' he insisted. 'You had Sally to deal with… and Paul… and the bank… the solicitors…'

Christine looked as if Steve had lost his senses.

'Have they been giving you a hard time?' Steve asked her.

'Ha… no,' laughed Christine as if nothing could be further from the truth.

Now it was Steve's turn to look puzzled.

'The bank phoned me last week to see if we still wanted the loan after making such a large deposit.'

Steve frowned.

'Large deposit?' he said. Thinking that fifteen thousand pounds did not seem that large.

'Yes,' said Christine. 'From America... some educational foundation or something.'

Steve just looked at her as the penny dropped.

'A million dollars,' said Christine excitedly. 'Steve, that's over half a million pounds.'

Steve's voice seemed to have deserted him once more.

'However did you wangle that one?' asked Christine. 'What's the interest like? When do we need to pay it back?'

Steve did not answer at first. He just turned to look across the studio to the young man fielding the barrage of questions from overexcited journalists. And as he did so Psimon glanced up. Just for a second he looked at Steve with his stone grey eyes then he nodded and smiled as if to say 'you're welcome'.

'I don't think we need to pay it back,' said Steve turning back to his wife.

'What?' said Christine 'I don't understand.'

'It's a long story,' said Steve. 'I should have called to tell you what was going on… I shouldn't have just walked out like that.'

'But you didn't,' said Christine. 'There were the flowers…'

'Flowers?'

'Yes,' said Christine, fishing inside her pocket for the note that she had kept. 'And the Nemo toy for Sally.'

Steve took the note and read it…

Hi darling.

So very sorry for what happened. Please tell Sally that it wasn't her fault and that daddy was very naughty for losing his temper. Just had a call from someone who could get us out of the mess we're in but I need to go away for a few days. Don't try me on the mobile, the network doesn't cover this region. Will be in touch when I can.

See you a week on Tuesday.

Love Steve

PS Give Nemo a kiss for me

Even his signature was exactly right.

'I was desperate to speak to you,' Christine went on. 'But there were your texts and your colleague called us to let us know you were okay.'

'My colleague?' said Steve.

'Psimon,' said Christine. 'He called us several times.'

Steve put a hand to his forehead.

'He sounds like such a nice young man.'

Steve turned once again to look at Psimon on the stage. The press conference was being brought to a close. Psimon was being ushered from the stage; Chatham stood beside him. Then the chairman addressed the room.

'Thank you… thank you…' he said as he struggled to quieten the excitement in the room. 'That's all we have time for just now.'

There was a collective groan of disappointment from the world's press.

'You will have the chance for more questions in just over a week's time.'

The journalists simmered down a little at this.

'From here Psimon will be going to the research facility at Portland Down, where an international symposium has been convened to begin the study of his remarkable abilities…'

Steve felt a sudden wrench as he realised that Psimon was moving out of his life.

'Who is that?' asked Christine as she stood with her arm around her husband.

Steve lifted Sally so that she could also see.

'That...' he said, 'is Psimon.'

'Your colleague?' said Christine in surprise. 'The guy that's been calling us?'

'That's right,' said Steve. 'He's the one who arranged the money.'

'But where are they taking him?' asked Christine as Psimon was bustled from the room.'

'He's off to meet some of the top minds in the world,' said Steve. 'But don't worry, I'm sure you'll get a chance to thank him.'

'Well I can thank him a week on Friday,' said Christine.

'What?' said Steve.

'I invited him to dinner,' said Christine. 'I was going to do lamb.'

Steve just stared after Psimon as he disappeared through the door at the far side of the studio.

'Who is he?' asked Christine, for it was clear that Psimon was more than just a colleague of Steve's.

'He's a psychic,' said Steve.

'What?' said Christine. 'A real psychic?'

'Yep,' said Steve. 'The first and only.'

EPILOGUE

Friday March 18th

'Stop fretting,' said Steve as he stood with Sally and Christine at the foot of their drive.

'But I'm nervous,' said Christine. 'He can read people's minds… what if I fancy him?'

Steve just laughed as the car pulled up beside them.

'How's it going freak?' he said as Psimon emerged from the back seat of the car. He crossed the pavement to greet his friend. 'The men in white coats figured out what's wrong with you yet?'

Psimon smiled as he took Steve's hand.

'Terminal case, I'm afraid,' he said.

Steve laughed and after a brief appraising look the two men embraced and held each other tight.

'It's good to see you looking well,' said Steve as two young boys ran up to them.

'Are you the psychic man?' one of them asked.

Psimon and Steve exchanged a look of amusement.

'Yes I am,' said Psimon.

'Told you,' said one of the boys.

'Can we have your autograph?' said the other.

Psimon looked embarrassed but Steve just laughed.

'You've only yourself to blame,' he said.

Psimon looked round for something to write with then turned as the driver's window of the car slid down.

'Thanks Ben,' said Psimon as the driver held out a pen and a piece of paper.

Psimon leaned on the car to sign the piece of paper.

'And yours too,' said one of the boys, looking up at Steve. 'You're the one who caught that killer, the SAS man.'

Steve blushed and Christine's eyes shone as she smiled at her husband's discomfiture.

Steve took the paper from Psimon and was about to sign it when he stopped and paused, looking at Psimon's name as he had written it on the page.

To Max and Stuart
From Simon, the world's first psychic

'What's the matter?' asked Psimon as Steve continued to stare at the paper.

'Nothing,' said Steve. He added his name to the paper and handed it back to the excited boys. 'It's just that I...'

'What?' said Psimon as they turned towards the house. 'Not imagining things that aren't there, are we?'

Christine linked her arm into Psimon's and Sally held his hand.

But Psimon glanced back at Steve.

'Maybe there's something of the psychic in all of...'

'Don't give me that bollocks,' said Steve cuffing Psimon smartly round the back of the head. 'You're the only psychic in the world, thank God.'

Psimon laughed as he was escorted up the drive. Steve followed close behind, and as they stepped through the door he heard Sally's voice.

'How did you hurt your face?' she asked.

'Your daddy cut me with a knife.'

'Did he really?' asked Sally as if Psimon were teasing her.

'Yes he did, the nasty brute,' said Psimon with a smile. 'He really did.'

Dear reader

Thank you for buying First and Only. If you enjoyed it I would be immensely grateful if you could mention it to your family and friends and maybe consider leaving a review.

If you did not enjoy it then thanks for giving it a go. Some people have objected to the level of violence, the religious references and the assertion that there are no real psychics in the world. If you feel this way then I apologise. I never meant to offend anyone's beliefs or sensibilities.

I have always been interested in paranormal phenomena and my religious upbringing remains a significant source of inspiration for my writing. For me the book is about the triumph of faith and friendship over fear and evil. I would like to think that other people perceive it as such.

But whatever the case, thanks again for taking the time to read it and I look forward to meeting you again soon (when I finally get round to finishing another book!).

Sincerely
Peter

First and Only the Movie!

Following the success of the novel, First and Only is now making a bid for the big screen. To learn more about this exciting development and to see how you could get involved please visit:

http://www.firstandonlymovie.com/